DIPLOMAT

In the dark Marcel t... kissed her willing lips... through the thin silk. He felt the tip of her tongue slide between his lips and at once he reached under her frock and put the palm of his hand on her bare belly. She sighed into his mouth, her wet tongue touching his. Under his hand the skin of her belly was like satin and at any other time he would be on his knees to kiss it. But time was short, and so he slid his hand down inside the tiny briefs she was wearing until he touched short and springy curls.

'Mein Gott!' she murmured in the dark, her mouth pressed hotly against his.

Also available

- CHAMPIONS OF LOVE
- CHAMPIONS OF PLEASURE
- A MAN WITH A MAID, VOLUME I
- A MAN WITH A MAID, VOLUME II
- A MAN WITH A MAID, VOLUME III
- THE ROMANCE OF LUST, BOOK ONE
- THE ROMANCE OF LUST, BOOK TWO
- SUBURBAN SOULS, BOOK ONE
- SUBURBAN SOULS, BOOK TWO
- OH WICKED COUNTRY!
- BEATRICE
- EVELINE
- MORE EVELINE
- 'FRANK' AND I
- THE ALTAR OF VENUS
- THREE TIMES A WOMAN
- THE MEMOIRS OF DOLLY MORTON
- THE ADVENTURES OF A SCHOOLBOY
- LAURA MIDDLETON
- THE BOUDOIR
- ROSA FIELDING
- RANDIANA
- THE LUSTFUL TURK
- INSTRUMENT OF PLEASURE
- SENSUAL SECRETS
- CAROUSEL
- BLANCHE
- THE FANTASY HUNTERS
- SABINE
- THE GENTLE DEGENERATES
- THE SALINE SOLUTION
- LETTER FROM MY FATHER I & II
- EROTICON
- EROTICON II
- EROTICON III
- EROTICON IV
- LASCIVIOUS SCENES
- PARISIAN FROLICS
- INDISCREET MEMOIRS
- CONFESSIONS OF AN ENGLISH MAID
- VIOLETTE
- A NIGHT IN A MOORISH HAREM
- FLOSSIE
- THE EXPLOITS OF A YOUNG DON JUAN
- THE SECRET WEB
- THE LIFTED CURTAIN
- REGINE
- UNDER THE ROOFS OF PARIS
- A GALLERY OF NUDES
- THE PLEASURES OF LOLOTTE
- ROMAN ORGY
- DREAMS OF FAIR WOMEN
- THE LASCIVIOUS MONK
- THE PRIMA DONNA
- THE TWO SISTERS
- MY SEX, MY SOUL

DIPLOMATIC PLEASURES

Antoine Lelouche

NEXUS

A NEXUS BOOK
published by
the Paperback Division of
W. H. Allen & Co. plc

A Nexus Book
Published in 1990
by the Paperback Division of
W. H. Allen & Co. plc
Sekforde House, 175/9 St. John Street,
London, EC1V 4LL

First published in Great Britain by
W. H. Allen & Co. plc in 1989

Copyright © Antoine Lelouche 1989

Printed and bound in Great Britain by
Cox & Wyman Ltd, Reading

ISBN 0 352 32316 7

This book is sold subject to the condition that it shall not, by way of trade or otherwise, be lent, re-sold, hired out, or otherwise circulated without the publisher's prior consent in any form of binding or cover other than that in which it is published and without a similar condition including this condition being imposed on the subsequent purchaser.

Contents

Author's Note		7
1.	A Celebration of Liberty, Equality and Fraternity	9
2.	Nightingales in an Embassy Garden	25
3.	The Comforts of the Grand Hotel Orient	41
4.	Frolics in Shah Jehan's Bed	57
5.	A Party at Madame da Silva's	73
6.	Storm Above and Storm Below	90
7.	A Night of Satisfactions and Resentments	106
8.	A Martyr's Crown is Worth a Fortune	122
9.	Secrets Under the Fig-tree	138
10.	The Fastest Gun in the West	154
11.	Nothing so Constant as Inconstancy	171
12.	The Tranquil Pleasures of the Countryside	187
13.	To Encourage the Others, as Voltaire Put It	203
14.	The Gates of Paradise are Opened Wide	220
15.	Gratitude is Often a Hope for Further Favours	237

16. When Everyone is Wrong, Everyone is Right   253

By no means an author's diplomatic apology – more a tribute to the exuberance of his youth

That diplomats have the same appetites and frailties as other men, enjoy the same pleasures and commit the same improprieties, is a matter of simple logic. Yet it is well understood that diplomats in retirement do not publish accounts of their misadventures abroad in the service of their country, particularly not the more intimate episodes.

The reason for this reticence is easily explained. It is the conventional view of governments that a diplomat in a strange bedroom is in some way bringing disgrace on his country. Apart from being the most obvious nonsense, this view is also hypocritical, for no group rivals the notoriety of politicians in the matter of clandestine sexuality.

There are aspects of my own years abroad in the service of France which are well worth the telling. Not that they illuminate our international policies in those years, nor expose any great secrets of State – it was my dearest though unrealised ambition to have nothing to do with such dangerous matters. The sole reason for my wish to relate the events which befell me is that they were very amusing.

So that no over-zealous person may accuse me of publishing anything which ought to remain confidential, I have cast my memoirs in the form of a novel. The casual reader is at liberty to assume that the Marcel Lamont who appears in these pages is a wholly fictional person and only my friends know how closely his escapades correspond with my own, over thirty years ago.

It has not been necessary to rely on memory alone for the reconstruction of my time on the island of Santa Sabina, for it has been my lifelong custom to keep a detailed journal. Though the names have been changed to protect the guilty and innocent alike, the facts were written down at the time and can be confirmed. As to the conversations, the broad outlines are authentic and I have recreated the details as best I can.

Yet even with the cloak of fiction to protect the reputations of those who feature in my little book, I have been advised not to put my own name to it, since that might enable ill-disposed persons to identify some of *Marcel Lamont*'s close acquaintances whose activities were not entirely blameless. I therefore recommend my little volume of fictionalised memoirs to the public under the *nom-de-plume* of:

Antoine Lelouche,
Paris, 1988

1

A Celebration of Liberty, Equality and Fraternity

It was at the Fourteenth of July celebrations at the French Embassy in the Republic of Santa Sabina that Marcel Lamont made up his mind to become the next lover of Trudi Pfaff, a German woman he hardly knew. They were on the terrace overlooking the Embassy gardens, pretending to seek a refreshing breath of air from the sea, though for Santa Sabina it was a tolerable evening – the temperature not much above 30C now that the sun was down. As ever, the air was clammy and the sluggish breeze off the sea much resembled the vapour in a steam-bath.

Marcel was sweating lightly in his formal evening clothes, but everyone sweated all the time in that climate. Like the other European women at the reception, Trudi was wearing as little as was consistent with propriety and fashion – a short evening frock cut low over her full breasts. It was of the thinnest possible silk, its colour between dusty pink and pale orange. The effect of her frock and her straw-blonde hair was to remind Marcel of the huge exotic flowers in the Embassy garden.

He had been in Santa Sabina less than a year and he had met Frau Pfaff perhaps seven or eight times altogether. Mostly they had encountered each other at the never-ending round of diplomatic functions, but twice he had talked to her on the Reserved Beach. It was named that because it was reserved for those who could afford to pay the entrance fee and buy the cold drinks on offer. This meant in effect that it was used almost exclusively by the foreign diplomatic corps and any travelling businessmen misguided enough to visit the island.

It was on the Reserved Beach that Marcel had become fully aware of Trudi Pfaff's very considerable personal charms and his imagination had suggested that a closer acquaintance with her would be pleasurable in the extreme. She was about the same age as he was, he guessed, which was twenty-six, and she was very beautiful in a heavy and blonde Teutonic style. Sprawled on a beach-towel in the sun, she was flagrantly provocative, the upper part of her white swim-suit almost inadequate to contain the fleshy delights within it.

The boys employed as beach-attendants found it impossible to keep their eyes off her, jostling each other for the privilege of serving her with a glass of iced mint tea or lemonade when she beckoned. The lucky boy who won the tussle would present her with a tiny dish of dried figs or cashew nuts or some other local delicacy with her cold drink. When at last he retreated reluctantly back to the palm leaf-thatched hut under the trees where the refreshments came from, the evidence of his youthful arousal was plainly visible through his tight shorts. The other boys would greet their friend's return with grins and fingers pointing at his bulge, then follow him behind the hut to watch him relieve his tension by hand – the inhabitants of Santa Sabina being totally without shame in sexual matters.

When Trudi rolled over on her towel, her breasts moved in a way that brought a smile of delight to the lips of any man fortunate enough to be observing her. The sight of her golden-skinned thighs gleaming with sun-oil aroused the most extravagant fantasies. If the venerable old Cardinal-Archbishop of Santa Sabina had ventured near the beach when Trudi was sunning herself, not even a lifetime of prayer and celibacy could have saved him from temptation.

It was not because Trudi was married that Marcel had so far controlled his natural inclination to become more closely acquainted with her. A senior colleague at the Embassy had warned him that she had an understanding with the Minister of Commerce and Fine Arts of Santa Sabina, and that to risk annoying so important a member of the host government would be highly imprudent. For the honour of France, Marcel directed his attentions elsewhere.

She arrived at the Fourteenth of July reception with her husband and was soon lost in the crowd of guests. Some time later Marcel found her in front of a large landscape painting supposed to be by Antoine Watteau, though anyone interested in art could see it was a copy. She was talking to Mr Hakimoto and Mr Kamizaki of the Japanese Embassy – neither of them taller than her bare shoulder. Both men had solemn expressions, but the glint in their jet-black eyes proclaimed that behind the inscrutable exterior there burned the fires of fierce Oriental lust for the beautiful body they were careful not to look at directly.

The Minister of Commerce and Fine Arts, with whom Frau Pfaff was said to have an understanding, was not present, though he had naturally been invited. But he had been dismissed from the government since the invitations were sent out and was now under house arrest. No official announcement of the reason had yet been made, but politics in Santa Sabina were volatile by European standards and ministers came and went in rapid succession. Only the President of the Republic was permanent, the office being hereditary in his family for well over a century.

Marcel bowed and said *bonsoir* to Trudi, well pleased that there was nothing to prevent an approach to her now that the misfortunes of political life had removed an admirer from her side. He glanced in admiration at the full breasts moulded by her colourful frock and then up into her pale blue eyes. He smiled with meaning. She smiled back in a way that suggested she was not unaware of his charm. A quarter of an hour later they were on the terrace, listening to the music through the open french windows. It was regrettably second-rate, being the offering of a string quartet on a cultural exchange visit. But then, Santa Sabina did not rate the highest quality in anything, not even in the champagne that was being served.

'It is a very pleasant party, Monsieur Lamont,' said Trudi in a correct but heavily-accented French.

'You are enjoying yourself, Madame? Often these occasions can be too formal, but I find myself in agreement with you – this evening is different.'

'Perhaps it is the champagne,' she suggested.

'Perhaps,' Marcel agreed. 'There is something which makes the heart beat a little faster in the sight of a champagne bottle being opened. The way in which the wine gushes out – only the French nation could have devised such an entertainment.'

They had somehow progressed right down to the end of the terrace, well away from the others. As usual the sky was dark and overcast. Strings of coloured lanterns had been looped between the palm-trees in the garden to give it a festive air, but they were small and dim.

'In Germany too we have sparkling wines,' Trudi said. 'They are very popular.'

Marcel moved to put Trudi between himself and the nearest guests further along the terrace. He reached out gently to touch her hip and stroke it through the thin silk of her frock. It was an approach which might have earned him an instant rebuke from another woman. But as he guessed, she was waiting for him to indicate his intentions and did not move away from him. On the contrary, his directness seemed to please her.

'I have heard of your sparkling wines,' said Marcel as his hand caressed her hip and moved towards her thigh. 'Perhaps they are good enough in their way, but there is only one champagne in the world and it is made exclusively by the French.'

Through her thin frock his fingertips skimmed lightly for an instant over a plump and fleshy mound at the join of her thighs.

'I have visited Paris twice,' said Trudi, a little breathlessly, as well she might be at a moment of such exquisite anticipation.

'With your husband, no doubt?'

Every electric light in the city flickered and went out. No one was in the least surprised, for the ancient generator which supplied power to the capital failed two or three a times a week. Inside the Embassy the musicians stopped playing, a few laughs could be heard, and then conversation resumed normally. It usually took twenty minutes or half an hour for the employees of the generating station to get their antiquated machinery started again, but Marcel knew he had at most five minutes to exploit his advantage. The Embassy servants had already gone to get the bottled gas-lamps kept for these occasions.

In the dark he took a step towards Trudi and kissed her willing lips while he fondled her breasts through the thin silk. He felt the tip of her tongue slide between his lips and at once he reached under her frock and put the palm of his hand on her bare belly. She sighed into his mouth, her wet tongue touching his. Under his hand the skin of her belly was like satin and at any other time he would be on his knees to kiss it. But time was short, and so he slid his hand down inside the tiny briefs she was wearing until he touched short and springy curls.

'*Mein Gott!*' she murmured in the dark, her mouth pressed hotly against his.

Her feet moved apart to separate her thighs. Marcel's hand slid a little deeper into her silk underwear and caressed the fleshy lips he found. In his experience no woman refused a man after his hand had been between her legs. Trudi responded by groping for the hard shaft inside his black evening trousers.

'You are adorable,' he whispered as the kiss ended, his fingers gently busy down below.

'Marcel!' she breathed ardently, her grasp very tight.

'Do you know what the Santa Sabinans call the part of me you are holding?' he asked tenderly.

If, as rumour insisted, Frau Pfaff had been on terms of intimacy with the Minister of Commerce and Fine Arts, then it was certain that she knew the word. But this was a game they were playing together and it had its rules. One was that they should both pretend and behave as if she were a faithful young wife falling in love for the first time with a man other than her husband.

'Tell me,' she whispered.

'You are holding my *zimbriq*,' he said, 'and I am caressing your beautiful *kuft*.'

He heard her sigh of pleasure, but time had run out. Lights appeared inside the building and were moving toward the terrace. Marcel gave her a fond squeeze and removed his hand to let her frock fall back into place. The servants were setting hissing gas-lamps along the terrace and Marcel moved to a polite distance from Trudi.

'Meet me tomorrow,' he said, 'at three in the afternoon.'

Trudi nodded, her beautiful face slightly pink in the gaslight.

'Don't look round, but your husband is coming to look for you,' Marcel warned her.

'Where shall we meet?' she asked quickly.

'At the Grand Hotel Orient. It is in San Feliz Square.'

'Who shall I ask for?'

'For me, of course! Do you believe that I wish to love you anonymously?'

'But is that sensible? There is so much gossip here.'

Herr Pfaff had spotted his wife and was halfway along the terrace towards her.

'Then ask for Mr Smith,' said Marcel with a grin, 'Mr John Smith – I believe that our British colleagues use that name for assignations in hotels.'

Trudi began to laugh, a full-throated laugh that made

her sumptuous breasts quiver inside her frock. Then Herr Pfaff was at her elbow, smiling politely.

'You have amused my wife, Monsieur Lamont,' he said. 'May I also hear the joke?'

'But of course,' Marcel answered with a shrug. 'I was explaining to Madame that only a small accident of history prevented the celebrated Marquis de Sade from becoming a leader of the Revolution we are celebrating today – as celebrated as Danton or Robespierre, perhaps.'

Herr Pfaff looked puzzled.

'You cannot mean the depraved person who wrote the obscene books, surely?' he asked.

'The very same! He was imprisoned in the Bastille for his sexual experiments. But the governor of the prison concluded that the Marquis was more insane than criminal and transferred him to the lunatic asylum at Charenton.'

'Insane or criminal – there can be no difference where such a pervert is concerned,' the German exclaimed.

'But consider – one week later the Bastille was stormed and captured by the revolutionaries. If the divine Marquis had still been there, he would have been liberated by the mob and hailed as an oppressed victim of the old regime. He could have become a national hero. His *120 Days of Sodom* would have been promoted as a great revolutionary work, like your own German countryman's book *Das Kapital*.'

Gunther Pfaff was not amused by the reference to Karl Marx.

'It is not correct to make jokes about degeneracy,' he said primly. 'Excuse me, Monsieur.'

He took Trudi by the arm and led her away. Marcel stayed on the terrace for a few more moments, recalling the sensation of Trudi's warm flesh under his fingers. That had been real; pleasure was real; delight between men and women was real. Most other things on Santa Sabina were sham.

Until a few years before, no government in the world had thought it worthwhile to maintain any kind of diplomatic representation on so insignificant an island as Santa Sabina. But that changed instantly when survey teams indicated the possibility of a vast oilfield off the west coast, and massive quantities of gold and rare minerals – including uranium ore – in the mountains of the interior.

At the same time it was realised by all the nuclear powers that Santa Sabina was extremely well-sited geographically as a base for long-range bombers, rockets and submarines, if permission could be obtained to set up bases on the island. Almost overnight the United States, the USSR, the Japanese, the French, the British and a score of other nations were offering Santa Sabina help and friendship, technical assistance, modern weapons, development loans, cultural exchanges and all the other benefits of modern diplomacy.

Not a new story, of course, but the essence of the joke in Marcel's view was that the President of Santa Sabina was wily enough to accept everything that was offered free, and at the same time remain completely unaligned and independent. Indeed, in his first week on the island Marcel had discovered that there was nothing whatsoever to be achieved. As he saw it, the foreign powers were like so many rich old men bidding for the favours of a desirable young woman. But she was too clever for them. She took all their expensive presents and in return gave them no more than a smile and a quick feel to keep them interested. Her legs remained firmly together.

A more urgent problem than the future of high diplomacy on Santa Sabina was that Marcel's moments with Trudi had aroused him to the point where something must be done. There was, of course, Madame da Silva's establishment on the Avenue of the Constitution, where the girls were pretty and well-experienced in the ways of love. But Marcel knew from past visits that if he started to play with one of Madame's girls he would stay all night and be too drained of nervous energy to meet Trudi at three the next afternoon.

Naturally, there was an answer to his problem. He

left the terrace and circulated inside the Embassy, looking for Eunice Carpenter of the Consular section of the British Embassy. He found her chatting to the daughter of the American Ambassador about horses and riding. The American girl seemed to Marcel to be a textbook example of healthy young Californian womanhood. She was nineteen or twenty, tall, with long straight yellow hair, perfect teeth, and large, perfectly-shaped breasts.

There was about Sherri Hazlitt an air of cleanliness so antiseptic that Marcel had never given a moment's consideration to her potential as a woman. It was not possible to imagine her well-showered body sweaty and slippery with the passion of love-making. Nor did she give much impression of intelligence. The most charitable theory as to why she was in Santa Sabina with her parents was that she had been expelled from every fashionable college in the United States, had nowhere else to go, and was incapable of earning a living.

By contrast, the English woman was into her forties and showing streaks of grey in her dark hair. She wore clothes which were too tight, so that being plump, the protuberances of her heavy breasts and belly had an air of defiance, as if to compensate for the sad truth that she was no longer young. That aside, Marcel had discovered soon after his arrival in Santa Sabina that Eunice Carpenter extended a warm welcome to young men. It was perhaps discourteous to compare her to a taxi, always available for the next passenger, but she turned few men away.

Marcel had first become aware of Eunice's availability on the Reserved Beach, late one afternoon when the heat was almost overwhelming and he had gone to plunge into the sea to cool himself down. There were only a few people left on the beach, it being the hour when wives who had little to do but spend their afternoons on the sand were on their way home to prepare for their husbands' return. Marcel closed his eyes against the light and the gentle hiss and splash of the little waves lulled him to sleep.

When he awoke there was a woman sitting beside him – a plump woman in a tightly-stretched bathing-costume of bright yellow. Marcel shaded his eyes with his hand to stare up at her round and chubby face and she grinned at him. She was at least forty years old he thought, and her body was big and flabby inside her too-tight costume. But she had a humorous smile that he found pleasing.

'Bonsoir, Madame,' he said, smiling at her politely.

'Hello,' she answered in English, 'were you having a nice dream?'

'I was not dreaming,' he said, not understanding the point of her question.

'Yes, you were. I've been sitting here ten minutes watching *this* twitching,' she said.

To Marcel's astonishment she tapped the long bulge in his swimming-trunks with a fingertip. Another man might have felt some sense of embarrassment at having his attention drawn to his condition of sexual arousal by a stranger. But women had shown a lively interest in Marcel's body since his adolescence and he took it as normal for them to be fascinated by his male part when it stood hard.

'There is an aphrodisiac drug in the air of this island,' he said, hoping that he was using the right English expressions. 'Since the day I arrived here I have thought of little else but making love. My *zimbriq*, as the natives call it, has been in a permanent state of arousal. Can you explain this, Madame?'

She chuckled, a hearty little sound that caused her belly to wobble inside its bright yellow covering.

'I know just what you mean, my dear,' she told him. 'I've been here nearly three years myself and I've had more men in that time than in all my life before. Don't you think that's tremendous?'

Her pleasure in this casual revelation of her amours made Marcel smile. There was something engaging in her lack of embarrassment, he thought, and a moment later she displayed her candour even further by laying the palm of her hand over the bulge in his swimming-trunks. He glanced round quickly and saw that they were the only two people on the beach.

'You can't leave here in this state,' she said. 'Would you like me to help you make it lie down?'

'Here on the beach?' he asked incredulously.

'No, silly – in the changing-hut. Come on!' and she heaved herself to her feet and held out her hand to him.

From where he lay at her feet, Marcel saw the plumpness of the mound between her chubby thighs and the overhang of her breasts above him. At another time he would have declined her offer politely, but she was offering a service at the very moment he needed it. He stood up and accompanied his new friend across the sand to where a row of trees made a natural boundary, and below them stood a line of changing-huts. They were roofless and built somewhat precariously.

'My name's Eunice,' said the woman leading Marcel along by the hand. 'What's yours?'

She opened the door of a hut and he saw her clothes hanging on a hook and her shoes on the bench-seat at the back.

'Marcel Lamont,' he said, pulling the door to behind him.

'It's a pleasure to make your acquaintance, Marcel,' she said – her hand down the front of his swimming-trunks to take hold of his *zimbriq* and shake it as if it were his hand.

Marcel laughed at that and she laughed with him. He put his hands on her bare shoulders and slid off the straps of her costume so that he could pull it down to her waist and feel her over-size danglers.

'Ah,' he murmured appreciatively, 'I adore women with big soft breasts.'

Eunice let him play with them, her round face wreathed in smiles, while she pushed his shorts down his legs and massaged his *zimbriq* with one hand and his warm pendants with the other.

'I've been dying to get my hand round this since I watched it going stiff in your shorts,' she said. 'I knew you'd be in the mood for a quickie when you woke up. Do you believe in long engagements? I don't.'

'What do you mean?' Marcel asked, not understanding at all.

'I got hot and bothered waiting for you to wake up. I'm trying to tell you that I'm ready,' she answered, grinning at him.

She let go of him to push her bathing-costume down her legs and step out of it. When she straightened up again Marcel put a hand between her thighs to clasp the plump and hairy mound he found there.

'Now you've got the idea,' she said, giving his throbbing part a strong stroking that made him gasp.

He was assessing the ways of making love in the confines of the tiny roofless changing-hut. Standing face to face, his back was brushing the planking behind him and her full moon of a bottom was resting against the wall at her back. The only possibility was to push her feet apart and take her standing up, but he had the gravest anxiety that the flimsy hut would collapse if too much weight was put against it. Eunice saw his momentary hesitation and guessed the reason.

'I'll show you how,' she said, and turned to bend over and put her hands flat on the bench built across the back of the hut.

'You have made love in these huts before,' Marcel exclaimed, grinning as he contemplated the big bare cheeks thrust towards him and the dark-haired split below.

'Many a time!' she said cheerfully.

He stood close behind her and opened her neatly.

'Oh yes – right in!' she gasped as he pierced her with his stiff shaft and pressed his belly against her bottom.

He reached forward and under to take hold of her big flabby breasts and squeeze them while he rode her.

'That's absolutely fantastic!' she sighed. 'You're going to make me very happy in about five seconds!'

Perhaps, as Eunice had suggested, his stiffness when he awoke on the sand *was* due to a forgotten dream that had stirred his fantasies. Whatever had brought it about, the truth was that Marcel was highly aroused even before Eunice had put her hand over his bulge. After that it was merely a question of time and opportunity – and both had presented themselves at once in the privacy of the changing-hut. He slid rapidly in and out of her wet warmth, on the brink of a delightful crisis after no more than five or six strokes.

'Oh my God, yes!' Eunice exclaimed loudly and joyfully as her climax overwhelmed her and her body shook uncontrollably.

Marcel responded with an incoherent *ah, oui, chérie, oui!* his hands clenched tight in the soft flesh of her breasts. His head was thrown back as he felt his golden moments rushing towards him, so that he was staring up at the sky. Above him, less than half a metre away, two faces grinned over the hut wall from the next cabin. Marcel's excitement was too advanced to halt and a moment later the boys were giggling at the expression on his face and the furious jerking of his body as he spouted his ecstasy into the Englishwoman's belly.

By the time he recovered the boys had disappeared. His sense of outrage at being spied on was soon dispelled when he found that Eunice was amused by it. Another woman would have blushed for shame to know that someone had observed her being penetrated by a man, but not Eunice. She offered at once to bend over again and let Marcel do it unobserved, if he had any sense of grievance. But he suggestd that they leave and he took her to a bar and then to dinner. Later on, in the privacy of his bedroom, he made love to her again, this time on her back and more thoroughly.

In the months which had passed since that day, Marcel had come to know how obliging Eunice was in times of urgent need. With this in mind, he detached her as soon as he reasonably could from her conversation with the American girl and led her out to the terrace. Only a few guests were still outside, now that dancing had begun in the Embassy ballroom, and the coloured lights between the trees had not come back on after the power failure. They stood by the steps which led down to the dark garden, and waited for the right moment to arrive before going any further.

'I haven't seen you all evening,' Eunice said cheerfully, 'where have you been?'

However adventurous her exploration of the pleasures of love with men of various nations, she spoke no language but English. Like many others before him who had followed her well-beaten path to pleasure, Marcel had to use her language and hope that words could soon be abandoned in favour of those actions which were understood in every part of the world.

'One has duties on these official occasions,' he answered. 'There are guests to be greeted and entertained. I am sure that you understand.'

'Oh, I understand all right! I saw you greeting and entertaining the German woman with her bosom hanging out.'

A quick glance around showed Marcel that no one was looking their way. He took Eunice by the elbow and led her down the stone steps into the garden until they were well away from the building. She giggled when he turned off the gravel path to pull her behind a tree and stand her with her back to its trunk. Though she had sneered at Trudi's extensive *décolletage*, her own frock was equally low-cut and Marcel had no difficulty in putting a hand down the front of it to fondle a bare breast. One of Eunice's many idiosyncrasies was that she never wore a brassière, even though a certain sagging would have made it advisable at her age.

'You mean Frau Pfaff, I suppose,' Marcel said casually, his fingertips stroking the warm bud of a breast to make it stand up.

'I suppose you had your hand down her clothes too, you beast, when you took her outside in the black-out.'

'Dear Eunice, I swear to you that yours is the only bosom I have had the honour of caressing today,' said Marcel with complete truthfulness.

'I say!' she exclaimed, as his fingers stirred her very easily aroused passions, 'I believe that you've got something very undiplomatic on your mind, you handsome devil!'

'You are right,' he answered, transferring his attentions to her other breast, 'we find ourselves, you and I, involved in an international incident of formidable proportions.'

Eunice unzipped his trousers with the skill of long practice and put her hand inside to clasp his upright *zimbriq*.

'Formidable is right!' she said. 'You *are* in a state!'

'I was overcome by such powerful emotions that my only thought was to invite you out into the garden,' he murmured.

'Poor thing!' she said, stroking him so pleasurably that his knees trembled. 'It needs a woman's touch. What's got you into this state – are you sure you didn't give that German woman a good feel?'

Marcell pushed her back against the tree and lifted her frock. Her feet were already well apart and his hand between her plump thighs touched curly hair and moist lips. Eunice giggled again.

'I never wear knickers at a party, darling,' she informed him. 'There's always a chance that some lovely man like you will push me into a dark corner for a quickie.'

Marcel's fingers were deep between her warm and very wet folds, flicking over the little bud that triggered her passion. Inside his trousers Eunice's hand was pumping steadily.

'But you've already done it this evening,' he whispered.

'Twice,' she agreed, her voice quavering. 'It's a lovely party – this will be my third thrill tonight.'

'Be quiet!' he whispered urgently. 'Someone is coming!'

'Oh, yes!' she gasped, her parted legs trembling against him.

To silence her, he pressed his mouth over hers, his eyes turning awkwardly in his head to see who was approaching from the terrace. In the darkness two figures passed by along the path, almost within arm's-reach. They were talking very softly to each other and the man's arm was round the woman so that he could fondle her bottom as they walked. They were too involved with each other to notice Marcel squeezing Eunice tightly back against the tree-trunk to muffle her climactic spasms.

2

Nightingales in an Embassy Garden

'That *was* nice,' said Eunice Carpenter, her face a pale oval in the darkness as she looked up at Marcel.

'I was afraid that they would see us here under the tree with my hand up your clothes,' he explained.

'Who do you mean? They can't see us from the terrace.'

'I mean the couple who came down from the terrace and walked past us.'

'I didn't see anyone,' said Eunice. 'The way you were fingering me, I wouldn't have heard a bomb go off.'

'But I think that a little bomb did go off,' said Marcel, 'inside your belly, yes?'

'Who was it that went past?' she asked.

'It was too dark to see properly. The man was in uniform, I think. They were both tall.'

'And now they're having a nice *knee-trembler* further down the garden,' said Eunice.

Marcel had not heard that English expression before and the image it evoked in his mind brought his attention back to the reason why he had brought Eunice into the Embassy garden. Certainly it was not to look at the stars, for the almost permanent cloud-cover over Santa Sabina meant that they were invisible on most nights of the year.

25

'I want to *zeqq* you furiously,' he murmured, his mouth close to her ear. She chuckled to hear him use the Santa Sabinan word for what men do to women.

'About time too,' she breathed.

His feet were inside hers and she guided him to the wet lips between her thighs. He bent his knees and straightened them again slowly.

'Ah!' he sighed as he pushed into her. 'How good that feels, Eunice!'

With his eyes closed and his hands clenched on the bare cheeks of her bottom he tried hard to persuade himself that he was making love to blonde and beautiful Trudi Pfaff rather than middle-aged and overweight Eunice Carpenter. He sighed at feeling Eunice's belly jammed hard against him to meet his thrusts.

'Yes . . . lovely . . .' she murmured.

The fact was that his encounter with Trudi on the terrace, when the lights failed, had aroused Marcel very highly. The fragrance of her expensive perfume lingered in his nostrils, rather than Eunice's unimaginative English lavender water. His fingertips still tingled, at least in his memory, from when they had touched Trudi's soft *kuft*. With his cheek against Eunice's cheek and his eyes tightly closed, he created an image of Trudi in his fantasy and the erotic energy with which he was charged enabled him to believe that he was embedded most delightfully in Trudi's warm belly.

Needless to say, Eunice was unaware that Marcel's restless imagination had transformed her into another woman while her avid reception of his attentions pushed him to the brink and then headlong over it. She moaned and gripped his shoulders hard as he pounded at her and erupted in jolting spasms of delight. Long after he had finished, she was still shuddering and ramming her belly against him, until a final sigh signalled the culmination of her pleasure. Marcel waited until she was calm again before he withdrew from the wet clasp that held him.

'That was beautifully brutal,' she said. 'You must have been utterly desperate.'

'Utterly,' he agreed, grinning in the dark at her British choice of words. 'You are an angel of mercy, dear Eunice.'

'Lend me your hankie,' she said. 'I need to dry my rag and ruin a bit before we go back into the party.'

'Stay very quiet,' Marcel whispered urgently, hearing footsteps behind him.

They both held their breath and stood completely motionless by the tree-trunk as the steps came closer and two people went past, not more than five paces to the right, heading for the steps up to the terrace.

'It didn't take *them* long,' Eunice commented with her little throaty chuckle. 'He must be one of the South American speed-merchants. Can you see who it is?'

The electricity had been switched on again while Marcel and Eunice were occupied with more interesting matters. As the couple went up the steps to the terrace Marcel saw that the man was in dress uniform and the woman was wearing a full-length and backless evening gown.

'It is Colonel Hochheimer, the American Military Attaché,' he said.'

'And who's the lucky girl who's had him up her?' Eunice asked, a touch of envy coarsening her expression.

'I couldn't see,' Marcel answered.

It was a polite lie. The only woman at the reception in a ball-gown like that was Madame Kristensen, the elegant and beautiful wife of the First Secretary at the Danish Embassy. It was not a question of sparing Eunice's feelings, however obvious it was from her tone that she had designs of her own on Colonel Hochheimer. Marcel thought it dishonourable to identify any lady in such circumstances, even to the one who had just obliged him. He zipped up his trousers and kissed Eunice on the cheek.

'Are you content now that you've enjoyed four thrills this evening?' he asked her. 'Or will you look for more?'

'When was once ever enough for *you*?' she retorted,

her arms round his waist to keep him with her under the tree.

'Alas, I am not free to make my own arrangements this evening. I am *on duty*, as you English say. My Ambassador expects me to entertain his guests.'

'I'm a guest and you've entertained me very nicely so far,' said Eunice, 'I'd be happy for you to carry on.'

'Someone else entertained you before I did,' Marcel countered. 'For all I know, you came out into the garden with him and stood with your back against this same tree!'

'No we didn't,' said Eunice, chuckling again. 'I sneaked him into the downstairs ladies' cloakroom and he had me with my back to the door . . .'

'My God!' Marcel exclaimed in mock horror. 'Who is this criminal who has grossly abused the hospitality of the Republic of France?'

'None of your business! Besides, the hospitality was British, not French. And it was abused beautifully!'

'I meant the Embassy facilities. Do you imagine cloakrooms are provided so that guests can enjoy casual *knee-tremblers* with each other?'

'Why not?' Eunice asked. 'It's private and comfortable in there – come with me and see for yourself.'

'I know who you were with! I saw you talking to him in the hall – that Dutchman, Pieter van Buuren. The man's a monster of depravity!'

'It sounds as if you know him well. He must be a friend of yours.'

'We know each other pretty well,' Marcel agreed, 'I must return you to the party now, dear Eunice.'

'Don't be in such a hurry,' she said. 'There's something I want to say to you.'

'Of course. What is it?'

'All the times you and I have done it together it's usually been a hit-and-run job. Not that I'm complaining – I enjoy it with you anytime and anywhere. But I've got this feeling that you might be the man to see me off properly.'

'See you off? What do you mean?' Marcel asked.

'*Zeqq* me senseless,' she explained. 'Shaft me to a standstill. Ruin me for life.'

'Dear Eunice, you flatter me.'

'It's never been done yet, but I think you're the right man for it. Come home with me tonight.'

'I regret that is impossible. The last guests will not leave until very late and even then the Ambassador will want me to stay longer, so that he can pass on any important items of information he has picked up during the evening.'

'I don't mind how late it is. I'll be naked and waiting for you in my little apartment even if it's three in the morning.'

'The offer is enchanting,' said Marcel, easing himself out of her encircling arms and kissing her hand to soften the refusal, 'but I shall be too tired by then to do you justice. We must postpone this marathon of love until some other time.'

'I suppose you're right,' said Eunice with reluctance. 'Come round one evening and I'll make sure you enjoy yourself. Any evening you like.'

'I will see what can be arranged.'

He almost meant it, certain that Eunice's unabashed lubricity would guarantee an immensely pleasurable encounter. But, at the same time, intuition warned him that anything more than the most casual of contacts with her might lead into undesirable complications. However greatly he enjoyed her complete and most un-British lack of inhibition, he guessed her nature to be more complex than he either understood or wished to understand.

Towards midnight he found himself dancing with the Ambassador's wife, at her invitation rather than his. Madame Ducour was approaching fifty, but had spent so much of her adult life caring for her appearance that she remained attractive. She was slender, had a good complexion, and kept her short sleek hair dyed a lustrous black. Her clothes were made in Paris by the very best couturiers and sent out in the diplomatic bag. For this evening's grand occasion she was wearing a knee-length evening frock in shiny black satin, entirely backless and cut low on her well-preserved bosom. Her admirably narow waist was nipped in tight by a sash with a bow at the back, and below that the frock flared out stiffly.

Indeed, so dramatic was the flare of Madame Ducour's frock that dancers behind her were afforded a glimpse of the backs of her thighs as she swayed and turned in Marcel's arms. And looking over her bare shoulder as he whirled her about in a dashing Viennese waltz, Marcel observed for an instant in the gilt-framed mirrors that lined the ballroom a flash of pale skin above Madame's black silk stockings. Pleased with the effect of white skin gleaming between the transparent black of her stockings and the richer black of her frock, he whirled her in fast and tight turns right round the ballroom.

Marcel's pleasure was aesthetic rather than sensual, for he had been privileged to see more of the Ambassador's wife than the backs of her thighs, charming though they were. No one who had seen her on the Reserved Beach could possibly deny that her legs were a good deal more shapely than those of most women half her age. Naturally, Marcel had seen her sunning herself often enough. But apart from that, there had been other occasions when he had seen even more of her than was revealed by a fashionably tight bathing-costume. To be exact, he had seen all of her, including the plaything concealed between her thighs. And more than once.

The truth was that, behind her careful facade of good manners and hauteur, Jacqueline Ducour was a predator of handsome young men. Marcel had not been long in Santa Sabina when she had, with effortless grace, seduced him. It was not until she lay naked beneath him, making little sighing sounds in the aftermath of a genteel climax, that he realised what had happened to him. His amazement rendered him speechless at the time and the image that remained in his memory was Jacqueline, dressed and departing, turning at the door of his room to give a little farewell wave with her white-gloved hand. Her lips pouted in an amused kiss to see him lying naked on his bed with his exploited *zimbriq* limp against his thigh.

After she had gone, Marcel laughed uproariously to think that he had been cajoled into bed as if he were a young girl. His respect for Jacqueline was boundless and he waited her next visit with great interest. Over the next month or two she dropped in on him at the Grand Hotel Orient two or three times a week. The hotel owner was so impressed by Marcel's connection with the wife of an Ambassador that he asked whether it would be considered appropriate to extend his establishment's name to *Grand Hotel Orient de France* and he was very disappointed when Marcel persuaded him that it would be unwise.

For Jacqueline's first few visits to his room Marcel was content to play along with her expert little game of seduction. She would lie gracefully on his bed, having removed all her fashionable clothes except fragile knickers of silk and lace, displaying her slack but still attractive breasts and her slender thighs. *Kiss me, chéri*, she would murmur, *I can only stay a moment*. And as he lay beside her, fully clothed at her insistence, to kiss her half-parted lips and then the small tips of her breasts, she would sigh *Tell me that you love me or my heart will break*.

How exciting was the fragrance of the perfume she had sprayed in her hair and on her neck and breasts! How sensuous the expression in her large brown eyes! Her fingers were long and thin and sensitive and she understood very expertly how to use them to bewitch young men into doing what she wanted them to do. Her fingertips traced little patterns round the corners of Marcel's mouth and down the sides of his neck, until he shivered with sensation. Those wheedling fingers of hers found their way into his shirt to tickle his flat nipples with such gentle skill that his back arched and he sighed continuously. Jacqueline watched his expression closely, her red-painted mouth open and curved in a beatific smile.

Madame Ducour was no ordinary woman of fifty who parted her legs to persuade young men to pleasure her. In a lifetime of sexual adventure she had acquired a kind of magic. Without permitting Marcel to do more to her than kiss her breasts, she mesmerised him into a state of erotic delirium. By the time she unzipped his trousers and put her hand inside, his emotions were so intense that he thought he was about to discharge his passion into her hand. But he was wrong – Jacqueline had no intention of letting him achieve anything other than her own pleasure.

Those long and sensitive fingers of hers with their red-painted nails and gold and diamond rings caressed his twitching *zimbriq* with a light and sure touch. She made him lie on his back while she pulled his trousers down to his knees and ran her fingertips over his engorged part until his sensations were so devastating that pleasure was hovering on the threshold of pain. *You are so beautiful, chéri,* she murmured, *tell me that you love me, or I shall die.*

She knew well enough how to recognise when his nervous system was so heavily overloaded that in another few moments it would burn out completely. Only then did she condescend to permit matters to proceed to their natural conclusion, her thin tantalising fingers releasing him as she murmured that he might remove her knickers. His hands were trembling as he slid them down her slim legs to bare her brown-curled delight.

'Come to me, Marcel,' she said softly, her knees up and wide apart.

After so astonishing a degree of stimulation it required very little to bring about his climactic release. He kissed the thin pink lips between her thighs in fervent gratitude, but even then she did not relinquish her control of him. She took his throbbing shaft between her exciting fingertips and guided it slowly to the opening she had exposed for him. *Slowly, chéri, show me how you love me slowly*, she sighed as he slid into her.

But matters had already gone beyond any question of fast or slow, and Jacqueline knew it. The very act of sliding into her precipitated Marcel's climax instantly. He could do nothing but writhe on her belly while his passion squirted into her. Nor did Jacqueline desire any other outcome. Not for her the ordinary pleasures of long penetration and wet skin rubbing on wet skin. Her pleasures were of a different sort.

At the instant she felt Marcel enter her, she uttered a soft moan and dissolved into gentle ecstasy. For her, that was what she wanted – she had achieved her purpose in seducing a handsome young man to the point where he was helpless in her hands. And not only her hands, of course, he was even more helpless in her belly, for she had made him give up the very essence of his youthful virility at the exact moment she had enticed him into her.

After two or three episodes of this type, Marcel began to assert his natural male dominance when Jacqueline came to see him. She found that he was no longer content just to kiss her slack little breasts while she played with him. He clasped them tightly and felt them thoroughly. And the next time that she lay on his bed and held his hard shaft in her long and sensitive fingers, he slid his hand down into her pretty silk knickers.

Ah no, chéri, you will break my heart if you touch me like that she murmured, her lean bottom wriggling on the bed as his fingers explored the warm lips under her tuft of brown curls.

'But I love you, Jacqueline, I love you to distraction,' Marcel countered, untruthfully, of course.

He stopped any more complaints by pressing his mouth over hers in a long kiss while his fingers pressed gently into her. And soon after that she cut short her teasing to push her knickers down and pull him on top of her. In this way it came about, because Marcel wished it so, that by stages they changed roles in their love-games. *He* was the one who teased her with his fingers until *she* begged him to mount her and bring about her pleasurable release.

Eventually the day came when he was able to persuade her to let him make love to her twice before she got up and dressed – previously she had never wanted or permitted more than one brief connection. As far as Marcel could judge, she did not share his second climax, and all the while he was on her this second time, her mesmerising fingertips roamed from his face to his groin to ensure that she was at his mercy for as brief a time as she need be.

Even so, by gentle persistence he finally achieved a moment which charmed him more than he would have thought possible. On her next two visits he accustomed her to being penetrated twice and then, the next time, he deployed all the skills of love he had learned in the beds of Paris and succeeded in reducing her to ecstatic sobbing in the first convulsive climax he witnessed in her. Afterwards she was utterly devastated and it was necessary to send down for a glass of cognac from the hotel bar to revive her a little before she was strong enough to put her clothes on and go home in a taxi.

After that, she never came to his room again. He made discreet enquiries and found that she had a new interest – a recent arrival at the Brazilian Embassy. This was twenty-two-year old Captain Gonzales, who had got himself into trouble at home and put his influential family to the trouble of having him sent abroad in the diplomatic service. He had a weak chin and a thin black moustache that failed to disguise the girlish prettiness of his face. It was Marcel's opinion that Jacqueline had found a very suitable partner for her teasing game.

'Oh, Jacqueline,' he said, as they waltzed round the Embassy ballroom, 'you will break my heart if you look at me like that.'

At the echo of her own words Jacqueline's eyes closed for a moment and she drew in her breath sharply.

'Dear Marcel,' she responded, 'you broke my heart long ago. You cannot imagine how lonely I am now.'

'But where is the handsome Captain Gonzales tonight?'

'Do not mock me, Marcel – I cannot bear it.'

'But I assure you that I have the greatest respect for you,' he said – and meant it.

'No, really – haven't you heard?' she asked. 'He got into trouble and was sent home in disgrace a week ago.'

'He is a more enterprising man than I gave him credit for,' said Marcel. 'How can anyone get into trouble in Santa Sabina? There is nothing to spy on and no secrets to sell. There is no money to steal. Rape is out of the question when the women welcome every kind of approach. And I do not believe the baby-faced Captain is capable of killing anyone, in spite of his uniform.'

'It's too hot to dance,' said Jacqueline, 'let's sit over there by the windows and have a glass of champagne. It is most surprising that my poor Alfonsino's misadventure isn't being gossiped about – I did not think that Latin Americans were capable of so much discretion.'

They sat on an imitation Second Empire sofa under the open window and amused each other with speculations on what the transgressions of the gallant young Brazilian Captain might have been. There were many couples out on the terrace now, vainly searching for a breath of cool air. And after so much champagne had been drunk it was possible, Marcel thought, that every tree in the garden sheltered a couple enjoying vertical love-making. Or in Eunice's colourful phrase, *having a nice knee-trembler*.

On the way back to the ballroom Jacqueline said that there was something of importance she must confide. She glanced round quickly, opened a door half-concealed under the main staircase, and pulled Marcel inside. The room was, as he knew very well, a small office with a desk. Jacqueline did not turn on the light, and that confirmed his suspicion that what she had to confide was of an intimate nature. Any lingering doubt vanished when she took his face in her hands and kissed him delicately.

While it was true that the hot desires aroused in him

by Trudi Pfaff had been temporarily satisfied in the Embassy garden by Eunice, Marcel found that his carnal appetite was being rapidly reawakened. Partly it was Jacqueline's body pressed against him, partly her perfume and the feel of her bare back under his hands. But in the main it was due to those clever fingers of hers, caressing the corners of his mouth and the hollow of his throat. In his dark evening trousers his shaft stirred itself and rose to its full height.

'Jacqueline – this is madness!' he whispered, wondering how she would cope with the situation if someone walked in on them.

'Yes,' she agreed, 'divine madness! Oh Marcel, how beautiful you are, my dear. I loved you to distraction and you broke my heart when you demanded too much of me.'

That he was beautiful Marcel knew very well. He was a little above average height, with very dark and curly hair and a profile that had a devastating effect on women. He wore his clothes with style and moved with an assurance that impressed others. To hear Jacqueline Ducour testify to his attraction was pleasing in its way, but of no great significance to a man who had heard the same sentiment from more women than he could easily remember. Jacqueline's warm tongue touched his lips and her hand slid down to trace the long bulge in his trousers.

'If only I could trust you,' she sighed.

Whether she did or not, the outline and dimensions of his bulge fascinated her. She stroked its swollen head through the thin cloth, deliberately arousing Marcel in the way she knew how. He put his hand under the hem of her black frock and touched the silk of her knickers between the legs.

'Jacqueline – I must make love to you!' he said urgently.

He pushed her gently towards the desk, intending to sit her on it and stand between her legs.

'I adored you, but your demands were too cruel,' she

sighed. 'Why were you not content to love me and let me love you in my way – it was so very beautiful.'

While she was speaking she unzipped his trousers and felt inside with her long tantalising fingers.

'It shall be as you wish,' Marcel murmured, almost giddy with delight as his stiff *zimbriq* throbbed between her fingers, 'I adore you still, Jacqueline!'

Though she pretended to a sentimentality that confused the youthful victims of her passions Jacqueline was a predator without conscience. Just as Marcel's hand found its way into her flimsy underwear and touched her between the thighs, she let go of him and stepped back, out of his reach.

'But this is absurd!' she exclaimed, in complete control of herself. 'You must compose yourself at once, my dear Marcel.'

Her voice was as distant as if she had no responsibility for his condition of high excitement.

'Jacqueline!' he pleaded, unable to understand her change of mood.

She opened the door to the hall, flooding the little office with light.

'Perhaps we may discuss this at a more convenient time,' she said over her shoulder as she went out of the door.

Marcel understood at last that she had been amusing herself with a kind of revenge on him and had no intention of letting him regain her intimate favours. He sat on the edge of the desk, his *zimbriq* poking its outraged head stiffly up out of his open trousers. He zipped himself up and breathed deeply to calm his nerves. After a time, he even smiled to himself as he contemplated Jacqueline's shameless effrontery. It was impossible not to have the highest respect for her.

When he was calmer, he returned to the reception, though not to the ballroom where Jacqueline would be, and drank more champagne with acquaintances from other Embassies. His excuse to Eunice for not going home with her, that the party would continue until a late hour, proved true, so that it was after two in the morning when he at last went to bed, and by then he was more than a little drunk.

He fell asleep thinking of his forthcoming rendezvous with Trudi Pfaff and he dreamed of dancing with her at the Embassy party. Although she was wearing her white swim-suit instead of a frock, she said she was very hot, slipped the straps off her shoulders and peeled the costume down to her waist.

'But your husband will think that we are lovers,' Marcel exclaimed.

'He may think what he likes,' Trudi answered, her superb breasts bobbing against his shirt-front as they danced.

No one else in the ballroom paid the slightest attention to her charming state of semi-nakedness.

'You must be hot too,' she said, 'open your trousers.'

As is the way in dreams, his trousers vanished immediately – and his underwear too. He felt no embarrassment, even when his stiff shaft prodded into Trudi's swim-suit, as if trying to poke right through it and penetrate her belly-button. The sensation of rubbing against the thin fabric of her white bathing-costume was extremely pleasant.

'My dear Trudi – in the interests of your country and mine, I must request the honour of making love to you,' he found himself saying with absurd formality.

'But not tonight,' she answered. 'You've been with another woman.'

And then, in the unaccountable way of dreams, yellow-haired Trudi vanished from his arms and he was dancing with the Ambassador's wife. She was fully-dressed and most elegant in her short black satin frock, but Marcel was naked except for his shirt and bow-tie. Jacqueline was holding his hot *zimbriq* and stroking it with her long and sensitive fingers in a way he remembered very well.

'But Marcel, you have allowed yourself to become impossibly aroused!' she said in a tone of reproof. 'It is fortunate that you leave off your underwear at a party.'

'I learned that from Mademoiselle Carpenter,' he

explained. 'She never wears knickers at a party. Twelve men have had her tonight besides me.'

The music stopped at once and the dancing couples stood motionless with their arms round each other to stare at Marcel and Jacqueline. The touch of her fingers was so insistently arousing that he knew it was only a matter of moments before his crisis of pleasure arrived.

'But not here!' he gasped. 'Come to the little office.'

'Everyone here is a friend of mine. They understand my little ways perfectly,' said Jacqueline, still waltzing him round the floor as she stroked him. 'I wanted to make love to Captain Gonzales in the garden, but he cannot be here tonight.'

In the silent circle of spectators, Marcel picked out Eunice in her over-tight pink frock. She had been dancing with her Dutch admirer and they stood face to face, van Buuren's hands up her clothes. As Marcel and Jacqueline danced past she grinned at him over her shoulder.

'Pieter won't take more than five minutes, then it's your turn to have me again,' she called out.

Further round the circle stood Madame Kristensen in her long blue backless ball-gown. The American Colonel had an arm round her to fondle her bottom and her hand was thrust into his open trousers.

'Jacqueline – I knew you would come back to me,' Marcel murmured, stroking her bare back with both palms, 'I have never ceased to adore you and your little games.'

'Look at Colonel Hochheimer!' she answered. 'He has been too, too long in Santa Sabina and has squandered his strength on local girls. Poor Inge can do nothing! She is desolate!'

Madame Kristensen had pulled a long limp *zimbriq* out of the Colonel's trousers. Shaking it produced no response and she raised her evening gown to show off elegant knickers of pale blue silk, then pushed them down her thighs to display a tuft of chestnut curls.

'But how adorable,' said Marcel.

'That's not her natural colour,' Jacqueline informed

him in a tone of disapproval. 'Although she and I are friends, there are times when she seems to lack refinement. As if tinting her *kuft* with henna isn't enough, she let Colonel Hochheimer abuse it this evening in the garden.'

Marcel was most surprised to hear Jacqueline use the common patois word *kuft*.

'I've never heard of a woman who tints the hair between her legs,' he said. 'You must be mistaken.'

She murmured *tell me that you love me, Marcel*, her lips brushing against his cheek and her teasing fingers bringing on sudden contractions of his belly. She flipped his *zimbriq* lightly and his frothing champagne gushed three metres across the room to spatter Inge Kristensen's bare thighs.

'But Monsieur – I hardly know you!' she protested.

'But I know him!' Trudi exclaimed, completely naked as she reappeared from nowhere to push Jacqueline aside and take his leaping shaft between her hands.

Marcel awoke bathed in perspiration, his loins still jerking upwards to rub his sticky shaft against the thin bed-sheet that covered him. *But this is absurd*, he muttered to himself, *I am not falling in love with Trudi Pfaff – am I?*

3

The Comforts of the Grand Hotel Orient

The day after the Embassy reception was a holiday for Marcel and he slept until nearly ten. He took breakfast on the hotel terrace, overlooking San Feliz Square, and told the waiter to enquire if Monsieur Costa had a moment to discuss a matter of business with him. The Costa family owned the Grand Hotel Orient, where Marcel had lived since he arrived on the island, and Baltazar Costa ran it. He came out smiling, a fat man of forty, to take a seat at Marcel's table, dressed as always in a white linen suit and an open-necked shirt.

As he sat down, Costa waved his fist threateningly at a beggar who was edging too close to the terrace. It was no more than a strip of pavement, divided from the rest of the pavement by a line of green shrubs in wooden boxes, but its faded awning gave a touch of dingy bravado to the front of the hotel.

In Baltazar Costa could be discerned traces of all the nations and peoples who had ruled Santa Sabina before it became an independent Republic. His name was of Portuguese origin, the island having been at one time a colony of theirs. But his hooked nose was a reminder that before the Portuguese came to the island it was a settlement and staging-post of the Arabs for the slave-trade. The darkness of Costa's skin testified to some element of African blood – the captives brought by the Arabs to breed and trade in.

With all this, Costa spoke excellent, if old-fashioned French, as did all the townspeople, for the French had occupied the island for much of the eighteenth century. And still there was another layer to be seen in this medley of a man. Around his neck and visible against his hairy chest, he wore besides an ivory crucifix, a small *zimbriq*-talisman carved from pink coral. This was a religious emblem of the original people who had inhabited the island before the Arabs, Portuguese, and French added their own layers of culture and custom.

'*Bonjour*, Monsieur Lamont – everything is to your satisfaction?' the hotelier enquired with great respect.

'Perfectly, Monsieur Costa. I am grateful to you for sparing me a moment or two from your busy day.'

'Ah, the enormous problems of managing an international hotel!' said Baltazar Costa, shaking his head sadly. 'You may find this impossible to believe, but I have so much to do that I can allow myself no more than two or three hours sleep each night and a mere half-hour siesta in the afternoon.'

This was nonsense and both of them knew it. By any civilised standard the Grand Hotel Orient was fourth-rate or worse and it was run by plump Madame Costa. Baltazar spent his mornings checking the cash receipts, his afternoons in bed with his wife, as their eight children testified, and most of his evenings at Madame da Silva's establishment on the Avenue of the Constitution. Nevertheless, between men of the world there are certain civilities to be observed. Marcel addressed Baltazar Costa as if he were the head of the Ritz Hotel in Paris, and Costa returned the compliment by treating Marcel with the courtesy due to a visiting foreign President.

'At three this afternoon a lady will call upon me to discuss certain matters of mutual interest,' said Marcel.

'I understand perfectly. You wish to entertain the lady in a distinguished manner.'

'You are most perceptive. Is it possible that your Shah Jehan suite is available?'

Baltazar Costa pretended to give the question his careful consideration, though Marcel knew the suite had been unused for some time. The last occupant was an American Senator on a global fact-finding mission, so confused by continuous air-travel that he thought he was in Taiwan.

'To my great satisfaction I find I can accommodate you in the luxury of the Shah Jehan suite,' said the hotelier, beaming cordially. 'You will require refreshments, of course.'

'Two bottles of your best champagne,' Marcel agreed.

'It shall be as you wish. In the past you have been kind enough to say that my arrangements for your private meetings have given every satisfaction. Shall I add the cost to your account, or would you prefer to settle it now?'

The bank-notes of Santa Sabina were highly impressive in appearance, perhaps to compensate for the ambiguities of their value in comparison with any other known currency. To assist Costa with his tax obligations, Marcel paid in cash with 50-tikkoo notes, each worth about five francs. Small though their value was, the bank-notes were almost the size of a pocket handkerchief and carried a brightly coloured portrait of the President of the Republic in military uniform.

'By the way,' he said, 'the lady will ask for Mr John Smith, not for me. Will you explain this to whichever of your charming daughters is at the reception desk today?'

'Mr John Smith!' Baltazar exclaimed. 'Such discretion! How charming to encounter such delicacy! Will you join me in a little glass of green absinthe as a token of my respect?'

'With pleasure, Monsieur Costa.'

Ramshackle though it was, the Grand Hotel Orient suited Marcel better than an apartment or a bungalow outside the city. For a remarkably small sum of money each month he had a comfortable room with a shower, food provided whenever he asked for it, and no difficulties with servants of his own. The hotel had recommended itself to him by being the setting of his first intimate encounter on the island of Santa Sabina, on the very day he arrived from France to take up his appointment.

He had been invited to dine with the Ambassador and the senior Embassy staff by way of welcome to the island. About midnight he returned to the hotel where a room had been reserved for him until he made his own arrangements. Up till then his impressions of the Grand Hotel Orient had been unfavourable, but events were in train which revised his opinion of it. Before going to bed he took a seat on the terrace overlooking the Square and ordered a small cognac. And no sooner had the waiter gone to fetch it than a girl seated herself at his table. She had a shock of black hair and wore a tight scarlet frock that displayed much of her bare thighs.

'*Bonsoir, Mademoiselle,*' said Marcel pleasantly.

There was little difference between the bars of Paris and those of Santa Sabina he saw – a man alone was a fair target.

'I have not seen you here before,' said the girl in very acceptable French, treating him to an amiable smile.

'I arrived only today.'

'Then you must buy me a drink to celebrate your arrival in my country.'

The waiter returned with the cognac, but before Marcel could ask his new friend what she would like to drink, she and the waiter said good evening to each other. Evidently he had served this one before and knew her taste.

'May I ask your name, Mademoiselle?'

'I am Johana. And you?'

'Marcel. I have never met anyone named Johana before.'

'You have never been to Santa Sabina before.'

Her drink was cherry-coloured and in a tall glass with cracked ice and diced cucumber. It was brought not by the waiter but one by one of Baltazar Costa's many daughters. She set the glass on the table, exchanged smiles with Johana and retreated only as far as the hotel entrance, well within earshot.

'To you, Johana,' said Marcel, clinking glasses with her.

As yet a stranger in Santa Sabina, he was intrigued by the passionate intermingling of races that had produced so very exotic a girl. He could recognise the Arab and the African blood in her features, but her short nose and high cheek-bones suggested a dash of Chinese as well.

'Why do you stare at me? Am I ugly?' she demanded.

'You are enchanting. Forgive me if I seem impolite.'

'*Enchanting* – I like that,' she said, smiling at him again. 'I will come to your room for 250 tikkoos, Marcel.'

He was not yet accustomed to local prices and the very moderate fee surprised him. While he hesitated, Johana appealed to Costa's daughter, as if to a referee.

'Concepcion – tell Monsieur Marcel that it is a fair price,' she said.

'It is fair, Monsieur,' Concepcion Costa agreed, 'only the best girls are allowed in this hotel. My father is very severe in keeping out the 50-tikkoo women.'

'But naturally,' said Marcel, half-laughing.

'Johana and I went to school together,' Concepcion added. 'She is a very good girl. Show Monsieur your *gublas*, Johana.'

The word meant nothing to Marcel until Johana unfastened two buttons at the top of her scarlet frock and pulled it open to give him a glimpse of her breasts.

'Very pretty!' he said, almost laughing at the eagerness of the two girls 'Which school did you and Mademoiselle Costa attend together?'

'The Convent of the Precious Blood,' she told him.

'And how old are you, Johana?' Marcel enquired curiously.

'Seventeen – the same as Concepcion. Am I too old for you?'

Marcel smiled reassuringly and addressed Costa's daughter.

'Am I to understand that your father has no objection if guests take young women to their rooms?'

'But of course not. There is an extra charge of 50 tikkoos for clean sheets tomorrow. That is the house rule.'

'What is money to you?' Johana asked, her hand on Marcel's thigh. 'You are a rich stranger. And for 250 tikkoos I stay all night with you – not just once and go. Do you want me?'

'Certainly,' said Marcel, feeling his shaft growing stiff, 'you shall be my welcome to Santa Sabina.'

'One small word, Monsieur,' said Concepcion, 'please do not disturb the other guests. I am sure you are a considerate man and will do nothing to make Johana scream and wake people up.'

As soon as she was in Marcel's room, Johana went about her business in a matter of fact way. She kicked off her high-heeled shoes, hoisted her scarlet frock over her head and stood to let him see what he had contracted for. She was not very tall, but her body was well-proportioned, her belly broad and smooth. But it was her lion's mane of dark hair and her complexion that gave her so exotic an appearance. Her skin was coffee-coloured, unblemished and gleaming, and the buds of her breasts were not pink or russet, but a rich copper-brown.

'Do you think I'm pretty?' she asked.

'You are delightful!' he replied. 'Your *gublas* are enchanting. I must kiss them at once.'

She grinned to hear him use the Santa Sabina word and corrected his pronunciation while cupping them in her hands to demonstrate what a superior pair of *gublas* looked like. Marcel reached out for her, but she stepped away, turned and poked her bare bottom at him.

'You pay first,' she said firmly.

'But naturally,' and he counted out the money and handed it to her, fascinated to know where she would put it for safety.

She squatted on her haunches to tuck the colourful bank-notes into the toe of one of her discarded shoes and grinned at him. Then she was standing close to him and accessible. He stroked her hips to feel the warmth of her body and stared in admiration at another exotic delight – between her legs she had a profusion of black curls such as he had never seen on a woman before.

'It is a little echo!' he said softly, his fingers twining in the crisp fleece.

'What do you mean?'

'It is an echo of the hair on your head, Johana. The colour is the same, a beautiful shiny black, and both are so thick!'

'It pleases you?'

'It is magnificent!'

She was in no hurry now that she had her money. She stood naked and smiling while Marcel ran his hands over her belly and breasts, enjoying the satin texture of her skin. For him these were precious moments, the anticipation of pleasure building itself to a maximum before he proceeded further. Inside his trousers something else built itself to a maximum also. He led Johana to the bed, fondling her bottom, and she slipped a hand into his trouser pocket and pinched his shaft, until he was so aroused that he asked her to lie down.

She posed on her back, her legs crossed at the ankles and her hands behind her head, while he took his clothes off. It was when he lay naked beside her that he learned another word of the old language of Santa Sabina – she took hold of his swollen part and said he had a strong *zimbriq*. The word amused him and he made her repeat it. After all, where better to learn a foreign language than in bed with a pretty girl? No language school could compete with that! And as he was to discover, even educated Santa Sabinans forgot French and reverted to the old language in moments of high emotion.

He stroked Johana's brown-skinned belly and slid his

hand between her legs to feel her mound through the shock of black curls.

'What is this called?' he asked her.

'That is my *kuft*,' she said with a grin, rubbing it against the palm of his hand.

Kuft, he repeated, and leaned over her to kiss it. Her thighs moved apart, to let his lips touch warm folds of flesh half-hidden in her shiny black fleece. He became exquisitely aware of the scent of her body – a sensual and spicy scent, a little like cinnamon. Exotic was an inadequate word to describe it – erotic was more suitable. He kissed his way up her belly to her coffee-coloured *gublas* and licked their dark buds, savouring the same cinnamon spicy taste of her.

'What is the word for what we are going to do?' he asked.

'You haven't said what you want to do to me. Do it first and I will tell you the name for it.'

'But what do men usually do with you?' he exclaimed.

'Who can say?' she answered. 'Some want to make love in my *kuft* and some in my mouth. A few want to do it in my *buztan*.'

To make sure that he understood all that was on offer, she rolled on her side to show the cheeks of her bottom and used both hands to part them and show him the dark knot of muscle between. To Marcel it was incredible that anyone who had purchased the freedom of Johana's exciting young body would divert his interest away from the most usual manner of making love. But that is a naive thought, he told himself – *chacun à son goût* as the saying has it.

'Do you have a preference yourself?' he asked.

'To me it is all the same. Do what pleases you best.'

His hand moved down to her belly and then to the join of her thighs, to the rich dark fleece he found fascinating. He combed his fingers through it and then parted the fleshy folds under the curls to caress the moist pink interior.

'You want to do it in my *kuft*, yes?' Johana asked placidly.

Marcel had intended to spin out the new pleasures of this encounter, but he reckoned without the simple approach of the girl herself. She tugged at his shoulders until he stretched himself along her belly. Her legs were widely spread, her hands pulled at his bottom and he felt himself drawn smoothly into her. With each thrust he felt her bush of hair rub his groin and the sensation was so enthralling that he could not slow down, much as he wished to. Johana's legs came up off the bed and crossed over his back to pull him deeper into her. Her arms round his neck held his face to hers and her wet tongue was vibrating inside his mouth.

'Ah, ah!' he gasped, as ecstatic spasms shook him and he jettisoned his passionate flood into the girl's belly.

'Very good,' she said approvingly, 'very good, Marcel!'

She released the grip of her arms and legs and with warm admiration told him that he was very strong for his age.

'But what do you mean?' he asked, when he was again capable of rational speech. 'I am twenty-six, is that old?'

'Not *too* old,' she said, smiling as she stroked his face, 'but you are almost thirty, and still very strong.'

'It is because you are so young that you think twenty-six is old.'

'I am grown up,' she said, 'I am a woman, not a child now.'

'You have demonstrated that most adequately. But in France we do not regard a girl of seventeen as fully adult, even though the law says that she is old enough to make love.'

'But of course she is old enough! How can it be against the law to make love?' Johana asked in astonishment. 'We have no laws against it here.'

'I am sure you are wrong about that,' said Marcel. 'Some of the many expressions of love are forbidden in every country in the world that I know of. Between brother and sister, for example.'

'Not here,' she said firmly. 'Brothers and sisters do it all the time when they are children. Everybody knows that.'

'Then at least there is a law forbidding rape,' he said.

'What do you mean?' she enquired.

'I mean if a man should overcome you by force and make love to you against your will. That would be a crime, I think, even here.'

'Yes,' Johana agreed. 'I would report him to the police and he would be arrested as a thief.'

'A thief?' said Marcel, his eyebrows rising up his forehead in surprise.

'But naturally! It is the same as if he went into a shop and stole what they sell from the counter. If he wants me, he must pay for me, like the shop.'

'But suppose this man took another girl by force – one who does not sell her services. That would be rape.'

'I don't understand you,' said Johana, her pretty face creased in puzzlement. 'Why does this man take girls by force when he can have them by asking?'

With his hand between her warm thighs, Marcel had no desire to become involved in long explanations or comparisons of legal systems.

'Perhaps it is different in Santa Sabina,' he told her. 'When did you first make love, Johana?'

When she was ten, she told him. Before then she and her friends did no more than play with each other. *I'll let you hold my snake if you'll let me feel your turtle*, the little boys offered, and the girls accepted immediately and, as often as not, posed the offer the other way round themselves. Eventually progress was made to a more advanced version in which a boy and a girl stand face to face with the boys' stiff snake clasped tightly between the girl's bare thighs. They felt each other's bottoms while the boy jerked to and fro.

One day, said Johana, she was playing this game with her cousin Joaquim behind a tree where nobody would disturb them. Joaquim cried out suddenly and she felt a warm spurt of wetness between her legs.

'It made me laugh,' she said, 'I was happy because I

must be nearly grown up if a boy did it between my legs instead of in my hand.'

'How old was he, your cousin?' Marcel enquired.

'A year older than me. Eleven.'

'I am sure he played that game with you often after that.'

'Yes, but not standing up,' she said. 'We went behind the house and lay down on the grass. Joaquim told me to open my legs and he pushed his *zimbriq* right in me.'

'Were you frightened?'

'No – I wanted to know what it felt like.'

'And did you like it, the first time?'

'It made me very excited to have him inside me,' she said, 'but he was so quick – he was finished in three seconds! It was his first time inside a girl and he was too excited.'

'You were disappointed,' said Marcel, unconvinced that she was telling him the truth about her escapades at the age of ten.

'When Joaquim got off me I rubbed my *kuft* to pleasure myself and it made him hard again to watch me and he put it back inside me. He was slower the second time, and we both felt the pleasure at the same moment.'

It seemed to Marcel that eleven was a remarkably early age for the boys of Santa Sabina to begin the serious devotions of love. But as Johana explained, the vigour of the local youths was not of long duration. They were at their best at fifteen, she said, but by the time they were twenty they were past their peak and incapable of pleasuring a woman more than once a day. Or sometimes twice if they were exceptional. At twenty-five they needed a great deal of stimulation to stiffen their resolve to any worthwhile degree.

'It is hard work for the woman,' she said. 'She must play with his *zimbriq* and shake it and lick it to make it stand up. Sometimes it takes half an hour to get it hard.'

'Alas. How desolate a fate!' said Marcel, trying not to let Johana see his amusement. 'And at thirty, what then?'

'They are finished,' she answered, rolling on her side to face him. 'A few can still do it once a week perhaps, but not easily. Their wives will have nothing to do with them, because it is too exhausting.'

'But the thirty-year-old wives,' said Marcel, 'what do they do when their husbands have become useless to them?'

'They get young boys to visit them while the husbands are away, of course!' said Johana, amazed by his question. 'A boy of fifteen can love a woman six times straight off.'

Her hand slid up his thigh and felt his hard shaft.

'Ah, it is strong again!' she said with appreciation. 'This time I teach you our way of making love.'

'And how is that different from what we did a moment ago?'

'In Santa Sabina we make love the proper way,' she answered, 'with the woman on top. This foreign way of yours of the man on top is uncomfortable.'

Before he could reply, she was on her knees to straddle him and feed his *zimbriq* into the dark-skinned lips between her thighs. Marcel stared in admiration at the fleece of black hair over her *kuft*, and reached up to handle her breasts and their coffee-berry tips. Johana rode him hard and fast, her face split in a grin of concentration.

'Slowly, *chérie*!' he gasped.

But she bounced on unchecked, sliding rapidly up and down his embedded shaft until it spat its tribute into her and she too was carried away by her own sensations. Her hands clamped over his to make him squeeze her breasts tighter and she bucked furiously on his spurting *zimbriq*. She uttered a long wail of delight, her eyes rolling upwards until only the whites showed and her body went into muscular spasms so severe that Marcel feared his captive stem would be torn from his body. With a final shudder she came to a halt and slumped over him.

'Very good,' he said, copying her own words of approval.

He took her by the arms and eased her forward and off him, to lie at his side on the bed. Her beautiful dark skin shone with perspiration which trickled down between her breasts towards her gleaming belly.

'Tell me now, Johanna,' he said, using a corner of the bedsheet to wipe her belly and breasts, 'what is your word for what has just happened to you?'

She smiled contentedly as he thrust the wet tip of his tongue into her round belly-button and taught him another word of the mixed-pedigree language spoken by the ordinary people.

'*Zboca*,' he repeated after her, wondering what the origin could be. 'Is that a noun or a verb?'

'Noun, verb – you sound like a schoolteacher! I make you *zboca* and you make me *zboca*, that's all.'

'To the satisfaction of both of us,' said Marcel, grinning at her. 'Is it always like that for you, Johana – so fast and violent?'

'How else could it be?' she asked in surprise.

'For many women it is otherwise,' he told her.

'Not in Santa Sabina,' she said with conviction. 'That is how we *zboca* here. Perhaps in your country the women are weaker than us and lie whimpering like kittens under you when they *zboca*. Or perhaps before you came here you only made love with girls of ten, not grown-up women like me.'

'You are delightfully uncomplicated, Johana. I am truly glad that we met this evening. You have opened up for me a new perspective on the emotional responses of women. I have every hope that my stay on your island will prove to be highly educational.'

'I don't understand any of that,' she said, 'but I think that you like me because I pleased you well.'

Marcel stroked her thigh, enjoying the smooth feel of it.

'So all the women of Santa Sabina *zboca* like wildcats?' he asked.

'Don't you believe me? You can find out easily enough. All the women here will go with you if you ask, especially the wives. You can have as many as you have strength for.'

'My dear Johana, how can you expect me to believe that.'

'You are a stranger,' she said. 'You have much to learn about us. A woman with a husband over twenty needs another man because her own can't keep her happy. And if the husband is over thirty, she will drag you into a doorway, if you smile at her when you walk past. She will have your trousers down round your ankles before you have time to ask her name.'

'But if that is so,' Marcel objected, 'how is it possible for you to make a living, Johana? Why should a man pay 250 tikkoos for what he can have for the asking?'

'Because I am very pretty,' she said angrily, pushing his hand away from her thigh. 'Men want a pretty girl to love, not a woman who is fat and ugly from having babies every year.'

'My apologies,' said Marcel hastily, 'the question was not intended as an insult, I assure you. This is my first day here and I do not know the ways of your country yet. Of course you are pretty, Johana! More than that – there is a wild beauty about you which I have never encountered before. To have you here with me tonight gives me more pleasure than I can easily tell you.'

'Strangers!' she said with contempt in her voice. 'You think we are not as good as you because we are different!'

'No, no – I would not want you to be like anyone else. I want you to be yourself, Johana. That is what is so exciting about you.'

'You find me exciting?' she asked, her tone friendly again.

'Immensely so, I assure you.'

'But does your *zimbriq* find me exciting?' she asked, taking hold of his limp tassel. 'No, it is asleep.'

'I shall be thirty in a few years,' Marcel reminded her with amusement.

'That is true. I must help you to grow strong again.'

He gasped as she went to work with both hands

on his dormant part, her fingernails running along its length.

'How is it that *you* do not have babies every year, Johana?' he asked, and she told him that she chewed qagga leaves.

It meant nothing to him then, but later on he learned that girls who wished to avoid becoming pregnant chewed the leaves of the qagga bush – its sap having contraceptive properties. But as he became aroused again, Marcel's thoughts turned to a more interesting subject.

'Is it true that there is no law here against brothers and sisters making love to each other?' he asked, his hands on her plump breasts.

'Ask anyone if you don't believe me,' she said. 'After my first time with Joaquim, I made love to my brothers whenever I felt like it. Didn't you make love to your sisters?'

'I have only one sister,' Marcel told her. 'I dreamed of making love to her when we were children, though I have never told anyone before.'

'And it was the same as with any other girl,' said Johana.

'I never dared. It is forbidden in my country.'

'You have harsh laws,' Johana commented. 'Your *zimbriq* still wants to make love with your sister – see how quickly he woke up in my hand when you were talking about her.'

'Less than a hundred years ago, French girls could be married and bedded legally at twelve,' he answered, 'but not if she was your sister.'

'If we had crazy laws like yours everybody would be in prison,' said Johana, 'including the police.'

He shivered in delight as she clasped his *zimbriq* tightly in one hand and shook it, her other hand on his chest to pinch his nipples. Under her assault his body responded quickly and waves of pleasurable sensation rocked him.

'That's very good,' Johana announced. 'He's properly awake now and wants to get inside me again.'

'Yes,' Marcel sighed, his bottom squirming on the bed.

'But why should I let him in?' she demanded. 'He wants to *zboca* in me, but he didn't like it when I did, because I'm too violent for him and he's not used to that! What is he used to – do you cut holes in ripe melons for him?'

'Johana!' he exclaimed, almost overwhelmed by the thrilling sensations that shook his body.

'He is throbbing in my hand!' she said. 'Is he shaking his head to disagree with me? Is he trying to tell me that he would like to *zboca* in my hand? No? So what is it he wants, I wonder – to make love to my *buztan*, maybe? Shall I turn over and lie face-down for you?'

Marcel seized her shoulders and toppled her sideways. In an instant he was on top of her, his hot belly on hers, and he was stabbing between her parted thighs.

'We'll do it the foreign way – with me on top!' he gasped.

Johana chuckled and opened her legs wider, to let him plunge into the slippery depths of her black-maned *kuft*.

'So strong, so strong!' she exclaimed.

Her ankles crossed over his back, her hands twined in his hair and pulled his mouth forcefully to hers. Marcel was thrusting very quickly, unconscious of everything but his urgent need. Even so, it was Johana who arrived first at the culmination of desire. For Marcel it felt as if a bomb exploded beneath him – a frenzied convulsion of movement that smacked her belly hard against his. Her heels drummed on his back and her tongue in his mouth seemed to be halfway down his throat.

Ecstasy took him in its grip and he cried out round Johana's gagging tongue as he emptied his frantic desire into her belly in gushes that racked him from head to toe.

4

Frolics in Shah Jehan's Bed

Stretched out naked on the embroidered cushions of the huge bed in the Shah Jehan suite, yellow-haired Trudi Pfaff was a truly enchanting sight. Her smooth skin was golden from the sun and glowed with health and well-being, inviting the onlooker's hand to slide gently over it and savour its delicate texture. She lay on her back with her yellow hair spread round her head on the cushions like a saint's halo. Her blue-grey eyes were innocent and untroubled, but the curve of her scarlet-painted mouth suggested she was eager for sensations no saint would entertain. Her arms were folded carelessly beneath her head – throwing into greater prominence the magnificent pleasure domes of her breasts.

This sumptuousness embraced the whole of her body. She was too elegant to be *plump*, but she was enticingly well-fleshed. There was a graceful rotundity in the curve of her belly, a pleasing roundness to her hips, a proportionate fullness to her long thighs and the tuft of fair hair between them had been trimmed to a neat triangle. Marcel was in a daze of delight as he kissed her passionately from head to toe, again and again, his hands trembling as they roamed over her satin skin, over her breasts, across her belly and between her legs. As for Trudi, she sighed in appreciation and lay back to let him do whatever he liked to her.

And there was so much to do, so much of her to fondle and kiss and stroke! Marcel's *zimbriq* had been standing up like an iron bar from the moment she had arrived for their rendezvous in the Shah Jehan suite. She came dressed in a big straw sunhat and a sleeveless blouse of white silk tucked into a close-fitting scarlet skirt. A bottle of champagne stood ready in an ice-bucket and it was Marcel's intention to drink most of it with her before doing more than kiss her hand. Then after he had made love to her the first time they would finish the bottle as they lay naked side by side.

That at least was his usual way of proceeding with pretty ladies on intimate occasions. The champagne lifted their spirits and saved them from qualms of conscience about their husbands during the preliminaries. It maintained their vivacity and interest after their first or second little climax of delight. And when Marcel had given his all, the champagne ensured that his companion did not subside into foolish remorse over the secret pleasures they had enjoyed together.

But today events moved with such unexpected speed and with so overwhelming an impact that Marcel's well-tried and useful procedure was abandoned. Trudi was shown to the suite where he was waiting for her, took off her sun-hat, and devastated him with her grey-blue eyes. He kissed her hand in the briefest of polite salutations and took her in his arms, his mouth hard on hers. In another instant his tongue was in her hot mouth and his hands were stroking her back through the thin silk of her blouse.

'Trudi, *je t'adore!*' he whispered, ending the long kiss at last, and she murmured *Marcel*.

She was almost as tall as he was. Her eyes were half-closed and she sighed slowly into his open mouth as her hands on the cheeks of his bottom pulled him hard against her to squeeze his upright *zimbriq* against her soft belly. Evidently the hardness pleased her, for she let go of him and stood back a little to get her hands to the buttons of her blouse. Marcel stared down, wholly entranced, while she opened it wide to show him her superb breasts. They were slung in a fragile half-brassière of white lace and he bowed his head to kiss the magnificent cleavage between their rotundities.

After that, events followed their natural course. With the skill of long practice Marcel unfastened the lacy brassière so that he could feel her breasts and kiss their pink buds. In some manner not apparent to him, he and Trudi moved across the suite until they found themselves standing beside the elaborate bed – his hands still clasping her breasts.

By then she was breathing sensually through her open mouth, her eyes closed and her body trembling, as if she were about to faint with pleasure. But for all that, she had somehow opened Marcel's trousers to get his *zimbriq* out and massage it with a firm and slow stroke. There was no question of drinking a glass of champagne – indeed, all that had gone completely from Marcel's mind. He undid her scarlet skirt and pushed it over her full hips until it slid down her legs and she kicked it out of the way.

'I've heard it said that the French are fiery and impatient when they make love,' she said, and smiled at him in a way that showed her pink tongue, 'and now I see it is true. You intend to throw me on the bed and ravish me!'

Her accent was strongly Teutonic, but in the delightful circumstances in which he found himself, Marcel found it charming.

'You are so beautiful,' he responded, 'how could any man not be inspired to the very height of passion?'

Banal as it was, his answer pleased her. She let go of his shaft to strip off her blouse and brassière while Marcel was sighing in admiration over her knickers of white silk and black lace. His *zimbriq* was twitching wildly and Trudi smiled as she reached out for it, but Marcel moved close, his feet between her parted feet, to rub himself voluptuously against the silk over her belly.

'It feels so hard!' she murmured, her open mouth seeking his in an endless kiss.

They stood pressed together, mouth to mouth, Marcel in a daze bordering on ecstasy, his fingers clenched in the soft flesh of her bottom while he rubbed himself against the silk of her knickers. Her arms were round his waist at first, but she too was affected by the emotions that were shaking him. She managed to get both hands inside his open trousers so that she could hold him as he held her – grasping the cheeks of his bottom and squeezing hard.

'You must stop or it will be too late!' she gasped as she felt the pressure grow stronger and more insistent against her belly. 'You are making love to my underwear, not to me!'

With great reluctance Marcel let go of her and sank down on to his knees.

'Then I shall strip you naked!' he exclaimed. 'There must be nothing between us, nothing!'

He eased her elegant knickers down her thighs and over her round knees to her ankles. She put a hand on his shoulder to steady herself while she stepped out of them and Marcel stared adoringly at her neat little triangle of blondish hair. A moment later he was kissing the smooth pink lips between her thighs and then using the tip of his tongue to thrill her.

'Take your clothes off and we will lie on the bed,' she suggested, her hands on his shoulders pushing him gently away.

And there they were, he and she, naked on the carved wooden bed, Trudi with her hands under her yellow-haired head and her flawless body fully exposed to his adoration. How he adored her that first time they were together as lovers! He adored her with his lips, with his wet tongue, with his fingers, his mind wiped out by a continuous blaze of near-ecstatic sensation. In truth, he adored her for so long and with such intensity that the moment came when she cried out as her back arched and her bottom lifted off the embroidered cushions.

It says much for the strength of sensation gripping Marcel that Trudi's climactic release took him by surprise. It ought not to have surprised him, of course, for at that particular moment he was stroking the insides of her thighs with his fingertips and her soft *kuft* was pressed wetly to his mouth. Her loins lifted off the bed in furious spasms while his tongue flicked at her bud, until her cry trailed off into a long sigh and she collapsed on the cushions.

'Marcel, Marcel,' she murmured, her fingers twining in his curly dark hair and pulling, so that he slid up from between her open legs to lie on her superb body and kiss her with tenderness.

'I did not realise that you were so aroused,' he murmured in mild apology, while his eager part rubbed itself against the satin skin of her belly, almost without his awareness of what it was doing.

'That was fantastic!' she said. 'I thought I was fainting.'

'You were magnificent, *chérie*,' he murmured.

He was dazed by the feelings that rippled through his entire body from his gentle rubbing against her belly. He gazed down into her blue-grey eyes and felt that he was drowning in sensations and then her scarlet-painted mouth opened in a little smile and she said softly: *Marcel, I think that you are going to zboca in another two seconds*. Nothing of what she said registered except the Santa Sabinan word. Its meaning focused his attention on his slowly-sliding part and he realised that his excitement was so intense that it was irreversible! His hands clutched Trudi's bare shoulders and he writhed in abandon on her body as his desire squirted on to her belly.

His sensations grew keener as her fingernails dug cruelly into the flesh of his bottom and his head jerked up until he was staring blindly at the carved walnut head-board of the bed. Trudi's nails sank deeper and rocked him backwards and forwards on her while he poured out his ecstasy in a seemingly endless flood. But all too soon the delightful throes faded and Marcel's gasping slowed to long sighing exhalations and then he lay still, feeling the slippery wetness between her belly and his own.

'Why did you do that?' she asked, spreading her legs more comfortably.

Marcel eased himself off her and lay propped on an elbow to look at her. He touched his fingers to her wet belly and traced down to her meticulously trimmed tuft and then clasped her between her open thighs, his palm covering the tender folds of pink flesh there.

'My intention was to make love here in your pretty *kuft*,' he told her, quite certain that she understood all the Santa Sabina words that applied to bedroom games, 'but I do not understand what is happening to me since I met you. My body is reacting as if it were that of a boy with a woman for the first time, and so excited that he reaches the peak of his pleasure too soon. Do you know how beautiful you are, Trudi?'

'They say the French are great flatterers of women,' she answered, smiling at him. 'I am not ugly, but it would be very conceited to think I am beautiful enough to make a man like you *zboca* just by letting him see me naked.'

Under Marcel's fingers the warm and moist lips between her thighs were pouting open. He felt inside until he touched her secret bud.

'But I made you *zboca* when I kissed you here,' he said, rolling it under his fingertip.

'That's not the same thing at all,' she answered, her bottom squirming on the cushions of the bed as his caressing fingers excited her again. Her face turned towards him and her eyes were half-closed as she asked *are you going to do it to me again, Marcel*?

He stared in fascination at the sumptuous breasts and shiny-wet belly spread out beneath him and became strongly aroused again. In spite of the forcefulness of his climactic feelings of only a few minutes ago, he had regained his hardness and was trembling in anticipation of the pleasures to come. He leaned over her to flick the pink tips of her breasts with his tongue until she gasped and then he licked them hard.

'Marcel – you're making me *zboca* again!' she gasped.

Her hand gripped his thigh and her fingernails were biting into the flesh. In another moment she was clasping his dark-haired pendants and rolling them in her palm. Marcel mounted her quickly, guided his distended *zimbriq* to the wet and pouting lips he had been playing with and, in one long push sank himself deep into her warm belly.

'*Mein Gott, mein Gott!*' she moaned as he rode her with great assertiveness.

In her delirium of pleasure she lost her grasp of the French language altogether and gasped out German words of endearment and encouragement to even more fervent efforts. Her knees were bent double until they almost touched her shoulders and in this way she had made herself as wide open to him as the anatomy of a young and healthy woman allowed. He slid in and out of her slippery cleft with extraordinary speed and vigour and, as they climbed together up the slope of bodily sensation towards release, they panted out each other's name.

The slope was steeper and shorter than is usual when a man and a woman approach their second climax within a very short time. Before Marcel had slammed into her for long, there occurred an explosion in his belly that annihilated him. And not only him – evidently there was an explosion of equally devasting force in Trudi's heaving belly, for she screamed and bucked wildly under him.

It was some time before either of them became aware of their surroundings again. Marcel's heart was still beating fast in his chest and he felt enormously content and at the same time elated. Trudi lay very still under him – her legs had slid down to lie outside his and her arms were loosely outstretched. Marcel thought of the giant white starfish he had seen washed by the sea, lying exposed and helpless on the sand. He climbed off her, his belly sticking for a moment to hers. Her yellow hair was tousled and there were tiny beads of perspiration on her forehead and her short upper lip.

'It is not possible to live through sensations so intense!' she told him. 'You have killed me, Marcel.'

Her legs moved together as if to bar the way to delight. Marcel kissed her face while he tried to organise his scattered thoughts.

'We have much to talk about, you and I,' he said, to give himself more time, 'we will refresh ourselves with a glass of champagne first.'

He got off the bed and put on his green-striped dressing-gown, brought here from his own room for this purpose. The Shah Jehan suite, so called, was in reality one large room, but carved and polished wooden arches divided it across the centre and so gave the appearance of two rooms connected to each other. One half had windows from floor to ceiling, the windows discreetly covered with coloured blinds on which were painted tigers and peacocks.

This window section of the suite was furnished as a sitting-room, with a crimson upholstered divan and gilded oriental chairs arranged about a large and very low brass-topped round table. It was on this that the ice-bucket stood with two bottles in it and two elaborate long-stemmed glasses with gilded rims. Marcel took the glasses and a bottle back through the carved archway to where the bed stood – a piece of furniture so large and ornate that, after the first time he entertained a lady on it, he had enquired where it came from.

Baltazar Costa had informed him with pride that he had seen this remarkable bed, by chance, on a visit to Sumatra and found it so enchanting that he bought it and shipped it to Santa Sabina, regardless of expense. He did not say where in Sumatra he had encountered it, but it was Marcel's firm opinion that it had been in an establishment of a certain kind. As to its origin, that was open to guess. Its uniqueness made it possible for it to have been built in a dozen places – Hongkong,

Macao, Shanghai, Singapore, Djakarta, Rangoon or Calcutta.

It was made of walnut, so much could be established. In shape it was square, measuring almost two and a half metres top to bottom and from side to side, so that there was no lack of space for even the most energetic love-making. Indeed, the thought occurred to Marcel that perhaps it had been designed for some Indian Maharajah or Chinese war-lord whose pleasures required several women at a time.

At each of the four corners, a polished walnut column, as thick as a woman's thigh, rose to a height of just over two metres. These posts supported no canopy, as might have been expected, but terminated in smooth round knobs. There were carvings round the columns, all the way from the foot to the top and a close inspection revealed that the unknown craftsman had depicted naked couples and trios engaged in vigorous love-making in all of the known positions except one.

The busy and athletic lovers expertly carved on the bedposts were standing up, kneeling down, squatting, bending over, forwards, sideways, backwards and upside-down, and all the apertures of the female body were made use of by the smiling men. Yet although Marcel had on more than one occasion examined every carving on all four columns and discussed them with whichever lady was with him, nowhere could he find a couple making love with the woman lying on her back.

The usual European posture evidently had little appeal in whatever exotic country the bed came from. There were depictions of men lying on their backs and women kneeling or squatting over them, but the nearest approach Marcel could find to the time-honoured tradition was a coupling in which a woman rested on her shoulder-blades. She had hooked her legs over the shoulders of her standing partner and his hands were under her bottom to lift her to the most convenient height.

When Marcel had first laid amused eyes on the decorations of the columns they had reminded him of illustrations he had seen of carvings in certain Indian temples and for this reason he had at first assumed that the bed had been looted from a Maharajah's palace. But the women depicted were not the heavy-breasted and full-hipped type usually shown in Indian art. They were slender of limb and had pointed little adolescent breasts, so that Marcel then concluded that they were Chinese. But that theory failed too when he looked more closely at the men and saw that their *zimbriqs* – where they were not plunged deep into the women – appeared to be clipped. That suggested an Islamic country of origin.

In the end, he was compelled to accept that the provenance of the bed was a mystery he was unlikely to solve. There was a panel joining the two head columns, and it displayed not more loving antics but beautifully carved flowers and fruit. Even this was of little assistance – the fruits were of the sort that were grown across the tropical half of the world and the flowers, though exquisite, were unidentifiable.

Trudi was sitting cross-legged on the elaborate handwoven bedcover, among the many embroidered cushions. Marcel handed her a glass of chilled champagne, sat on the side of the bed and touched glasses with her. She pouted her lips at him in a kissing motion, drained her glass and held it out for more.

'I've never seen a bed like this before,' she said. 'Is it typical Santa Sabina work, do you know?'

Marcel told her what he knew of it and helped her, with an arm round her bare waist, to inspect the carvings on the nearest column.

'Oh!' she exclaimed, putting her forefinger to a grouping to direct his attention to it.

He looked closely and thought it pleasant enough, though far too energetic for anyone not trained in a circus from early childhood. It was a sideways view of a standing man, his knees bent slightly and an enigmatic smile on his face. His *zimbriq* was embedded in his partner, who stood on one leg facing him. Her other leg was raised and supported on the man's right shoulder, so pulling herself wide open for him.

'If we did not already know that the bed was imported here, that position would be conclusive proof that it was not made in a Santa Sabinan workshop,' he said.

'Why do you say that?'

'It is well known that the men of this island lose their capabilities extremely early in life,' he explained. 'Their precocity as children is extraordinary, but by the time they are twenty-five their energies have been drained. It is not possible to estimate with any certainty the age of the man who is shown obliging his friend in this little carving, but at least we can say that he is an adult and not a child. Therefore it follows that he is not an inhabitant of Santa Sabina.'

'Yes, I see what you mean,' she said, looking again at the carving, 'the men here are more likely to be found in this position,' and she pointed to a man on his back with a girl squatting over him.

'And not even that, when they reach their thirties,' said Marcel, 'or so I have been informed.'

'You should not believe that everything you are told is literally true,' said Trudi,' I believe that some of the more cultured of the men here retain their strength longer than you think.'

It was in Marcel's mind that she was talking about Ysambard D'Cruz, the former Minister of Commerce and Fine Arts. The moment did not seem appropriate to pursue the question of her friendship with the fallen Minister, interesting as Marcel found the matter.

'Two or three weeks ago,' he said, to amuse her while he refilled their glasses with champagne, 'an American Senator visited Santa Sabina as part of an idiotic world-tour that had been arranged for him. He has been for many years a representative of one of the more backward States and it would be fair to describe his attitudes as provincial.'

'I was introduced to him at a reception at the United States Embassy,' said Trudi. 'He was drunk at the time.'

'He stayed in this suite,' Marcel continued, grinning at her. 'He was so confused by alcohol and travel that he believed himself to be in Taiwan and kept asking why the local people did not look at all Chinese.'

'He stared at my bosom the whole evening,' she said, 'and he pinched my bottom when Gunther was not looking.'

'He felt it was his duty to expand his horizons by sampling local customs all along his route. Or so he told the proprietor of this hotel one night. He had dined too well at the American Embassy, this Senator from the backwoods, and it was necessary to help him up the stairs when he got back here. But he was not too incapable to instruct the obsequious Baltazar Costa to send a suitable young lady up to his suite.'

'*Pfui!*' Trudi exclaimed in distaste.

She rolled over face down, her chin supported on one hand, and Marcel was given an opportunity to admire the smooth-skinned and perfect globes of her bottom. He dipped two fingers into his champagne glass as if it were holy water in a church and touched the crease between her cheeks lightly, as if blessing them.

'The girl selected by my friend Costa for this important act of international co-operation is named Johana,' he continued, 'she is seventeen, convent-educated and a young lady of considerable enterprise. The Senator is well into his fifties and was full of whisky and so she was not surprised that he encountered difficulties in completing the act of love, even though she straddled him and did all the work.'

'Where's the enterprise in that?' Trudi asked. 'I have made love in that way myself.'

'But of course,' said Marcel, astonished to feel a pang of jealousy now he was certain that she was referring to her relations with D'Cruz. 'The enterprise was not in how she relieved the tired Senator of his tensions but what she did afterwards, when he recognised what the carvings on the bedposts were. He was so amazed by them that Johana knew she had an innocent on her hands. She told him that this is the standard marriage-bed in Santa Sabina and that on their wedding night every couple were expected to imitate every one of the carvings.'

'And he believed her?' Trudi asked with a laugh.

'More than that – he gave her five hundred dollars, which is a fortune here, and said he wanted it to be his wedding-night. So Johana gave him a dose of *datra*, washed down with more whisky and set to.'

'The local aphrodisiac? I have heard of it.'

As an intimate friend of the now-dismissed Minister of Commerce, Trudi's acquaintance with the effects of *datra* was closer than she pretended, in Marcel's private view.

'It's made from a species of thorny shrub that grows wild up in the hills,' he told her, sure that she knew this already. 'They break off the branches when it comes into flower and pound them between stones to extract the sap. They dry it in the sun until it congeals and grate it to a powder for the use of men whose abilities are waning.'

'And does it work?' she asked with seeming innocence.

'I am assured that it works very well. The sap contains alkaloids of some kind which act as a stimulant on the nervous system. According to the sales-talk, an erection is provoked that lasts for hours. The Senator was able to enjoy five of the many ways of love displayed here before he collapsed from nervous exhaustion or so Johana claimed. They had to let him sleep it off for several days before he was strong enough to be shipped home.'

Trudi turned over and stretched herself out on her back again, her yellow hair spread out round her head on a cushion. Her legs were together and she was cupping her magnificent breasts in her hands.

'Have you ever tried this – what did you say it was called – *datra*?' she asked, smiling at him.

'I have never had reason to,' he answered, smiling back at her, his hand stroking her thigh slowly. 'No beautiful lady has ever yet asked more than I was able to give her.'

'Oh, you are conceited!' she exclaimed. 'I would teach you a lesson if I had the time! But I have to be home again by six o'clock, otherwise I would take the starch out of your *zimbriq* for you and leave it limp for a week!'

Her golden-skinned legs were beginning to ease apart gently to the caress of Marcel's fingers. He slid his hand between her thighs and stroked slowly upwards until he was touching the soft lips between them.

'Would you destroy me with this delicious *kuft*?' he asked. 'Surely it is too well-bred for any such violence. After all, it is so sensitive that when I kissed it not long ago it made you *zboca* almost at once.'

His middle finger lay along the moist folds and he parted them casually.

'Yes, my *kuft* is high-born and well-bred,' she agreed, her blue-grey eyes half-closed. 'It does not tire easily, Monsieur, and it is quite ready to take you on again now – if you're up to it. But I suppose that your two little adventures have sapped your strength. Your *zimbriq* is so soft and useless that you hide it for shame under a dressing-gown.'

'By no means!' Marcel exclaimed.

He untied the cord round his waist and pulled open the whole front of his green-striped dressing-gown to show her that the part she had maligned was standing proudly upright. He insisted that she owed him an apology and that the only way to win his forgiveness was to do as he said. With his fingers caressing inside her, she agreed at once and he instructed her to reach behind her head and touch the nearest bedpost. Whichever posture her hand fell on, that was how she must agree to let him proceed. She giggled and put her arm above her head.

'Excellent!' he said, and smiled down at her faintly flushed face. 'Turn and see how you have chosen to be loved.'

By great good fortune she had not chosen one of the more impossible positions. Marcel took off his dressing-gown and sat on the side of the bed, his feet planted firmly on the floor, while Trudi straddled his thighs with her bent knees resting on the bed. He pierced her deeply and with ease, for her *kuft* was very slippery, and devoted himself to a full-handed fondling of her superbly plump breasts, while she slid up and down on his embedded *zimbriq*.

'You'll need a dose of *datra* before I've finished with you,' she murmured, 'several doses in fact – it's not true that it keeps a man hard for hours on end.'

'Ah, that's interesting,' Marcel breathed. 'You speak as if you have observed its operation on a friend. How many times can a man take it before it ceases to have any effect at all?'

'It doesn't always work the second time,' she sighed, 'and there is no possibility of a third time.'

'But perhaps that depends on whether the man is a local or a European,' he suggested.

'Yes, I always forget that,' she said, her up and down movement slowing to a stop on his lap. 'By our standards a Santa Sabinan may seem to be in the prime of life, but he is sexually exhausted. Why is that – do you understand it?'

'The doctors say that it is a question of genetics. The men and women of Santa Sabina come into earlier blossom than we do and they fade earlier. But their flowering is more intense than ours. If a man has become almost incapable at thirty, we must remember that he was making love five or six times a day when he was fifteen. And not only to young girls – he was being exploited by married women as well.'

Marcel applied himself to stimulating the prominent pink buds of Trudi's breasts until she gasped and began her rhythmic ride up and down again. Then for no reason he could think of he recalled Jacqueline Ducour's way of arousing the victims of her passion to uncontrollable fervour. He ran his hands lightly down Trudi's body to the join of her widely-parted legs and fluttered his fingertips in her groin. She gasped loudly and rode him faster. His palms lay flat on her magnificent thighs and his thumbs stroked the fleshy lips into which he was so comfortably inserted.

'Marcel!' she exclaimed and plunged up and down at breakneck speed, sending tidal waves of sensation surging through him. 'You're making me *zboca*!'

'Wait for me!' he gasped.

The balls of his thumbs rolled over the bare and wet folds of flesh between her thighs until she wailed in ecstatic sensation. Her back arched to push her hot belly towards him and the vigour with which she jolted herself up and down caused her breasts to bounce against his chest in a manner that was wholly delightful.

'Yes!' he cried out. 'Now, Trudi!'

Her arms were round his neck and her mouth pressed tightly to his in a wild kiss of consummation. Marcel gasped into her open mouth while his passion spurted so strongly up inside her that, in his climactic frenzy, he believed that she must be able to taste it on her tongue.

5

A Party at Madame da Silva's

Overlooked by the bureaucracy in Rome, Francesco Busoni of the Italian Embassy had served longer in Santa Sabina than any other member of the diplomatic corps. Not that he was displeased by this lack of promotion – he was a firm believer in the Neapolitan doctrine of *dolce far niente* and the life of the island suited him very well. His good nature made him many friends and the lack of anything definite to do at his Embassy gave him all the time he could wish for to pursue his two main interests in life – the translation into Italian verse of Homer's *Odyssey* and the pursuit of pretty young women.

Only after Francesco reached the age of retirement was his Ambassador able to stir Rome into recalling his long-serving Second Secretary for the purpose of pensioning him. Francesco's friends arranged a testimonial dinner at which over fifty were present, an immense amount of wine was drunk and innumerable speeches of tribute were made in a variety of languages. The event took place at Paladio's open-air restaurant down by the harbour and the sight of so many formally-dressed foreigners attracted an audience of Santa Sabinans. They stood in rapt attention, cheering and clapping their hands at the speeches, not one word of which did they understand.

Towards midnight, when the party broke up, five or six of the younger men accompanied Francesco to Madame da Silva's establishment on the Avenue of the Constitution, where Madame's naked girls greeted them with bare breasts and bottoms to be fondled as the party settled comfortably in the salon and champagne was brought.

'My dear friend,' Madame exclaimed, holding out both hands to Francesco, 'I cannot believe that you are leaving us!'

Serafina da Silva was in her forties, tall for a Santa Sabinan woman, long-faced, with black eyebrows raised in arches of permanent surprise. As befitted her position, she alone of the women wore clothes – an Empire-style frock in white. It was designed to expose most of her bosom and, as she was without hips or *embonpoint* to fill it, the frock had a tubular look.

Indeed, it could be said that everything about Serafina gave the appearance of being stretched in the vertical dimension. Her face was long, her nose was long, her bare arms were long, the unsupported breasts inside her thin frock were long enough. When she seated herself beside Francesco her frock outlined her thighs and revealed that they too were long and thin. Marcel raised his glass to her, convinced that she had a long slit between those skinny thighs.

Marcel had once asked Johana why she didn't work for Madame da Silva, in view of the obvious attraction of a regular supply of well-to-do clients. One of Johana's objections was that Madame took half of everything her girls earned. The other was that Madame opened her doors at two in the afternoon and kept her girls busy until two in the morning, which Johana considered excessively long.

'I have arranged a little speciality for your last visit,' Serafina told Francesco and clapped her hands together for attention.

'Gentlemen, it is a great honour to have you in my

house,' she announced to the assembled company, 'and in honour of our dear friend sitting here beside me, whose charms and good nature we shall miss greatly when he leaves us to return to his own country, Mirella and Yzabel have devised a little entertainment for him to remember when in future years his thoughts turn to Santa Sabina.'

She clapped her hands again and two girls got up from clients' laps and advanced into the centre of the salon.

'Yzabel has been with me for only a week or two,' Serafina continued, 'and for that reason not all of you will have had the pleasure of making her acquaintance yet.'

Yzabel was nineteen or twenty and had an attractive face and body. Her skin was coffee-coloured – not the intermediate shade of *café au lait* but a darker and more interesting tone. Her breasts were of a good size for a man to hold in his hands and her belly was smooth and shiny. A most intriguing dark line ran downwards from her tiny belly-button, as if Providence had thought fit to indicate the shortest route to her slit. And with something of that in mind, Yzabel licked the tip of her middle finger and traced her line of darker skin colour down to between her thighs.

Marcel was almost holding his breath as Yzabel sank slowly to her haunches on one of the brightly-striped rugs. She was half-sitting, half-lying, her naked torso propped on an elbow, and all conversation stopped the moment she spread her thighs and displayed her pretty *kuft* and its tight little curls. The cause of so much interest was that Yzabel's nut-brown inner lips were long and plump, and protruded from her permanently-parted outer lips. In case anyone in the room had missed her unusual attraction, she stroked it with her wet fingertip.

'*Che bella!*' Francesco exclaimed, slipping into his native Italian as he grasped Marcel's arm. 'Have you been with her?'

There was a gleam of perspiration on the freckled

dome of his bald head and he pulled a coloured silk handkercheif from his pocket to dab his face lightly.

'No, not yet,' Marcel breathed. 'She is adorable!'

The other girl, Mirella, was very pale-skinned and had been chosen by Madame da Silva for that very reason, to provide a provocative contrast of flesh tones when the two girls were close together. She was a good deal more slender than Yzabel, with thin arms and thighs and very small pointed breasts set high on her chest. Between them on a thin gold chain dangled a small *zimbriq* carved from red coral – the little ornament worn by nearly every Santa Sabinan. Her hair was dark brown and long, and hung in thick strands well below her shoulders, though between her legs she had only untidy wisps.

'I have been with Mirella,' said Francesco. 'She looks thin and weak but she is like a tigress when she becomes excited. She rode me like a wild beast until she had satisfied herself.'

'And you?' Marcel asked in amusement. 'You lay on your back and suffered – is that what you are telling me?'

Mirella went down on her hands and knees between Yzabel's open legs. Her lean-cheeked bottom was thrust jauntily up, and, on an impulse, Marcel learned forward and touched her exposed *kuft*. She grinned over her shoulder and waggled her bottom at him.

'In a quarter of an hour,' she said, 'you can feel me as much as you like.'

Marcel sat back in his chair and Mirella forced Yzabel's thighs flat to the floor and put her mouth to the split between them. There was renewed sighing and even a stifled moan or two round the room as Mirella's wet, red tongue licked at the protruding lips of Yzabel's *kuft*. Yzabel's eyes opened widely, the whites almost luminescent against the sombre beauty of her dark skin, and her red-painted mouth gaped open in delight.

'*Madonna mia!*' Francesco murmured. 'What girls you have, Serafina! I must make love to Yzabel before I go home!'

'And you shall, my good friend,' she replied. 'After our little entertainment she is yours – my present to you.'

'Ah, Serafina, I shall miss you most of all!' he sighed.

Glancing sideways, Marcel saw Francesco lift one of Madame da Silva's long slack breasts out of her deep-cut frock and kiss it. Not the urgent kiss of desire, he noted, more of a kiss of amiability and friendship. But there was no time to take note of Francesco's little gestures of gallantry – the two girls out in the centre of the salon commanded close attention. Yzabel's legs spread wider and she grabbed a handful of Mirella's long brown hair to hold her face hard against her. Mirella squealed a little at having her hair pulled and pushed her tongue between the coffee-brown lips of Yzabel's *kuft*.

Yzabel began to utter staccato cries as she felt her critical moment approach. She let go of the other girl's hair and fell flat on her back, legs spread as wide as they would go, her fingers clawing at her own plump brown breasts. Mirella's red tongue flickered with all the speed of a snake's tongue until Yzabel screamed loud and long and her back arched off the floor. Quick as a cat, Mirella turned and lay with her head on Yzabel's belly, still contracting in spasms of ecstasy, her bony knees thrust upwards and outwards, to expose herself completely. She pulled her thin-lipped *kuft* wide open and stuck two fingers of each hand in it to rub herself furiously. She stared up at Marcel with a fixed grin, gurgled and went into convulsions of delight, her head rolling from side to side on Yzabel's belly.

When the girls had got their breath back after their little performance, Yzabel took Francesco's hand and led him away. Madame da Silva smiled graciously at Marcel and went about her business, while skinny Mirella sat herself on his lap and put an arm round his neck.

'You like me very much, yes?' she asked. 'You want to feel my *kuft*? Come upstairs with me.'

'By all means,' said Marcel, 'but not yet. There is

something I have to discuss with a colleague before he leaves. Wait for only ten minutes and I will accompany you upstairs and do some very nice things to you.'

Her hand was down between their bodies, gripping his hard shaft through his clothes.

'You want to *zeqq* me now,' she announced. 'You can speak to your friend later. Put your hand between my legs and feel me.'

That was the kind of invitation Marcel was totally unable to refuse. Mirella slid her thighs apart on his lap and he stroked between them, enjoying the touch of her now moist lips.

'Put your finger inside,' she murmured in his ear, 'you saw me *zboca* – feel how wet I am.'

Marcel was lost. He pressed a finger into Mirella's slippery folds of flesh and found her wet bud. She giggled at the touch and pushed her hand down inside his trousers until she could get hold of his *zimbriq* and squeeze it. When she repeated her invitation to accompany her upstairs he did not hesitate. Up in her room she took his money and flung herself on the bed, opening her legs to show what she had to offer.

'You can play with my *kuft* all you want now,' she told him, 'I knew you were crazy to have me when you felt me downstairs.'

Marcel stood at the foot of the bed while he contemplated the possibilites of what he had paid for. At a guess Mirella was eighteen or nineteen, pretty of face but much leaner than Santa Sabina girls were in general. Her breasts were so small that when she lay on her back they showed as not much more than prominent russet buds. Yet this unpromising girl had secured a place for herself in Serafina de Silva's highly-regarded establishment – no easy thing to achieve for even the prettiest of girls. And Francesco had testified to her abilities.

'Downstairs you put four fingers in your *kuft*,' he said, stroking her thin belly.

'I have a very greedy *kuft*.' she said. 'She wants to be fed all the time. Look!'

She used her thumbs to roll back the wispy-haired folds between her legs until Marcel could see into her pink and moist interior.

'Put your *zimbriq* in me,' she suggested.

If at that moment the house had blazed up in flames around him and he had only minutes to live, Marcel would not have noticed. There was room in his mind just then for only one thought – to push into the girl. In an instant he was kneeling on the bed with Mirella's ankles in his hands to lift onto his shoulders. He wriggled his knees apart and leaned forward to bring the tip of his trembling shaft to her waiting slit.

'What a strong *zimbriq*!' she said, taking hold of it. 'I shall fall in love with you when I feel it inside me.'

Marcel had no doubt she said that or something similiar to every client as part of her professional chatter, but it didn't change the fact that he had a fine strong *zimbriq*. She guided him into her and laughed up at him when she felt him pushing deep into her belly.

'That's good!' she said. 'Hold still for a moment and I'll show you something'

What she showed him proved to be of exceptional interest. Without moving the rest of her body, she was able to make her abdominal muscles contract and relax at will and this she proceeded to demonstrate. To Marcel it felt as if there was a soft hand inside her belly clasping his shaft and massaging it in a steady rhythm that made him gasp with pleasure.

'Mirella – that feels marvellous!' he murmured.

Her knowing brown eyes stared up at his face, assessing his degree of arousal expertly.

'You came to my room to *zeqq* me,' she said, 'but I'm doing it to you. I'll soon make you squirt in me!'

He pushed once or twice experimentally, but she shook her head and told him to be still. And in truth, the sensations rushing through him were so delightful that he was content to kneel passively, Mirella's ankles in his hands to hold her legs up, while she pleasured him in this unusual way.

'But this is marvellous,' he murmured, meaning that a certain part of her was. She understood him perfectly.

'I told you my *kuft* is greedy,' she said. 'She's sucking your *zimbriq* to make him feed her.'

She spread her arms out wide on the bed, palms down, to give herself a firmer base for her operations. Half-dazed with pleasure Marcel watched her pale-skinned belly clenching and unclenching to the internal movement of her muscles. His embedded shaft was jerking in involuntary spasms as his climactic moments overtook him.

'Yes, yes!' he moaned, feeling his essence sucked from him in long waves of ecstasy.

His eyes were open and he was staring down at Mirella, but he had not the least notion of which woman he was with. It could just as well have been Trudi or Eunice or any one of the multitude of women he had made love to over the years. All that he was aware of was that his hard member was gushing its passion into a warm and wet female slit. Which particular female body surrounded the slit and which particular female personality inhabited that body were matters of supreme indifference to him at that moment.

'*Very* good!' Mirella pronounced when he could see and hear again. 'Lie on your back now and I'll do it to you again.'

'Later,' he murmured, withdrawing from her. 'There is someone I must speak to, if he hasn't left already.'

He dressed quickly and went down to the salon. One of those invited by Francesco to join the party at Madame da Silva's was Colonel Hochheimer, the American Military Attaché and the opportunity was too good to miss. There were questions Marcel wanted to put to the Colonel, questions to which he thought he was unlikely to get answers. But where better to try than in the false camaraderie of Serafina's salon, surrounded by naked girls? Especially when Hochheimer had already been drunk when they left Paladio's restaurant.

In the past two weeks Trudi had visited Marcel at the

Grand Hotel Orient five times. Each episode of their love-making had been so magnificent that he had become infatuated by her superb body. But being an intelligent man, he had become aware that Trudi had deep-seated anxieties about something more than her husband discovering that she had a lover. As they talked together and explored each other's personality, Marcel came to believe that Trudi's anxieties stemmed from her affair with the disgraced Minister of Commerce.

What puzzled Marcel was why so lusty a young woman as Trudi, to whom four climaxes in an afternoon were very welcome – why she had thought it worth her while to let D'Cruz make love to her. He was a stockily-built man, light-skinned and not particularly good-looking. Trudi spoke of him with mild affection, but evidently had never been in love with him. The answer to this enigma had to be that she had been using him for some secret purpose of her own.

In the salon Marcel found the man who might know the answer, Colonel Hochheimer, inelegantly sprawled on a bamboo settee, his medal-beribboned uniform jacket unbuttoned and one of Madame's naked girls on his lap. There was the vaguest of smiles on the Colonel's face, occasioned perhaps by the girl jerking at the limp part she had taken out of his unzipped trousers. He looked up as Marcel paused by the settee, struck by the coincidence that in his dream the American had suffered the same disability.

'Hi, fella, you having a good time?' the American asked drunkenly. 'Take the weight off and tell me something.'

'But I fear that I am intruding, Colonel,' Marcel replied, putting his hand on the girl's smooth bare shoulder to indicate his meaning. She looked up at him and smiled in recognition.

'That's OK, sit right down. This little lady won't mind. Call me Errol – you're with the French Embassy, right?'

'That is so. We have met before. My name is Marcel Lamont.'

From his vantage point above the seated American Marcel saw that there was a distinctly bald patch appearing in his short-cropped sandy hair. Hochheimer was by no means as young as he liked people to believe. But his wits were sharp enough.

'Right,' he said, 'I saw you at the Fourteenth of July party – you were out in the garden screwing. I spotted you under a tree with somebody in skirts.'

'That is true,' Marcel admitted, 'and you took a certain Danish lady out into the garden for the same purpose.'

'Hey, your intelligence works better than I thought,' said Errol, 'that's classified information, fella, me and Inge.'

'But not you and Filumena here?'

'Filumena – is that your name, honey?' Errol asked the girl on his lap. 'That's a pretty name.'

'She's a pretty girl,' said Marcel. 'Do you want her?'

Errol peered at her uncertainly. Marcel's opinion was that Filumena was the most attractive girl in the house. She was olive-skinned and oval of face, with very long walnut-brown hair that was parted in the middle and hung down her bare back to her waist. For a girl of seventeen or eighteen her breasts were exceptionally full but her charms were wasted on Errol in his present condition of intoxication. He reached out to prod one of her breasts, but went no further. For her part, Filumena was losing patience with Errol's lack of response.

'What's wrong with you?' she demanded, dragging at his soft *zimbriq*, 'Why don't you want to *zeqq* me?'

'You are very beautiful, Filumena,' said Marcel, 'and I shall *zeqq* you myself in a little while. But there are things which the Colonel and I must discuss. Ask the waiter to bring another bottle of champagne and leave us in peace for ten minutes'

'Let's have a man's drink,' said Errol, slurring his words, 'no more of that gassy French soda-pop. Order a bottle of araq. That OK with you, buddy?'

82

'But of course,' Marcel responded at once, somewhat dismayed by the prospect.

The Santa Sabinans distilled araq from the sugary sap of palm-trees. It gave rise to dreadful hangovers and, when imbibed in large quantities, caused kidney failure, liver enlargement, brain damage, irreversible coma and death. In the Colonel's state, two small glasses would surely render him unconscious and that would be the end of Marcel's chance to get answers to his questions. Filumena gave Marcel an encouraging smile and departed to pass on the order. In her disappointment with Errol she left his trousers unzipped and his limp *zimbriq* dangling in plain view. Errol was too far gone in drunkenness to notice and Marcel thought it would be distracting to draw his attention to the exposure.

'You spoke a moment ago of intelligence work, Errol,' he said. 'It goes without saying that we have the greatest admiration for the work of the CIA.'

'Damn right,' Errol agreed vaguely.

'The budget is so enormous and the manpower so extensive that your agents can penetrate where no one else has any chance at all,' Marcel continued, laying the flattery on thick.

His real belief was that American espionage successes were not achieved by infiltrating highly-trained agents but by the crude bribery of employees of foreign governments with huge sums of money. Errol was nodding at him vaguely, either in agreement or as a prelude to falling asleep.

'Ysambard D'Cruz,' said Marcel softly. 'A most able man, by all accounts. A cousin of the President of Santa Sabina. A well-regarded Minister of Commerce and Fine Arts. Yet at this very moment while you and I sit here in the comfort of Madame da Silva's salon with naked young ladies to serve our every desire, the former Minister is under house-arrest.'

'Not any more,' Errot observed, his eyelids so heavy that he was having difficulty in keeping them open. 'He's in a cell in the Queen of Heaven jail-house.'

'Then his predicament is most serious and I am sure

that you know why he has been arrested and imprisoned,' said Marcel.

There was a long pause while Errol Hochheimer showed signs of waking up.

'What makes you think I know anything about it?' he asked, his voice clearer than it had been a few moments ago.

A waiter arrived with a long-necked bottle and two glasses on a silver tray. He opened the bottle and poured the pale yellow spirit for them. Errol emptied his glass in one long swallow and held it out for more.

'But of course you know why D'Cruz was removed from office,' said Marcel, shuddering at the taste of the araq. 'You are the head of American intelligence in Santa Sabina.'

'You know too damned much,' Errol muttered. 'Listen, fella, the US did nothing to destabilise D'Cruz. The guy did it all to himself. I hope they pull his toenails out.'

'It was because of his affair with a certain German lady,' Marcel said at random. 'Deny it if you can!'

'Why in the hell should I deny anything at all?' Errol asked, throwing back his second glass of araq. 'If D'Cruz wants to screw diplomats' wives that's OK by me. You know, I'm damned if I can figure out how a whorehouse makes a living when every girl you meet falls over on her back for you.'

'It is because this is the nearest thing to a men's club to be found on the island,' Marcel informed him. 'This is the one off-duty place where a man can be sure that he will not be followed or bothered by his wife or his mistress.'

'You're brighter than I thought,' said Errol blearily as the araq took its inevitable effect on him, 'but I'm not so stupid myself. I know you're screwing the German woman who got D'Cruz into trouble. So watch yourself or you'll find your *castazz* going through the wringer.'

The Santa Sabinan word for a man's precious pendants did not amuse Marcel at that moment.

'How is it possible for you to know that?' he asked.

'Are you having her followed? But why is she important?'

'Nobody's being followed,' Errol mumbled. 'The locals have a man outside every hotel to watch who goes in and who goes out. I just buy the stuff from them to keep up to date.'

'The beggar with the mandolin!' Marcel exclaimed. 'He's there every day. He works for the Santa Sabina secret police!'

'What's it to you?' Errol asked, trying to hold his glass still while he filled it again. 'Screw the ass right off your Kraut friend for all I care. You've got diplomatic immunity. It's locals like D'Cruz who wind up in the slammer.'

'Permit me,' said Marcel, taking the bottle from Errol's wavering hand and holding his other wrist still for him while he poured araq into his glass.

'Thanks – you're a good guy, at that. Have you screwed anybody tonight?'

'I have been upstairs with Mirella and it is my intention to go with Filumena before I leave.'

'Great, great,' Errol murmured, beginning to lean sideways towards Marcel, his drink slopping on to the floor as his wrist went as limp as his exposed *zimbriq*, 'damned if I can remember if I have or not.'

'How did Trudi Pfaff get D'Cruz into trouble?' Marcel asked urgently.

'Stupid deal he made,' Errol sighed under his breath, his head resting on Marcel's shoulder, 'I hope they yank his *castazz* right off and stuff them down his throat.'

'But why do you hate him so much?'

His question remained unanswered, for Hochheimer was unconscious and breathing heavily. Marcel eased his shoulder from under the Colonel's head and stood up, letting him topple over and lie along the settee. His *zimbriq* hung forlornly out of his open trousers and he began to snore loudly through his open mouth. To Marcel he looked middle-aged and played out.

Across the room naked Filumena was sitting on the lap of Mr Kamizaki of the Japanese Embassy. He was giggling and showing a lot of teeth as he played with her breasts and it was all too obvious that she would not be available for some time. Marcel thought he might as well leave, since neither of the other girls in the salon attracted him irresistibly, but Serafina da Silva entered the room, saw him hesitating and came to him smiling.

'Your poor friend the Colonel has fallen asleep,' she observed, her hand on Marcel's arm. 'A cultured man does not expose himself like that in company – it is very impolite.'

'He's not my friend,' Marcel excused himself.

Before he knew what was happening, he was sitting beside Serafina and the waiter was setting another bottle of champagne on the knee-high table before them.

'Benedito – go and fasten the Colonel's trousers,' Serafina instructed the waiter, 'then get Tomas to help you carry him into one of the small bedrooms to sleep it off.'

She turned towards Marcel and her loose breasts slid sideways inside her very low-cut frock as she handed him a glass of champagne.

'A little drink with me before you depart,' she said. 'I saw you looking at Filumena, but she is going up with the Japanese gentleman. Perhaps you would like one of my other girls?'

'Thank you, Madame, but I have been with Mirella.'

'I know – but when you have visited my house before you stayed all night. Are you sad tonight – or are you in love?'

'A little in love, perhaps,' Marcel confessed, 'but not too much to prevent my enjoyment of other women. If Yzabel comes down soon perhaps I shall go with her.'

'I regret that will not be possible,' said Serafina, leaning sideways again to refill his glass, and giving him a glimpse down her frock as far as her red-brown buds, 'Monsieur Busoni has decided to keep her to himself all night.'

'My dear friend Francesco is a connoisseur of women,' said Marcel, smiling at her, 'I was most impressed – though not in the least surprised – when I observed that he did *this*.'

With his free hand he scooped one of her pale slack breasts out of her bodice and bowed his head to plant a kiss on it.

'Oh Monsieur!' she exclaimed, sounding remarkably modest.

Marcel dipped the pointed end of her breast into his glass and then licked the champagne off it.

'You are so gallant, you French!' she murmured. 'You must go upstairs with one of my girls. Have you been with Terzia? She is very agile – she can balance on her head while you *zeqq* her standing up.'

'I don't want any more young girls tonight,' Marcel answered, 'they are without character or personality. Is it too presumptuous of me to hope that I might perhaps persuade you, dear Madame Serafina, to take pity on me?'

'But I am a woman of forty, Monsieur!' she protested. 'You have had too much champagne if you find me attractive.'

'It is my greatest desire to *zeqq* you, Madame,' Marcel told her a little drunkenly as he bowed his head to kiss her exposed breast again.

Owner of a commercial establishment though she was, Serafina was Santa Sabinan born and bred. She had never refused a man or boy since she was eleven and was not about to start now – particularly when the man displaying an interest in her was as handsome as Marcel. She smiled at him graciously, flipped her breast back into her frock and led him by the hand into her own elaborately decorated bedroom. He set down the glass he was carrying on her dressing-table and stood still while she undressed him and knelt to kiss his flat belly and stiff *zimbriq*.

His motives for wanting to make love to Serafina da Silva were obscure even to himself. Forty was not too old, of course – Jacqueline Ducour was more than that and she had little difficulty in getting young men to pleasure her. But in comparison with her own girls,

Serafina was not a man's natural choice. Marcel was mildly puzzled by his own excitement as he lay on the brass-posted bed and watched her pull her long white frock over her head and slide her lace-trimmed knickers down her legs. But his *zimbriq* jerked when she stood smiling at him in only her stockings and a narrow black suspender-belt.

He reached out to touch the dark-haired lips between her long thighs and she slid her feet apart on the floor to let him feel her. The prospect of what was to come had excited her and Marcel was able to slide two fingers into her with ease. Her narrow hips wriggled pleasurably and she cradled her sagging *gublas* in her hands and stroked their russet tips. Her tongue was sticking out and vibrating quickly to show him that she was impatient for the feel of his hard flesh inside her.

She started to breathe loudly and jerk her belly backwards and forwards, her *kuft* so hot and slippery that Marcel thought she was in the throes of a climax. He pulled her towards him with his fingers hooked inside her and she proved him wrong by sitting on the bed with her back to him to peel off her stockings. To recover the initiative, he put his arms round her to squeeze her long belly and slide his fingers into her.

She reacted at once by pushing him on to his back and straddling him, one stocking off and the other hanging loosely round her knee. She opened herself as deftly as if she were opening an oyster and forced his *zimbriq* up into her belly.

'Ah, Serafina,' he sighed in gratitude.

She rode up and down on him, leaning forward to hold the tip of a long and dangling breast to his mouth. He sucked it in and used his tongue on its tip while he stabbed upwards into her. Serafina was murmuring to him without a pause, but in her excitement she had lapsed from every-day French into the old language. She was telling him that he was the most beautiful man she had ever made love to and he could have her as often as he wanted without paying anything at all. But the only word Marcel could understand of all her loving babble was *zeqq*.

6

Storm Above and Storm Below

By the undemanding standards of Santa Sabina the Gran'Caffe Camille was regarded as fashionable. It was to be found on the ground floor of a once flamboyant but now crumbling baroque building across the square from the church of the Four Crowned Martyrs. Because of the oppressive heat, no one except the owner ever sat inside the café, even though there was a large wooden-bladed fan turning slowly on the ceiling to keep the air moving about. Camille's customers – the cream of Santa Sabinan society – sat at the little round tables outside in the square to drink mint tea or iced coffee or the vivid orange or violet drinks that were thought to be chic.

Two days after Francesco's party, Marcel was gossiping over a drink at Camille's with the Dutchman Pieter van Buuren. The long siesta hours were over but neither had any intention of returning to their Embassies that day – the damp heat was appalling, even for Santa Sabina. The good and great of the island capital evidently thought so too, for every table was occupied and the waiters were plying their loaded trays back and forth with whatever last shreds of energy they could muster.

Pieter van Buuren was a fair-haired, pink-skinned

and short-necked man of Marcel's own age, with the muscular build of an amateur boxer. They had struck up a friendship from the day they met, based to some extent on the shared joke of the cul-de-sac nature of their present posting. But apart from professional interests, both had a hearty appetite for the delights offered by pretty women. They were talking about Eunice Carpenter, with whom Pieter had spent the night recently.

'What a woman!' he said. 'She kept me at it all night. I can't remember how many times I had her.'

'You mean how many times she had you,' said Marcel.

'Maybe you're right. Every time I dozed off she woke me up by playing with me to make me hard again. The last couple of times I was too far gone and she climbed on top of me.'

'Yes, Eunice has learned the ways of Santa Sabina,' said Marcel. 'Can you imagine her doing that to a man in Britain?'

'This country is good for women,' said Pieter. 'Something in the air brings out the best in them. Do you know what time I woke up the next day? Two in the afternoon – alone in her bed. I was so exhausted I could hardly stand upright, and she'd got up to go to her office at nine that morning!'

'I've had invitations but I've never been to her apartment,' said Marcel. 'All the times that I have made love to her have been what she calls *hit-and-run*, and I do not want any more involvement than that.'

'You're afraid she'd be too much for you!' Pieter exclaimed with a grin. 'I never thought I'd hear you admit you'd met your match! But it's no surprise really – the French have a reputation for fire and flash and no staying-power.'

Before Macel could refute this disgraceful and insulting suggestion, Pieter tapped his arm and said *look over there!* He half-turned in his seat and saw Errol Hochheimer in uniform striding away from the terrace, his face set in a scowl. He was leaving a table set back unobtrusively against the front of the Gran'Caffe, and he had got up from it so forcefully that he had knocked his chair over backwards. A white-coated waiter bent to pick it up and Marcel saw that Madame Kristensen sat alone at the table, her pretty face pale with suppressed fury.

'A lovers' quarrel, do you think?' Pieter asked, grinning.

'Yes – the night you had Eunice in the Embassy cloakroom he took her out into the garden and had her against a tree.'

'You followed and watched them do it?' Pieter enquired. 'That's real degeneracy! But the French were always voyeurs – they invented the word!'

'At some other time I shall teach you not to defame your betters,' Marcel retorted with mock severity, rising to his feet, 'but at this moment I have important business with Madame Kristensen. *Au revoir*, Pieter.'

The waiter was setting the overturned chair upright again, when Marcel said *bonsoir, Madame* to Inge Kristensen. She stared at him as if she had never seen him in her life before, her hand raised to wave him and the waiter away. At once Marcel took it and kissed it respectfully, then sat down and ordered the waiter to bring another of the pink liqueurs that Madame was drinking and a tiny glass of cognac for himself.

Deserted by her lover, Inge Kristensen was upset, angry, hurt and insecure. Marcel had the ability to be very charming. He fixed his gaze on Inge's dark brown eyes and narrow face and exerted his inborn talent to the limit. Her suspicions were soon dispersed when she was reminded that he was with the French Embassy and she recalled that he had been introduced to her. In a quarter of an hour Marcel had dispelled her anger and coaxed a smile to her face, and they had almost become old friends.

A single drop of rain fell on his hand. He looked up and saw that the thick white cloud layer which so often covered Santa Sabina had turned a dirty grey and was darkening by the minute.

'There will be a storm soon, I think,' he said, reluctant to interrupt promising developments.

'I hope not!' Inge exclaimed sharply. 'I hate thunder – I must go home at once'

Marcel put money on the table for the drinks and led Inge by the arm across the square to where two or three carriages stood for hire outside the Martyrs' church. They were the open four-wheelers that the locals called a *barossa*. Elsewhere in the world they would have had horses between their shafts, but in Santa Sabina horses cost too much and the carriages were pulled by mules. Marcel felt several drops of rain on his face and noted that the coachmen were putting up the collapsible hoods that were supposed to keep the passengers dry.

He handed Inge up into the leading *barossa* and asked her where she lived. It proved to be a villa outside the town, on the coast road, but before he could instruct the coachman, it began to rain heavily. Marcel got in beside her and suggested that she should drop him off at his hotel. His interest in her stemmed from his infatuation with Trudi Pfaff – Hochheimer had hinted that some sort of *deal* between Trudi and Ysambard D'Cruz had brought about the Minister's downfall and her present anxieties. He thought it possible that Inge had learned something about Hochheimer's activities during the time she was his mistress.

What he wanted to arrange was a suitable opportunity to find out what Inge knew. Before he left her he intended to suggest they should meet again very soon. He had no doubts of his own ability to persuade her, with a little gallantry, to confide in him. Up on the box, the coachman pulled his straw hat down hard on his head and wrapped a cracked old waterproof sheet round his shoulders to keep the rain off. He seemed to be having a long, though one-sided, conversation with his ambling mule.

Marcel raised his voice a little over the steady drum of the rain on the carriage hood, but Inge was staring nervously about her and not listening to him. The *barossa* had turned out of the square and was rolling slowly along the broad and tree-lined Avenue of the Constitution, for the wet heat had disinclined the mule to go faster than a walk. Without warning there was a split-second of blazing light in the sky, followed by a deafening crack of thunder. The mule whinnied and jerked its head up in either fright or protest, its long ears laid back and its yellow teeth bared. The effect on Inge was equally dramatic – she shrieked and grabbed Marcel's hand in both her own.

'Don't be alarmed,' he said, 'it's only thunder.'

'I'm terrified of it,' she stammered, her pretty face pale, 'I can't help it!'

'There, there,' he soothed her, slipping an arm round her waist to comfort her.

She cowered against him, gripping his hand so tightly on her lap that her nails were digging into him. As if the thunder had been a signal, the steady rain changed into a rushing torrent of water falling vertically from the sky. The mule whinnied in displeasure yet again and broke into a trot when it felt the cascade on its back, while the driver disappeared under his waterproof sheet. The rain hammered noisily on the black hood of the *barossa* and splashed up so hard from the road that it came in the open sides of the carriage, soaking Marcel and Inge from the knees down.

The sky was illuminated from horizon to horizon with blazing white light and the simultaneous roar of thunder was ear-splitting in its intensity. The mule squealed and broke into a gallop that its driver did nothing to check.

'Too much storm,' he shouted over his shoulder through the noise of the rain. 'We must wait for it to end!'

There was no point in trying to compel him to take them to the Kristensen villa outside town. Even if the coachman had been willing, his mule evidently was not. It had already turned off the Avenue of the Constitution without instruction from him and was making at breakneck speed towards a goal of its own choosing.

'Get us under shelter,' Marcel shouted back.

Inge was trembling like a leaf as she pressed herself close against him. *Well, why not?* Marcel asked himself and slid his comforting arm up from her waist until his hand was cupping a soft breast through her cream silk blouse. She huddled against him even harder and he could hear her terrified gasping.

The carriage lurched and almost tipped over sideways as the determined mule turned sharply right through an open gateway into a yard. Marcel was thrown on top of Inge, his face against hers, her nose in his mouth and his tongue in her ear. Her legs were flung wide as she fell half out of the crazily tilting carriage, her skirt up her legs and Marcel's hand so far up between her thighs that his thumb was in her hot groin. The grip of his other hand dragged her blouse open, but neither of them had time or opportunity to notice.

With a jarring crash the *barossa* rocked back upright on four wheels and came to a halt at last. The mule had made its way to the lean-to which served as its stable and it stood steaming and snorting, safely out of the rain, while the carriage and passengers were still out in the yard.

'Damn clever mule,' said the coachman, in all the pride of ownership.

The rain was thumping on the *barossa*'s leaky hood with unbelievable violence. The instant Marcel stepped out he was under a deluge. In the few seconds it took to help Inge down and hurry her under the lean-to roof alongside the mule, his thin suit was soaked right through. The lightning flared again, the thunder roared like an avalanche sliding down a mountain. Inge flung herself bodily into his arms and clung wetly to him with all her strength.

'Where are we?' he asked over her bedraggled head.

'This is my house, Monsieur,' the elderly coachman answered. 'You can stay here until the storm is over, then I will drive you and your lady to where you want to go. It is dry here and you will be private.'

His light-brown face wrinkled in a grin as he winked

at Marcel and jerked his chin slightly at the open front of Inge's blouse.

'Put this round you and come with me,' he added, taking the old waterproof sheet from round his shoulders and handing it over.

His living-quarters were reached by a rickety wooden staircase up the outside of the white-washed building. Marcel put the waterproof over Inge's head and his own and draped it round them as best he could. She stared at him wild-eyed as, with an arm round her waist, he helped her up the steep climb behind the thoroughly saturated coachman. The room they entered contained the coachman's facilities for sleeping, washing, cooking and eating – all under a low roof of palm-leaf thatch placed over exposed wooden poles. The noise the rain made as it fell like a waterfall on the thatch was unnerving at first, but soon became a background roar.

'Tell me your name,' Marcel suggested, looking at the bed under the eaves by the back wall.

'It is Mateus, Monsieur. Is my house to your satisfaction? There is half a bottle of araq on the table if the lady needs it for her nervousness.'

Inge shrieked as the thunder rolled with terrifying loudness right overhead and wound her bare arms so tightly round Marcel's neck that he was afraid she would choke him. He took hold of her wrists and eased her grip a little.

'I can shut the lightning out for your lady,' said Mateus, and he closed a wooden-slat blind over the one small window.

'Thank you,' said Marcel, 'your house will satisfy our needs very well until the storm finishes.'

He took his sodden money from his back-pocket and peeled off five 50-tikkoo notes, bringing a warm glow to the coachman's eyes.

'Thank you, Monsieur. My house is yours for as long as you and your lady want it. When you are ready to leave, I shall be below with the mule to take you anywhere, but please do not hurry yourselves.'

With a deep bow and a flourish of his disintegrating straw hat he was gone, closing the ramshackle door leading to the stairs carefully behind him. Marcel unwound Inge's arms from his neck and led her gently across the room to sit on the end of the low bed. The only mattress was loose straw spread thickly over wooden slats, but the red and blue country-weave blanket over the straw looked clean. He took off his soaked white jacket, hung it over the back of a chair and spread out his paper money to dry on the square dining-table.

'I fear your clothes are soaked,' he said, sitting on the bed beside Inge, 'we must dry you before you catch a chill.'

It was true that the furious tropical storm had cooled the temperature to about 35C, but the prospect of catching cold was remote in the extreme. Inge looked at him vaguely for a moment and seemed grateful for his care. Certainly she did not resist when he unbuckled the patent leather belt round her waist, tugged her blouse free and eased her arms out of it. The skirt unclipped and came off with no difficulty, leaving her sitting in a semi-transparent slip. Marcel could see through the wet and clinging garment that she wore no brassière over her small and pointed breasts.

Inge's slip was interestingly short – its hem descended no lower than the top of her thighs – revealing the scarlet triangle of her tiny briefs. Like all the European women in Santa Sabina, she went bare-legged in the daytime because of the heat. Hardly able to believe the good fortune that had fallen to him, Marcel stroked from her knees up to her bare thighs, savouring the satin-smooth touch of her skin. He prised her legs gently apart and sighed in delight at what he saw.

In his dream on the night of the Embassy reception, Inge had pulled down pale blue knickers to show off a neat little tuft of chestnut curls between her legs. No doubt his dreaming mind had envisaged it like that because that was the colour of her hair. And indeed, the unconscious assumption had been correct – the fleece between Inge's legs *was* a rich chestnut. But it was far from being a neat tuft. It grew so thickly that the curls bushed out from both sides of her tiny briefs.

'But how charming,' Marcel could not prevent himself from saying, and Inge looked at him with a puzzled expression.

'What are you doing, Monsieur?' she asked, a frown creasing her forehead.

'Your clothes are soaked right through,' he told her again, 'I shall hang them up to dry while I rub you with a towel.'

Before she had time to consider the proposition, thunder exploded overhead. She screamed and grabbed for him, her arms round his waist and her face pressed to his wet shirt.

'It's all right,' he said, trying to soothe her panic by rubbing her back, 'the storm will end soon and I will take you home. But in the meantime I must get you dry.'

She was still trembling with fright when he removed her wet slip. She put her arms round his neck again and held on to him while he got her scarlet briefs under her bottom and down her long legs. Then he stood up and lifted her in his arms easily, feasting his eyes on her body, naked except for the bright red coral necklace round her neck.

'Promise you won't leave me alone!' she whimpered as he carried her round the side of the bed and laid her on the red and blue blanket.

Mateus' rough towel was hanging on a nail in the wall by a bamboo wash-stand. Marcel stripped himself to his striped underpants, thinking that a cautious approach was sensible in Inge's unnerved condition. She offered neither protest nor comment when he rolled her over face-down on the blanket and rubbed her back briskly with the towel. She had an interesting back, long and narrow, with a circular brown mole under her right shoulder-blade. He rubbed with both palms through the towel, dipping into the small of her back and up over the round cheeks of her bottom and down her slender thighs.

Her legs were modestly together and as he massaged down to her knees he pressed them slowly outwards and away from each other. Soon he was able to see the chestnut curls, thick and strong enough to conceal her *kuft* from his inquisitive eyes. *So beautiful*, he thought, hardly able to restrain himself from dropping the towel and feeling between her thighs with his bare hand. His *zimbriq* stood fiercely to attention in his underpants, but he forced himself to remain calm while he pretended to dry her thighs.

When his tension was too great to contain any longer, he turned Inge on to her back and applied the towel gently to her pointed little breasts. Perspiration had trickled down between them and her polished coral necklace was shiny from it. But her fear was not the only reason for that – the temperature was such that Marcel felt the drops running down his own dark-haired chest. He dried Inge's flat belly and saw that her legs were together again, which he found disappointing.

'But you are so hot, my dear Inge!' he said, trying to keep his voice level and not betray his state of excitement. 'You must be feverish – we must cool you before some harm is done.'

He had seen that there was a white enamel bowl on the washstand, filled with clean water. He brought it to the bed, dipped his handkerchief in it and wiped round Inge's breasts. That seemed to bring her a little relief and he got her to put her hands under her head so that he could dabble the wet handkerchief in the smooth hollows of her armpits.

'That feels good,' she said tremulously – her first rational words since the storm began. 'Where are we?'

'In a safe place,' he answered. 'We are waiting for the rain to stop.'

He dipped his handkerchief in the cool water again and spread it over her hot belly.

'Have we been here long?' Inge asked. 'What is the

time? My husband will wonder where I am. And my children.'

Marcel glanced at his wrist-watch and told her that it was almost half past five and there was no need for anxiety. The downpour had assuredly brought the whole of Santa Sabina to a total standstill and her husband could no more get home than she could.

His little attentions to her with the towel and the water had lulled her fears to a large extent. The constant rattle of the rain on the palm-leaf roof had become almost comforting and the dimness of the room seemed postively restful. When he squeezed out the handkerchief again in the bowl and touched her thigh to indicate his intention, she opened her legs for him to bathe her hot groin.

'Does that make you feel a little better?' he asked, dipping his handkerchief in the water once more.

'Much better,' she answered, opening her long legs wider.

From her chestnut-curled groin he progressed slowly to her *kuft*, parting the thick curls with his fingers to press the wet cloth to it. She gave a little cry of surprise at the touch and her legs jerked nervously. Marcel smiled at her reassuringly till her body relaxed, her bare feet turning outwards, while he dipped his handkerchief in the bowl and laid it between her thighs again. This time he did more than just hold the wet cloth against her. He used it to caress the fleshy folds between her legs, combing her thick curls out of the way with gentle fingertips.

For two brief heartbeats Inge's pale cheeks flushed a delicate pink, then she gave herself up to the sensations of the moment. She was breathing quickly and her eyes were closed, but she did not need her vision to tell her that the wet hankerchief lay on the blanket and that Marcel had separated the lips of her *kuft* to caress her little bud. Nevertheless, for reasons of female logic she thought it appropriate to ask about his intentions.

'What are you doing?' she murmured.

'Calming you, dear Inge,' he replied, 'the storm was making you hysterical.'

'You won't make me calm by touching me there,' she said, opening her beautiful hazel eyes to stare at him.

'Do you want me to stop?' he asked, feeling her legs tremble to the sensations he was stirring.

'You ask me that – your victim?' she exclaimed. 'After you've kidnapped me in broad daylight and dragged me to your hide-out to ravish me? Now you seek my opinion on whether you should continue or not – what kind of rapist are you?'

'The tender-hearted type,' he answered, his fingers deep in her warm and wet *kuft*.

'What lies!' she said, 'How can you claim to be kind and gentle when you are threatening me with that enormous thing bulging out of your underpants!'

Her hand darted through the slit of his shorts and extracted the long and swollen part she meant. It was with some justice that she called it enormous, for the excitement of his ministrations to her had aroused him to a high pitch and he was at an impressive full-stretch.

'Oh!' said Inge. 'It's monstrous – you cannot possibly stick *that* in me! You'll split me wide open!'

It spite of her protest, she did not appear to find the idea utterly out of the question, to judge by the way she flipped her hand up and down the hard shaft she had exposed.

'Resign yourself,' Marcel said firmly, 'there is no escape now that you are in my secret hide-out. After I have violated you to the point of unconsciousness I am going to tie you naked to the bed by your wrists and ankles.'

'No, I beg you not to use me for your depravity!' she gasped. 'Let me go and my husband will pay the ransom!'

'I shall keep you here for as long as I wish,' he insisted.

His body was shaking to the thrills caused by her busy hand stroking him, just as she was squirming under his stimulation of her *kuft*.

'Will you make me wear a black silk mask?' she asked breathlessly. 'I beg you not to – please don't tie me to the bed, naked, with a black silk mask to hide my face!'

'But of course you must be made to wear a black silk mask,' Marcel said at once, amused by her fantasy. 'I shall leave you here on your back with your legs wrenched wide apart by cruel bonds. And when you least expect it, I shall come back and ravage your helpless body, time after time.'

'Get it over with and let me go, please!' she begged.

'I shall keep you prisoner for weeks,' he replied, his fingertips skimming over her slippery bud, 'and violate you hundreds of times, and even when you have fallen into an exhausted sleep you will wake to feel me in your belly.'

Inge made a gasping sound, perhaps of terror at the fate which he was describing, but her manipulation of his shaft did not stop or even slow down.

'No, not again,' she pleaded, 'I'm not strong enough, it is too much! You will *zeqq* me to death!'

Her eyes were rolling up in her head to show the whites and Marcel could see she was on the threshold of a climax. But at that very moment the forgotten thunder crashed out above them in a mind-splitting explosion. Her mouth gaped open in an unheard scream and her body jerked up into a sitting position, her hands pressed flat over her ears to shut out the noise.

'No!' Marcel howled in frustration.

Unable to restrain himself, he slammed her down on her back and hurled himself on top of her while the thunder roared out again, throwing her into an instant hysterical seizure. Her head was hard back pushing her round little chin up sharply, and there was a trickle of saliva from one corner of her wide open mouth. She was uttering a continuous high-pitched shriek, her hands pressed over her ears to shut the storm out. Her body rolled from side to side, and her long legs were kicking out wildly. All this violent activity continued as Marcel slid into her wet slit.

He was so far gone that he hardly heard the thunder

boom out once more, but it had its effect on Inge. Her heels thumped up and down on his legs with bruising force and her perspiration-wet body squirmed in convulsions so frantic that Marcel had to pin her to the bed with all his strength to keep from being dismounted. Naturally, in his advanced state of arousal the writhing of her body under him brought on his crisis at once. With savage thrust he fountained his essence into her belly and cried out in the exaltation of release.

When he came to himself again, Inge was still making her shrill noises and heaving beneath him. He thought it best to stay on top of her and restrain her movements as much as he could, so that she did not accidentally hurt herself. Very gradually she slowed down, until at last she stopped shrieking and her hands fell away from her ears. He felt the fading tremors of her belly and prayed that the thunder would not start her off again. Slowly her hazel eyes opened and she looked up into his face. She took two or three deep breaths, licked her lips and gave him an exhausted smile.

'You're too much for any woman,' she whispered, hardly able to get the words out. 'I've never felt anything like that in my life before.'

Marcel kissed her cheek and climbed off her to fetch a glass of araq from the bottle on the table to revive her. It was evident to him that Inge was confused. The strong sexual sensations she had been experiencing from his manipulation of her mind and body had somehow become integrated and fused into the hysterical seizure brought on by the thunderstorm. As a result, she believed that she had experienced the world's most stupendous climax.

It would have been cruel to disillusion her. And besides, it might even be true – there was no way of knowing what she had felt. He put an arm round her shoulders to help her sit up while he held a cup to her mouth and persuaded her to take a few sips of araq. A rumble in the sky made her start and spill some of the spirit down between her breasts, but the thunder had moved a long way off and she was soon calm again. He eased her down on the bed again and heard her contented little sigh as he licked the spilled araq from her belly.

'The storm is going away,' he said, stretching out beside her. 'The *barossa* is waiting below to take you home when the rain stops. But first you must rest a little.'

'Yes,' Inge agreed. 'I must rest after what you've done to me. You are incredible, Marcel, truly incredible.'

'My love-making is not the same as Colonel Hochheimer's?' he asked, trying to steer the conversation in the direction that interested him.

'How can you ask!' she said, smiling faintly. 'You are a king in bed. I don't know how I ever got involved with Errol. It must have been the uniform.'

'I met him the other evening,' said Marcel, not bothering to mention where the meeting had taken place. 'He was talking about Ysambard D'Cruz in terms which made it clear that he was involved in his downfall.'

'Errol is terrified the Santa Sabina government will find out about him now that they've put D'Cruz in prison,' said Inge. 'The United States Embassy will deny everything, of course, but they'll send Errol home and he'll lose his job.'

'But what exactly was he involved in with D'Cruz? He did not explain that to me.'

'He didn't tell me either,' she said, holding the palm of his hand against her warm belly. 'It's Top Secret and political. And it's very important – I gathered that much.'

'What about Trudi Pfaff? How did she get involved?'

'She's been having an affair with D'Cruz, but she had nothing to do with Errol's project. He called her a bitch and a whore who'd ruin his plans. I think he even tried to get her out of the way by letting her husband find out about D'Cruz.'

Marcel digested the surprising information that Gunther Pfaff knew of his wife's love-affair. While he considered some of the many implications of that, he stroked Inge's belly thoughtfully, not to excite her but to make her feel cosseted and secure, so that she would talk freely.

'Errol was behaving in a mysterious fashion when we met,' he said. 'He gave me the impression that he detests D'Cruz and will shed no tears for his fate, however dreadful.'

'Yes, that's a mystery to me too,' said Inge. 'Right up to the day D'Cruz was sacked he and Errol were the best of friends. They used to meet and get drunk together at least once a week, sometimes in bars, and sometimes in brothels. There's one run by a woman called da Silva they used to go to.'

'Really?' said Marcel, trying to recall whether he had ever seen the American and the former Minister of Commerce together in Serafina's salon.

'That's what we quarrelled about,' Inge went on. 'He swore that the only reason he went there was to meet D'Cruz in private, but I never entirely believed him. Today when I said he doesn't have to go there again now that D'Cruz is locked up, he claimed to have another contact to meet there. So I lost my temper and told him that he's a pig and he can go and live with the whores for all I care, because he won't be seeing me again.'

She sounded so miserable that Marcel hugged her to him and kissed her eyes and cheeks to comfort her a little.

'Do not be sad for too long,' he murmured, 'love comes and love goes – that is how life is. You are beautiful and charming and soon there will be another to love you and make you happy.'

7

A Night of Sàtisfactions and Resentments

A little before seven o'clock the rain stopped falling with a dramatic abruptness. At one moment it was tumbling out of the sky like a waterfall, then it became a gentle drizzle and, only a moment later, it had stopped completely. Marcel assisted Inge to dress in clothes that were not yet dry – like his own they were clammy to the skin. He kissed her and took her down to the stable, where Mateus was asleep on the straw beside his mule.

'I shall remember this afternoon all my life,' she said, leaning out of the *barossa* to kiss him once more.

She drove off and Marcel strolled towards the town centre. Santa Sabina's antiquated drainage system was inadequate to cope with the quantity of rain that had descended on it in so short a time and the streets were ankle deep, even the Avenue of the Constitution. Marcel did as he saw others doing – he took off his shoes and wet socks and put them in his jacket pockets, rolled his trousers up to his knees and waded on through the warm water.

Inge had confirmed his suspicion that Colonel Hochheimer had been involved in some sort of secret arrangement with the fallen Minister of Commerce and Fine Arts. And because Marcel refused to believe that Trudi's liaison with D'Cruz had been a simple affair of love and desire, logic insisted that she was also involved in the plot. That D'Cruz was a corrupt politician came as no surprise – there was no other kind in Santa Sabina. And, in Marcel's view, precious few elsewhere.

Though he told himself repeatedly that none of this was his concern, the uncomfortable truth was that suspicions had entered his mind and were gnawing at him. That women found him pleasing he had no doubt, but did that alone account for the enormous love and delight which Trudi showered on him so very soon after she had been sexually involved with D'Cruz? He felt that he owed it to himself to find out more.

The bolting mule had carried his passengers a long way down the Avenue of the Constitution before turning off into the poor quarter where it was stabled. And as Marcel strolled back, he saw that neither the cloud-burst nor the steamy heat had done anything to depress the natural cheerfulness of the Santa Sabinans. Little groups of men sat on the public benches under the palm trees, swishing bare feet in the flood water while they chattered away. The irrepressible women were on the look-out for virile young men and Marcel declined more than one offer with a charming smile of regret.

The sad truth he had discovered was that lovemaking with the hot-blooded women of Santa Sabina usually proved to be a disappointment. They were too impatient and snatched at pleasure as if the world would end in five minutes. Unlike the European custom of the man mounting the woman, the island tradition was for the man to lie on his back and the women to squat over him.

Not that Marcel objected to a reversal of positions, except that, as soon as a Santa Sabina woman impaled herself on a *zimbriq*, she was transformed into a sort of human dynamo. She bounced up and down so furiously that both she and her partner reached their climax in seconds – out of curiosity he kept count with one beauty he had met casually in a shop and gone home with. Her plunging was so forceful that he had fountained his excitement into her on her seventeenth stroke!

All the same, he was tempted by a woman who waved at him from a balcony. She was in her early twenties and very pretty, with a fringe of jet-black hair combed down over her forehead. She smiled at Marcel as he stood in ankle-deep water on the very edge of the pavement to stare up at her and she made exaggerated kissing movements with her mouth. He smiled back and, encouraged by his response, she hoisted her loose lemon frock halfway up her bare thighs.

His interest showed in his face and without hesitation she pulled her frock waist-high and let him see that she wore nothing at all under it. The sight of her curly black fleece through the wrought-iron curlicues of the balcony was almost too much for him – his *zimbriq* bounded in his trousers and he almost began to shuffle through the flood-water towards the door of the apartment building. The woman above smiled more broadly, slid her feet apart and rubbed her *kuft* with one hand to indicate that extraordinary pleasures were in store for him.

When he was under the balcony and could not longer see her, some slight power of rational thought was restored to him. Experience of Santa Sabina women told him exactly what would happen. She would have the apartment door open and the instant he stepped inside she would rip his trousers open and lunge for his *zimbriq*. He would hardly have time to get her frock over her head before she had him on his back and spiked herself on him. And then it was a question of how fast she could slide her wet *kuft* up and down his shaft.

If two years ago a traveller had returned to Paris and told him of the prettiness and eagerness of the young women of Santa Sabina, Marcel would have assumed that Paradise had been discovered on earth. More than that, he would have bought a ticket and made the journey to experience the sensual delights of so very interesting an island. But now that he had availed himself of the enthusiasm of twenty or thirty of the island women, he knew enough about them to be sure that the woman on the balcony would exhaust him without pleasing him.

Since leaving the stable, he had been trudging through dirty rain-water for twenty minutes, and he decided it was enough. He was in no hurry to get anywhere and it would be better to wait for the drains to empty the streets before continuing to his hotel. Apart from the discomfort of paddling along the pavement, another reason for his decision was that the woman on the balcony had reminded him of the pleasures of love and he was not far from the building where Eunice Carpenter lived.

Her apartment was on the fourth floor and, needless to say, the electricity had failed and the lift had stopped working when the storm broke. He climbed the stone stairs and knocked at Eunice's door. There was a long pause that made him think that she was out, and he was turning away when he heard a bolt rattle. Eunice opened the door and looked both surprised and pleased to see him. She was bare-foot and in a light satin négligé of an unflattering electric blue shade.

'You invited me to drop in at any time,' Marcel reminded her, 'but I fear that I have arrived at an inconvenient time.'

'No, I'm all alone,' she said with a smile of welcome. 'Come in and dry your feet.'

Her apartment was in one of the older buildings and had a hardwood floor. Marcel felt pangs of guilt as he left wet marks the length of the passage from the entrance to the small bathroom. He washed the mudstreaks from his feet and joined Eunice in the sitting-room, not bothering to put on his shoes and socks. The french windows to her small balcony were wide open, but there was no breeze at all and she looked distinctly hot and uncomfortable, sitting on a wicker-work settee. Marcel poured himself a glass of whisky from a bottle on the sideboard, filled the glass to the rim with ice-cubes and sat down beside her.

For relief from the heat, or perhaps for another

reason, she had taken off her obtrusively-coloured négligé and was displaying herself in shiny satin pyjamas of a lavender tint. Marcel was constitutionally incapable of being alone with any woman under sixty, without making at least some preliminary advance. He laid his hand against her chubby belly. He found it to be very hot under the thin pyjamas and when Eunice turned her head to smile at him he saw drops of perspiration on her forehead.

'My poor Eunice,' he said, his success with Inge vivid in his thoughts, 'I must cool you down a little.'

He picked a couple of ice-cubes from his glass, put his hand down the waist of her pyjama trousers and rubbed the ice gently over her belly.

'Marcel!' she exclaimed. 'That's lovely!'

She raised her bottom from the settee to push her pyjamas down her thighs and opened the buttons of her jacket. Marcel rubbed her belly with a circular motion, enjoying the view he had of Eunice's brown-haired *kuft*. The fleshy lips were pouting slackly and gradually he let his hand circle lower until he touched the fast-melting fragment of ice to them. She gave a little shriek and giggled.

'Has someone been here already?' he asked with a grin. 'Am I following Pieter van Buuren yet again?'

The final speck of ice turned to water and she sighed to feel Marcel's fingers press inside and caress her in a short and rhythmic motion.

'I was so hot and sticky when I got home that I stripped off and stood under the shower for ages,' she said, 'but it didn't help much. I was sitting here in a day-dream fingering myself.'

'My apologies for interrupting you,' he said. 'It shall be my pleasure to make restitution at once.'

'The pleasure will be more mine than yours,' she murmured.

She slid her legs further apart on the settee cushion and her round face flushed slowly red from the sensations aroused by his busy fingers. She put an arm round his shoulders, to pull him tightly against her body.

'What entertaining little day-dream was in your mind when you sat here with your hand between your legs?' he asked.

'I was thinking how nice it would be if a lovely man like you pushed me on my back and ripped my knickers off,' she murmured.

'I am flattered!'

'You should be!' she answered. 'If you knew how many times you've had me on my back over a table at the Gran'Caffe with hundreds of people looking on!'

'What a beast I am!' he said. 'What else have I done?'

'You've had me naked across your lap in an open *barossa* dozens of times. You say you'll *zeqq* me all the way down the Avenue, but we never get past the Convent before I climax.'

Marcel pushed his free hand up inside her unbuttoned satin pyjama jacket to bare her big soft *gublas* and fondle them.

'I like this *barossa* ride of yours – it sounds amusing,' he said. 'I know a coachman who would drive us – late at night when there's nobody about? Dare you ride with me naked?'

'Oh, yes, yes! Tonight if you like!' she gasped, her chubby belly quaking in a sudden passionate climax.

Marcel continued to play with her until she exhaled a long sighing breath and stopped shaking. He gave her time to recover by fetching her another drink from the sideboard.

'You haven't cooled me down at all, but you've made me feel a lot better,' she told him with a broad grin.

'It was my pleasure . . .' he started to say, then changed it to *our* pleasure.

Eunice felt his long hard *zimbriq* through his trousers and said it was certainly going to be his pleasure in a minute.

'I'm glad I decided to drop in,' he said. 'I was passing your building and I thought how nice it would be to see you. And to find that you were caressing yourself and thinking of me is a most agreeable coincidence.'

Eunice put his hands on her fat breasts to keep them out of the way while she unzipped his trousers.

'Don't get upset,' she said, stroking his *zimbriq*, 'but for once you weren't the star of my day-dream.'

'You are unfaithful to me!' he exclaimed, trembling with pleasure as her clasped hand slid up and down. 'What was this other person doing to you?'

'We were in a changing-hut on the beach. He was making me bend over for him.'

'You were thinking of Piet,' Marcel gasped, 'he's on the beach nearly every day.'

'You're wrong,' she chuckled. 'And what difference does it make to you who I invite to *zeqq* me in my imagination?'

He had a soft *gubla* in each hand and tugged at them to pull her sideways along the settee so that he could mount her but she shook her head.

'It's far too hot to have you lying on top of me,' she said.

She handled his swollen *zimbriq* so expertly that he could feel that only seconds were left. He pulled her open pyjama jacket down from her shoulders and grasped at her *gublas* with feverish fingers.

'That's how I like to see it!' she murmured, 'hard as iron and with a head purple and swollen as a plum. You're going to *zboca* for me!'

He gave a long gasp and gushed his sticky excitement up the front of his white shirt.

'Nice!' Eunice exclaimed. 'Very nice, my dear.'

While he was getting his breath back she went to the sideboard for more cold drinks. Marcel took a long swallow of Scotch whisky and water and grinned at her.

'I know who you bent over for in your day-dream,' he said, 'it was Errol Hochheimer.'

'How did you guess that!' she asked in amazement.

'Remember the night he passed us in the Embassy garden? There was something in the way you spoke of him that suggested you would be happy to open your legs for him.'

'Him and a dozen others,' she said, 'I found out who was with him that night. Inge Kristensen – do you know her?'

'I've met her,' Marcel answered in a neutral tone, thinking it unwise to let Eunice know he had come straight to her from *zeqqing* Inge.

'You'd better take your shirt off and let me put it to soak for you,' said Eunice,' 'I can iron it dry before you go – if you stay the night, that is.'

Marcel stripped off his stained shirt.

'I was planning to take you out to dinner,' he said. 'How can I do that without a shirt?'

'It's too hot tonight to go out,' she answered. 'I'll make a light meal here. We've had the hors-d'oeuvres already.'

He half-turned on the settee to watch her walk across the room away from him and smiled to see the bare and heavy cheeks of her bottom roll below the lavender pyjama jacket. There was something enchanting for him in the way the two halves of a woman's rump slid up and down alternately in walking. More than one girlfriend in Paris had thought it an odd request but had pleased him by walking naked round the room while he sat and stared at her swaying cheeks. Even more enchanting was a pair of breasts bouncing up and down when a woman ran naked, but in a city this was not easy to arrange.

He sipped his drink while he amused himself with these thoughts and then went after Eunice into the bathroom. She was putting his shirt to soak in the hand-basin and he stood behind her, his arms round her so that he could dandle her breasts.

'You have the most shameless *gublas*,' he said, looking over her shoulder at her breasts reflected in the mirror. 'They are too big, too round, too soft, too plump – I swear it would *zboca* immediately if I put my *zimbriq* between them!'

'I'd love to see you,' she said, 'if it would only cool

down a bit! The first time I have you all night and it has to be so hot that even I'm wilting!'

He peeled her pyjama jacket off, slid his trousers down his sweating legs, turned on the shower and pulled Eunice under the cold water with him. In reality the water was not cold at all, merely tepid, but it brought some refreshment on hot flesh and Eunice was content to lean her back against the tiled wall while he soaped her body. When he let the water wash the creamy lather from her breasts, their red-brown buds were standing up very prominently. He put his head down and sucked them in turn.

'You think my *gublas* are too big and fat, do you?' she breathed, her eyes closed in pleasure.

'Big and round and soft and shameless,' he corrected her, one hand circling on her belly until she moved her feet apart for him to feel between her thighs.

'What is it about Errol Hochheimer that makes you eager to get him into bed?' he asked, his fingers titillating warm folds of flesh. 'Is it the uniform? You'll have to hurry up, because they say he may be recalled very soon.'

'I know,' she breathed, her hand clasped round his *zimbriq*. 'He's made a mess of his job and he's in trouble.'

There was no opportunity to question her further just then. Eunice tugged him towards her by his stiff handle and with a dip and a long slow push he slid up into her and heard her little moan of pleasure. Tepid water cascaded down between them, washing over her *gublas* and down between their bellies. It served to cool their skin a little while he see-sawed back and forth in a motion that conserved energy while producing delightful sensations.

On a night as hot and clammy as this it was going to be all too easy to *zeqq* Eunice to a standstill, he reflected. He had accepted Piet's challenge, but it would be no victory at all to see her collapse from the effects of the climate rather than his ability as a lover. Even moving as steadily as he was, her breasts were heaving and falling as she laboured to breathe. Her fingernails sank sharply into his bottom and she rammed her bulging belly against him in ecstatic convulsions, moaning and panting, her mouth wide open. The sight of a woman's climax never failed in its effect on Marcel – he stabbed into her with short quick strokes that brought on his crisis at once.

When they were calm again, they stayed where they were, under the shower, letting the water stream down over them. Marcel's *zimbriq* softened until it slid out of its warm hiding-place, to hang between his legs and be cooled by the water running down his body. He pushed Eunice's wet hair back from her face, and kissed her cheek.

'Since you're so interested in Errol Hochheimer, do you know about his agreement with Ysambard D'Cruz?' he asked casually.

Eunice gave him a sideways look. Her hands were still on his bottom and she massaged the cheeks thoughtfully.

'There are some things it's best not to know about,' she said. 'I've no interest in Errol's job, only in finding out what his *zimbriq* feels like.'

'Not as nice as mine,' said Marcel, 'but you do know what Errol's been up to, I think.'

'We have a special relationship with the United States,' she said, finding it difficult to sound formal while standing naked under a shower with a man who had just made love to her.

'Everyone knows of the understanding between Great Britain and America,' said Marcel. 'But alas, dear Eunice, you do not yet have the special relationship with Errol that you desire.'

He felt between her parted thighs to caress her lightly.

'This is where real alliances are made,' he told her. 'Alliances of pleasure and friendship and reliability, such as between you and me. I hope you will achieve your desire and get Errol Hochheimer inside you here.

But soon – perhaps in weeks, perhaps days – he will be gone. You and I will remain here.'

'You're right,' she breathed, pressing her wet cheek to his. 'But I can't tell you what he's been up to, because I don't know. That sort of information is classified and above my level.'

'You are a highly intelligent woman and you hear things not meant for your ears,' Marcel suggested.

'I have absolutely no information at all about Colonel Hochheimer,' she said, as primly as was possible in the circumstances, 'and if I had, I would not pass it on to a foreign national.'

'But of course, you have your duty,' said Marcel, and licked the corners of her mouth with the tip of his tongue.

'But if you want my guess . . .'

'Yes,' he said, his fingers inside her slippery *kuft*, 'I would be interested to hear what it is that you guess.'

'Well, it is only a guess . . .' she sighed, 'but I think he's been bringing guns in.'

'Impossible!' Marcel exclaimed, so astonished that he put his hands on her plump shoulders and stared into her face.

'I know it sounds silly,' she said defensively.

Marcel resumed control of himself, kissed her cheeks and suggested another drink now that the shower had cooled them down a little. She agreed and thought it was time they had something to eat – to keep his strength up, she said, flicking her hand across his dangler. Five minutes later they faced each other across her dining-table, Marcel with a green bath-towel wrapped round his waist and Eunice with a similar towel tied like a turban round her wet hair, but otherwise naked. They ate a cold roast chicken and drank a bottle of white wine, though Marcel turned up his nose when he saw that it was not French wine – not even of European origin.

He was sure that Eunice's *guess* about Errol Hochheimer was based on information she had acquired during the course of her work, but he thought it prudent to leave the matter for a while. He talked of the possibilities of arranging the naked *barossa* ride along the Avenue of the Constitution.

'You realise that if we're found out we'll both be sent home in disgrace,' he said, smiling at her across the table.

She laughed and her heavy *gublas* shook. 'So we won't let ourselves be found out,' she said. 'Can you arrange it? I get really excited when I think about being *zeqqed* in public! The changing-huts on the Reserved Beach get me going every time I'm there, though you can't really call it public – except when the beach boys watched you and me over the wall. The nearest I've ever got to performing in public was on the ship coming out here.'

'But tell me – it sounds amusing!' said Marcel, rubbing his bare foot over hers under the table.

'I was sunbathing,' she said, 'everybody else was on the sun-deck by the swimming-pool but I went up on the boat-deck to be alone because I wanted to pull my costume down and get my *gublas* brown.

Her feet caught his foot between them and squeezed. Marcel straightened his leg under the table, stroking up to her knees with his toes.

'There were no deck-chairs up there,' she continued, 'so I lay on the deck. I was there in the sun for an hour or more, costume down round my waist, doing my back and front in turn.'

'It is a front to be proud of,' said Marcel, his heel resting on the edge of her chair between her knees.

Eunice glanced down at the rotundities of her breasts and nodded her agreement. Her warm thighs clamped Marcel's foot.

'Just as I as rolling over on to my back, one of the ship's officers came up the steps and poked his head over the deck. He stared at my bare *gublas* and his mouth dropped open – he couldn't believe his luck. Now you may find it hard to believe, but I was different before I came to Santa Sabina. I'd only had three boy-friends in my life and I never lived with any of them.

Making love was something that happened once a week after we'd been to the theatre or out to dinner.'

'And so when this ship's officer saw you half-naked, it embarrassed you?' Marcel asked.

'I blushed scarlet! Before I could cover myself up, he was on his knees on the deck beside me. He yanked my costume off so fast I didn't know what was happening to me until he had his trousers undone and was lying on my belly!'

'My God – he raped you?' Marcel asked incredulously.

'I suppose he did, if you think about it,' she said, 'but it was a blazing afternoon and I'd got hot and bothered lying in the sun. I didn't know whether to scream or laugh when this sailor shoved it straight in me without a word. As soon as he began ramming away I knew that's what I wanted, so I spread my legs and let him have his way. And that's the only time I've been *zeqqed* in a public place.'

'What did he say afterwards?' Marcel asked, stretching out his leg to slide his foot up between her thighs on the chair. 'Did he apologise, for example?'

'He asked my cabin number and said he'd be there at ten-thirty that night,' she answered, laughing at his serious tone.

Under the table her legs opened wide to let the sole of his foot touch her belly.

'It's not ten-thirty yet,' she said, 'and we're not in the middle of the ocean, but I'm ready if you can think of a way we can do it without stifling from the heat.'

They got up from the table together and Marcel led her to the wicker-work settee. She sat on it and spread her thighs, while he removed the towel from his waist and knelt between her feet. She flicked at his stiffness with a fingertip and set it nodding.

'You're like me, Marcel – you can't get enough of it!'

She brought the head of his *zimbriq* to the loose lips between her legs and rubbed it up and down them. Marcel grasped her chubby thighs with greedy hands and started to push into her very slowly, while he and she stared down at his centimetre by centimetre penetration of her brown-curled *kuft*. When at last he was fully in her, they both remained still, enjoying the sight of what he had achieved.

'For me that's the best sight in the world,' she whispered.

Her arms hung at her sides and he kept his belly away from hers, to avoid the heat of contact.

'Do it slowly,' she murmured, 'I want to see myself being *zeqqed*.'

Marcel nodded and began a slow to and fro movement. He wanted to feel her breasts, but drops of perspiration were trickling down between them and to handle them would make her uncomfortable. Instead, he took their prominent red tips between his fingers and rolled them slowly. The sensation of being engulfed in Eunice's warm and wet *kuft* was so enjoyable, and the sight of its long lips forced open by his shaft was so exciting, that he knew his golden moments would come soon. He looked up at Eunice's face and saw her brown eyes gleaming with the intense emotions that were about to overwhelm her.

'I want to see your face when you do it,' she gasped.

He was so aroused that he hardly knew what he was doing – the heat and discomfort were forgotten as he gripped her heavy breasts full-handed and sank his fingers into them while he rammed into her. She took his face between her hands and held it firmly, her eyes waiting for the change in his expression when his crisis arrived. His chest swelled as he sucked in air in a sudden pang of pleasure and then the breath rushed out from his mouth and he gasped again and again while his ecstasy spurted into Eunice's shuddering belly.

When they separated, he was left sitting on the floor, his back against the settee. Eunice fetched a tray of ice-cubes and, imitating the way he had cooled her earlier, rubbed ice over his perspiring chest and down his belly. He gave her a smile of gratitude and spread his legs wider on the floor to let her press ice-cubes into his groin. When her hand was very cold, she clasped it loosely round his limp *zimbriq* and the sensation was very refreshing.

'I think it is for your own purposes that you are trying to revive me,' he said as her fat breasts swung near his face.

'I'd be a fool not to,' she answered. 'How do I know when you'll turn up unexpected on my doorstep again?'

Somewhat recovered from his strenuous delights, he made Eunice lie on the polished wooden floor while he washed the traces of exertion from her body with a cloth dipped in cold water. When she closed her eyes and gave every indication of enjoying his attentions, he asked her if she'd ever had a love-affair with a Santa Sabinan.

'I don't have love-affairs,' she said with a chuckle, 'I make love with any man who takes my fancy, which is not the same thing. But as you're interested, yes – I've had a Santa Sabinan or two, more out of curiosity than anything else.'

'Is it true that their strength is dissipated by the time they are grown up?'

'They rise to the occasion after a dose of datra, but compared with you they're non-starters. They say the fifteen-year-olds are insatiable, but I've never fancied young boys.'

'What I find difficult to understand is this,' said Marcel, washing with cool water between her parted legs and soaking her dark-brown curls, 'everyone insists that Ysambard D'Cruz is the lover of Trudi Pfaff. I'm sure you've heard this.'

'It's a open secret,' said Eunice, opening one brown eye to look at him curiously, 'the only person who doesn't know about it is her husband.'

'Perhaps he knows,' Marcel said, laying aside his cloth and pressing a light kiss on Eunice's belly, 'perhaps Herr Pfaff as well as Frau Pfaff has a reason for wanting the affair to continue.'

'If D'Cruz was rich, I'd say she was dropping her

knickers for his money,' said Eunice. 'It's not for fun, believe me.'

'I think that Hochheimer has involved her in his plot. She is the bait on the hook.'

'From what I know of Santa Sabinan men, *kuft* is the wrong bait to catch them with,' said Eunice. 'By the time they're thirty they've lost interest. They swallow their aphrodisiac and have a go out of pride, but that's all it amounts to.'

She pushed Marcel's head away from her belly and got up from the floor.

'Do you want another drink?' she asked, a trifle curtly.

When he nodded, she went to the sideboard to pour whisky into two glasses. She handed his down to him on the floor while she sat in silence on the settee, her plump legs crossed firmly. Marcel realised that he had been clumsy and had aroused either suspicion or resentment.

'Dear Eunice – I have hurt your feelings by this talk of another woman,' he said softly.

'Tell me something,' she said, 'and tell me the truth – were you ordered to come here and interrogate me?'

'Good God!' he exclaimed. 'Is that what you think? I swear to you that I had no other reason for coming here than the desire to make love to you.'

'You did that very well,' she said, glaring down at him over her bare breasts. 'You softened me up for your questions in record time. I suppose you think I'm a fat old fool.'

'No, no, no,' he said anxiously, 'I like you a lot.'

He reached out to put a hand on her knee but she pushed it away and stood up.

'I'm going to bed,' she said angrily. 'You can get your clothes on and clear out. I never want to see you again, you rotten Frog.'

She pushed past him and his last view of her was her rolling bare bottom as she walked out of the room, leaving him dumbfounded.

8

A Martyr's Crown is Worth a Fortune

The starting-point, terminus and turn-around for all the buses that ran in Santa Sabina was Vasco da Gama Square down by the harbour. There was a stone statue of the great voyager on a plinth in the centre, and palm-trees edging the pavement on all four sides. Small shops and cafés, where passengers could buy a glass of mint tea or a slice of fried sword-fish, surrounded the square.

The buses were army surplus trucks bought cheaply at the end of the war from former combatants. They had tarpaulin tops to keep the sun off, slatted sides, and were open at the back, with wooden steps for passengers to climb in and out. Inside, there was a long wooden bench along each side and passengers' belongings were stowed in what space was left between the two rows of knees.

The city of Santa Sabina stood at the extreme easterly corner of the island of Santa Sabina, for the excellent reason that here was a large and well-protected bay, in which the port had been built. There were two roads out of the city, one along the coast to the north-west and the other along the coast to the south-west. The north-west road traced a high and rocky coastline before turning inland to the town of Vilanova in the foothills of the Sierra Dorada mountains. The south-west road ran through groves of tall coconut palms and clumps of bougainvillaea and frangipani flowers, its final destination the fishing-port of Selvas on the west coast.

Soon after noon, while the thoughts of Santa Sabinans were turning towards siesta, Marcel climbed up into a bus, which he was assured was on the point of leaving. He said *bonjour* to the three on the hard wooden benches – two elderly men and a fat woman of forty, local etiquette requiring an exchange of greetings. The assurances of immediate departure meant nothing, of course.

It was three days since he had seen Trudi – their longest time apart from the time they had become lovers. That morning, while he was at breakfast on the terrace of the Grand Hotel Orient, Concepcion Costa brought news of a telephone call for him on the reception desk and his heart told him it was Trudi. He murmured words of endearment into the telephone and she responded with warm affection. He asserted that unless he held her in his arms before the day was over he would die of unrequited love. She sighed romantically and said that a day without his embrace was a day without joy and hope.

She then astonished him by asking him to come to her house that afternoon. To the obvious objection, she informed him that the Embassy had an important visitor from Germany and her husband would not be home until late that night. When Marcel still hesitated, she said that there were reasons why she didn't want to be seen in the city. At that, curiosity impelled him to agree to go to her house. He returned to finish his breakfast of water-melon and black coffee with a feeling that there were revelations in store.

There was never any problem in taking an afternoon off. Or a day off, or even a week off, there being no work to do at the French Embassy – or at any other Embassy, he thought, except perhaps that of the Americans, who were born to the work ethic and would invent things to do rather than enjoy themselves in idleness. This insane drive to be doing something all the time was very probably at the heart of Hochheimer's mysterious involvement with the disgraced Minister.

The bus started up with a growl and lurched out of the Square after Marcel had been sitting in it for only twenty minutes. The Pfaff residence was a little way out of the city along the road to Selvas, and the route through the suburbs went past the Reserved Beach. Through the fringe of palm-trees between it and the road Marcel could see ten or twelve people lying in the sun and two more floating lazily on their backs out on the sea.

There was a woman in a bright yellow bathing-costume lying face-down on the sand. Eunice Carpenter was the only person who wore that colour on the beach and he stared at the generously curved bottom thrust up towards the sun. *It must be Eunice*, he thought, waiting to see the woman's face, but the line of changing-huts obscured his view and the moment was lost. He felt badly about the way he and Eunice had parted and he had tried several times to reach her by telephone, but she refused to speak to him.

The Reserved Beach marked the city limits, and after it there was only a straggle of huts thatched with palm leaves. There were no adults to be seen at this time of the afternoon – they had gone to their beds, to make love in their impetuous manner and to sleep for an hour. Two or three little girls in bright colours sat in the shade plaiting palm leaves, giggling and waving at the bus as it passed. Further on, by a clump of banana trees, a boy of eleven or twelve and a girl of the same age were sitting on the ground facing each other. The boy had no shirt on, and his hand was up the girl's frock.

The Santa Sabinan woman sitting opposite Marcel in the bus grinned and pointed to the playing children, leaning forward to pinch his thigh and secure his full attention. *Amasta na zeqq-zeqq*, she said, nodding her head wisely, as if offering an explanation of everything. Marcel nodded in agreement, though the only word he understood was the last one.

It's the air of this island, he reflected, *just to breathe it is an aphrodisiac – I must rescue myself or this woman will disable me before I get to Trudi!* He was certain that she was capable of hurling herself across the swaying bus to rip his trousers open. But by good fortune the next kilometre-stone had the figure 5 on it, and Trudi's directions were to get off the bus at the fifth kilometre marker. He sprang to his feet and pulled the greasy rope that ran the length of the bus, setting a bell jangling in the driver's cab.

The Pfaff residence stood on a ridge of rising ground away from the sea, with its own rutted track winding up to it. It was a long single-storey house with whitewashed walls and a red-tiled roof – a house of some importance, as befitted a person of Gunther Pfaff's status. And there lay another mystery, Marcel thought as he followed the track from the road up to the house – why had Pfaff been relegated by his government to a posting as insignificant as Santa Sabina?

Marcel understood clearly why he himself had been sent to the island. At lunch one day an important member of the French government had drunk a little too much wine and gone home to sleep it off. His unexpected arrival in his own bedroom in mid-afternoon had disrupted an episode of tender passion between his wife and an exceptionally handsome and active young man. Madame X was naked on her back on the matrimonial bed, her legs kicking in uncontrolled delight as her young friend discharged his passion into her belly.

Apologies were out of the question. Marcel's hasty departure was the only possible course of action and the Minister proved to have an unforgiving nature. He took divorce proceedings against his wife and plotted revenge against her lover by using his influence to have Marcel posted to the most unimportant capital possible. And there he would remain, his career in the diplomtic service blighted for the sake of love. Or at least until the Minister and his friends lost office. Applying the lesson of his own misfortunes to Pfaff, Marcel concluded that he too had done something to bring himself into disfavour.

It went without saying that Pfaff had not been found in bed with someone's wife, for he was not the type. Indeed, to Marcel it was unfathomable that Pfaff had persuaded a woman as beautiful and desirable as Trudi to marry him. Presumably it was at a time when her prospects were dismal and Pfaff's had still been excellent.

The door was opened by a maid dressed neatly and plainly in a white cotton blouse and black skirt. She was seventeen or eighteen, with a pretty face and a pleasant smile, and a gently-swelling curve under her waist-band that announced her to be pregnant. She grinned when he told her his name and led him through the house to a shaded veranda at the back, gestured towards the cane chairs and left him to admire the view. On this side of the house the ground fell away down a dark green hillside of thick grass and bushes and then rose again slowly to a tree-lined ridge that formed the horizon.

A minute or two passed before Trudi came on to the veranda and held out her hand to be kissed. She looked ravishing in a house-coat of oatmeal-coloured silk. It had no collar and, what was of the greatest interest to Marcel, a row of gold buttons ran down the front.

'You are enchanting,' he murmured, turning her hand over to kiss the soft palm.

He put his arms round her to hold her close while he kissed her mouth with delicate passion. Her full breasts pressed against him and the kiss became prolonged and excited. Her wet tongue flickered in his open mouth and, very naturally, his hands slid down her back until he could stroke the plump cheeks of her bottom. The touch of her flesh through the silk of the house-coat was so voluptuous that he sighed and rubbed himself slowly against her belly.

'No, you don't!' she said, easing herself a little away from him. 'If I let you rub yourself against me like that you'll get so excited that you'll do it in your trousers.

Stand there and don't move till I tell you – and put your hands in your pockets out of the way.'

She moved back from him to sit on a full-length bamboo chair and swing her legs up to lie propped against the square crimson cushions.

'That wonderful look of desire on your face!' she said, her pale blue eyes staring intently at him. 'It excites me to see it! But what is it that you desire, my friend?'

Marcel gave a long sigh as her nimble fingers opened the gold buttons down the front of her house-coat. She stopped at her waist, put her hands inside and displayed her breasts cupped on her palms.

'Do you like my *gublas?*' she asked, smiling at the uncouth local word. 'No – stay where you are!'

He had taken a step towards her but, at her exclamation, he halted at once and put his hands back in his trouser pockets. She stared up at him in a calculating manner while she undid the rest of her gold buttons and showed him that she was naked under her house-coat. He stared in adoration at her golden-skinned belly and her neat little triangle of blondish hair.

'You are so beautiful, Trudi!' he sighed. *'Je t'adore!'*

The sight of her naked body aroused him to the point where he scarcely knew what he was doing. When she had started her teasing she had told him to put his hands in his trouser pockets – to keep them from touching her, he thought at the time. But her motives were more insidious – she wanted to know how far she could push him towards unreason by arousing him sexually – as evidenced by his inability to refrain from touching himself. She smiled to observe the movement of his concealed hand, unaware that it was Jacqueline Ducour who had conditioned him to respond to sexual tantalising.

Her magnificent thighs slid apart on the cushions to let him see the bare pink lips below her neat little tuft of curls and his hand moved faster. When she put her hands between her thighs and touched her *kuft*, he lost any lingering vestiges of control – his hand was deep in his pocket to grasp and rub his jerking *zimbriq*.

'Oh, Marcel, you're going to *zboca* in your trousers after all,' she said with a smile, her hands cupping her breasts again.

It seemed to him that she was offering him her breasts and immediately he unzipped his trousers and let his distended shaft jump out. It was the work of a moment to straddle Trudi on her long chair, seize her sumptuous breasts with hands that trembled and push his *zimbriq* between them.

'My God – what are you doing!' she exclaimed.

He squeezed her *gublas* together round his shaft and thrust fiercely into the fleshy pocket they made. Trudi stared up open-mouthed at his flushed face, surprised by the response she had provoked, and turned the situation to her own advantage. She dragged his trousers and underwear down his thighs and put her hands up under his shirt to grip the lean cheeks of his bottom and urge him on.

'Is that what you want, Marcel?' she demanded. 'To make love to my *gublas*?'

'They are superb!' he panted, his loins jerking backwards and forwards to her urging.

She proved to herself that she could still control him by pushing his hands away and squeezing her breasts together herself to accommodate his long sliding movements. He balanced himself with his hands on her shoulders and thrust hard and fast, feeling his crucial moments rushing towards him, while Trudi glanced down at the shiny purple head that was emerging and disappearing with great rapidity between the cleft of her breasts. Her blue eyes turned up in curiosity to his face.

'It's so big and hard,' she said calmly, choosing words to inflame his emotions. 'How can you get it into me without splitting me open – it's impossible!'

Marcel's hands clutched at her bare shoulders, his *zimbriq* slid hard on her satin skin and his body jerked to the hot torrent released between her plump breasts.

It was an extremely satisfactory climax and when it finished he sank to a sitting position on the floor of the veranda, his wet *zimbriq* poking out of his open trousers. Trudi put her hands under her head, spreading out her yellow hair on the crimson cushions, and lay with her flawless body fully exposed for his admiration. The evidence of his satisfaction trickled down between her oversized breasts and Marcel acknowledged to himself that he was completely infatuated by her body.

There was, he fully understood, an ambivalence in his feelings towards her that he had not encountered in his dealings with any other woman. He was sure that he did not like Trudi as a person – she was manipulative and scheming. But her beautiful body, that was a different question altogether! He had adored that since the first time he had seen her naked on Shah Jehan's bed. And knowing this, he knelt beside her chair and cupped a wet breast in his hand while he kissed her.

She put her arms round his neck and pressed her cheek to his.

'You're the first man who's ever wanted to *zeqq* my breasts,' she said. 'I am flattered. I think you must really love me, Marcel.'

'I love you to distraction,' he answered, 'I dream of you every night and I want to be with you all the time.'

'How you exaggerate!' she said. 'When you leave me you go back to your everyday life without a thought – until the next time *this* stands up,' and her hand moved down his body to hold his limp *zimbriq*.

'You are mistaken, Trudi,' he told her, 'I am infatuated by your beauty. It has become an obsession. If we were in Europe I should take you away from your husband to live with me.'

'Are you serious?' she asked, moving her head to look into his dark eyes.

'Completely. My whole being cries out to make love to you every day and every night.'

Naturally, there was no need to distress her by explaining that, since she was not available to him every day, it was more convenient to satisfy this need with other women. It went without saying that he would have preferred it to have been *her*, but that in dire necessity, one warm young *kuft* was much like another. Once entered, they became indistinguishable. Why that should be so was an abstruse philosophical question unsuitable for discussion with a woman, especially the loved one.

'If I thought you really meant what you say . . .' said Trudi.

'What would you do?' he asked. 'We cannot live together here – there would be too much scandal.'

'But if we went back to Europe we could be together,' she said. 'Gunther doesn't love me – I only stay with him because I have nowhere to go. But if you asked me, I would go with you.'

'It would be necessary to resign my post and take you to Paris,' he said. 'But what would we live on? I have nothing. Are you rich, Trudi?'

'No,' she said, 'but there might be a way.'

'Then tell me!'

'It is dangerous,' she murmured. 'Let me think about it.'

Marcel was certain that he was getting very close to the subject she had invited him to her house to discuss. But she was not completely ready yet to trust him with her dangerous secret, much as she wanted his help.

'I refuse to let you think about anything which brings that little frown to your beautiful face,' he said. 'You were made for love and pleasure, not for trouble and anxiety.'

He stroked her bare belly with his palms, making her tremble and sigh, and he caressed the long pink lips between her thighs until she turned on the cushions to put her feet flat on the veranda floor on either side of him. At once he leaned forward and penetrated her wet *kuft*.

'That feels so good!' she murmured. 'Oh, Marcel!'

Her bottom writhed on the chair to his strenuous thrusting and her high-heeled sandals drummed against the floor. Through it all Marcel plucked at her breasts, urging her to ever greater heights, while forcing himself to remain as unaffected as possible by the turmoil of her belly. Though the voluptuous feel of her flesh had soon siphoned his passion from him between her *gublas*, this time he intended to make her experience the extremity of climactic release.

'Marcel, Marcel, *je t'aime!*' she gasped as her crisis arrived and her belly rose and fell in rhythmic waves to the stab of his hard shaft.

His hands rolled and fondled her plump breasts until her throes subsided and she smiled up at him in gratification.

'My poor darling, I was too quick for you,' she said.

'No, I wanted to watch your face,' he said, smiling back as he continued his to and fro motion.

'And how did I look?'

'You were beautiful,' he replied. 'The expression on your face at your moment of climax was enchanting!'

He rolled the tips of her breasts firmly between his fingers and pinched them to make her gasp at the sensation. When they were firm again he touched the pink lips where his *zimbriq* was inserted and stroked gently.

'Ah, ah . . .' she exclaimed.

Her shuddering legs strained outwards to the limit – she stared up at him incredulously, spasms shaking her belly.

'What are you doing to me . . .' she gasped.

He paid no attention to her words, or her little cries, her gasps and moans. He maintained a strong and steady stroke, feeling his *zimbriq* growing harder and thicker all the time. Trudi passed totally beyond words and made gurgling sounds as she rolled and bounced beneath him, frantic for release from the overwhelming stimulation.

At the first throb of his climax he exclaimed *now, chérie! Now, now, now!* while he stabbed hard into her belly. Her climactic shriek was so piercing that the brown-skinned maid appeared at the open door to the veranda, thinking perhaps that her employer was being murdered. She was just in time to see Trudi's legs kicking in the air and Marcel's bare bottom driving to and fro between her spread thighs as he spurted his desire into her.

The little Santa Sabinan stood with a grin on her face to see her elegant employer in so wild a paroxysm. She laid one hand flat on her swollen belly and put the other up her black skirt to stroke her *kuft*, aroused by the long and noisy convulsions on the chair. When at last Marcel raised his red-flushed face, he caught a glimpse of bare thighs and black curls before the maid jerked her hand away and disappeared silently back into the house.

When they recovered from their transports of delight, Trudi suggested that they should have some refreshment while they talked. She fastened the gold buttons down the front of her thin housecoat and shook a small brass handbell that stood on a low bamboo table. Marcel rearranged his clothes and was sitting at a polite distance from Trudi when the maid appeared barefoot with a tray of cold drinks. Trudi said there was something she wanted to show him and went into the house. It was a good ten minutes before she came back and in that time she had made up her face, brushed out her yellow hair and changed from the creased house-coat into a sunflower-yellow silk blouse tucked into white linen slacks.

The time for pleasure is over, thought Marcel, and the time for business has arrived. Trudi sat down and handed him a large black and white photograph from an envelope she had brought with her. It appeared to be of a painting, but so dark that it was not easy to make much of it. Yet there was something familiar about the elongated figures in the picture.

'What do you think it is?' she asked.

'I know no more of art than anyone who visits public galleries from time to time,' he answered with a shrug, 'but this is reminiscent of paintings by the celebrated El Greco.'

'I know a lot about paintings,' she said, speaking with complete assurance. 'I studied as an art historian before I married Gunther. Your guess is correct – this is an original oil painting by Domenikos Theotokopoulos, the sixteenth century artist known as El Greco, who was born in Crete and settled in Toledo.'

Marcel tried without much success to make out the detail of the four robed men in the photograph.

'What is it a painting of?' he asked.

'The four Evangelists – the Saints Matthew, Mark, Luke and John. This picture is not catalogued anywhere in the world.'

'Then where is it?' he asked, his mind racing ahead.

'In a safe place,' she answered evasively. 'More to the point is where it came from. Would you like to know?' and when he nodded, she went on.

'For over three centuries it was hanging in a side-chapel of the Church of the Four Crowned Martyrs here in Santa Sabina. In that time it became so blackened by dust and candle-smoke that nobody knew what it was anymore.'

'But *you* recognised it,' said Marcel, with delicate irony, 'and you decided that it must return to Europe, where it will be appreciated by connoisseurs of fine art. And where its true value can be established in the sale rooms, and the proceeds deposited safely in a Swiss bank account. To accomplish this it was necessary to secure the co-operation of the Minister of Commerce and Fine Arts.'

'You have a quick mind, my dear. The problem now will be obvious to you – if Ysambard D'Cruz implicates me I shall be arrested. Gunther has diplomatic immunity, but I do not.'

'You are in serious danger,' said Marcel. 'You must leave Santa Sabina at once – this very day, if there is a ship sailing, no matter where to. I do not understand why you are still here.'

She shrugged her shoulders under her yellow blouse and handed him the envelope. In it were photographs of two other religious paintings – a seated Madonna holding on her lap a naked baby with a golden halo, and the other of a bearded John the Baptist standing up to his knees in the river Jordan.

'That's a Murillo,' she said, tapping the Madonna with her fingernail, 'and I am almost sure that one is a Velasquez.'

'But how did they find their way to this remote island?'

'The Portuguese brought them here for their churches. There were no Portuguese artists of the first rank and so they went to Spain to buy them. The Murillo is in the Church of Our Lady of the Immaculate Conception and the Velasquez has hung for centuries on the wall above the font in St Dionisio at Vilanova. The reason I am still here is that the arrangements for transporting these two pictures are not yet complete.'

'The Minister was arrested because the El Greco was missed?'

'No, it hasn't been missed,' she answered. 'We had it copied in Italy from a photograph and the suitably dirty copy has been on show in the Martyrs' Church for nearly three months.'

'Then why was D'Cruz arrested?' Marcel asked, unconvinced.

'I don't know and I've no way of finding out.'

'But the risk is enormous!' he exclaimed in dismay.

'The rewards are even more enormous,' she said with a tight little smile. 'The copies of the Murillo and the probable Velasquez are on their way by sea. That's why I am still here.'

'But how do you hope to make the exchange and get the originals away now that D'Cruz is out of action?'

'The right people have been bribed in the churches and the captain of the ship bringing the copies will take the originals out. But if I am arrested, the whole plan collapses.'

'Worse than that,' Marcel said earnestly, leaning across to take her hand, 'you will spend the next twenty-five years of your life in prison. I have not been inside the Queen of Heaven jail, but it is said that the conditions are deplorable.'

'So I have heard,' she said softly. 'Will you help me?'

'But this is theft on a grand scale,' he objected. 'What about your husband?'

'He knows nothing of this – he would send me home instantly and divorce me if he knew! This is my way to independence, do you understand? A way to become rich enough to leave him.'

'I see,' Marcel said thoughtfully.

'But do you see? Do you really see, my darling?' she asked, leaning forward to place her hand on his knee.

Her breasts rolled under the thin silk of her blouse in a way that caught Marcel's eye and brought a smile of pleasure to his face. Trudi noted his interest and did it again.

'You say you want me to live with you,' she said softly, 'this is the way. Help me now and we shall be rich when the pictures are sold. We can live together in style in Paris.'

'What do you want me to do?' he asked curiously.

'Nothing very difficult or complicated,' she said, trailing her fingers across his cheek in a loving caress. 'Make contact with the ship's captain when he docks, supervise the exchange in the churches and get the originals on board ship before it sails. I will give you the names of the men to contact.'

'And you – can you get away quickly?'

'There is a tramp steamer leaving for Madagascar at the end of this week. If you will take over from me, I can sail on it and be safe from arrest. I will wait for you in Paris.'

'Your husband will start a hue and cry when you vanish.'

'I shall write him a note telling him I am leaving him. It will not surprise him – he will be relieved rather than anxious, believe me. How soon can you and I be reunited?'

'Not so fast,' Marcel murmured, 'I must give this a moment of consideration before I abandon my career and reputation.'

Trudi moved across to sit facing him on the leg-rest of his chair and took his face in her hands.

'Is the choice so very hard for you?' she asked. 'You can have your boring job for the rest of your life or you can have me and be rich.'

With his mouth pressed to hers, Marcel undid the front of her sunflower-yellow blouse and put his hand inside to assure himself that she was wearing nothing under it. He ran his hands over her soft *gublas* and she leaned heavily against him.

'Do you really dream about me every night, Marcel?' she asked. 'Imagine how it will be when we are together – you can make love to me whenever you like.'

Under his fingertips her buds were warm and prominent. Her head was on his shoulder and she was sighing pleasurably. He found the side-fastening of her slacks, undid it and put his hand down the top of her knickers to stroke her belly.

'I want to make love to you for days and nights on end,' he murmured, pulling her slacks and small silk knickers down her legs so that he could fondle her soft bottom.

'I can make you very happy,' she promised and, to prove it, she had her slacks off in a moment.

His fingers probed her fleshy petals and she had his trousers unzipped and his hard shaft in her hand. Marcel eased himself down on his back on the crimson cushions of the long chair and she straddled him on her knees, leaning forward to make her bare breasts brush lightly against his chest.

'Ah, Trudi, I adore you beyond words,' he breathed.

'It will be like this always,' she promised.

He put the purple head of his *zimbriq* between her thighs, held her by the hips and urged her to slide down on him slowly. Halfway in he stopped her, almost dizzy with the excitement of what he saw, until Trudi squirmed, and forced him in all the way. He grasped the plump breasts in her open yellow blouse while she rode him – not furiously in the Santa Sabina way, but with tender deliberation.

'You are the only man for me, Marcel!' she panted, 'I swear I will make you happy for the rest of your life!'

'Trudi, Trudi – *je t'adore,*' he murmured.

She held him in a long kiss that sucked his tongue into her mouth. Her climax of pleasure was not long delayed and it was like an earthquake inside her belly. Her open mouth sucked the hot breath from him, and her slippery *kuft* gripped like a hand and milked him in exquisite throbs so that he rammed up into her as far as he could reach and made her cry out in ecstasy again and again.

9

Secrets Under the Fig Tree

The day after his first visit to Trudi's home, Marcel again took the bus along the coast road towards Selvas. This time the other passengers were a weary-looking young man, his plump wife, and five children, ranging from a boy of eight or nine down to a baby in arms, a chubby little creature – naked except for a thick cloth round its middle. While they were waiting for the bus to leave Vasco da Gama Square, the woman delved into a large wicker-work basket and brought out lunch for the family – thick slices of goat's cheese, cold legs of chicken and a litre bottle of the awful local beer.

For the sake of politeness she offered the stranger a piece of the yellowish cheese and for the sake of politeness Marcel thanked her and gave her a 10-tikkoo note 'for the children.' She undid the bodice of her red-striped frock to bare her breasts and held the baby to one of them. Without troubling to open its eyes, the baby applied its mouth to a long brown nipple and sucked contentedly, while its mother chewed at a roast chicken-leg.

There was no bright yellow bathing-costume to be seen on the Reserved Beach when the bus drove past. At least a dozen women lay on the sand, pretending that the sun was shining, though the sky was totally overcast and the humid heat was stifling. Marcel shrugged and decided to trouble himself no more with Eunice Carpenter. So much the worse for her if she refused to accept his apologies and overtures of friendship. No woman had the right to be so unrelenting and unforgiving.

The fifth kilometre stone went past and he stayed on the bus, for he was not visiting the Pfaff residence. He had agreed to join Trudi's conspiracy to steal the paintings, though not with a good heart. It was because he was infatuated and too weak to say *no*. He recognised all too clearly his own failings and was ashamed – yet he still submitted to her will. But to be weak was not the same as to be stupid. He guessed that Trudi had told him only what she thought he should know and a state of half-ignorance might prove dangerous to him after she had made her escape.

For his own protection, he needed to know more. And as a source of information, who better than the person who spent hours every day in the same house, had access to bureaux, desk and drawers, who saw everyone who called, and who spied on Trudi out of curiosity? In short, who better than Trudi's young maid to ask about her secrets? With this in mind, he had spoken to the girl when she showed him out. He gave her a 50-tikkoo note and stroked her bottom casually through her black skirt and asked her to meet him. She told him when her day off was and where he could find her.

Beyond the sixteenth kilometre stone the bus drove noisily into a small village and stopped outside an establishment with a faded wooden sign that declared it to be *Xavier's Bar*. The owner had made a perfunctory attempt at sophistication by putting two white metal chairs and a small table out in the street, and Trudi's maid was sitting there with a glass of lemonade. She waved and smiled at Marcel when she saw him getting off the bus.

Xavier came out of the bar – a fat and bald man whose concept of cosmopolitanism did not extend to dress, for he presented himself informally in a string vest and brown shorts. The strong taste of the goat's cheese lingered in Marcel's mouth and he ordered cognac with water and, seeing that the maid was impressed, the same for her. Xavier regretted that he had no cognac and suggested araq instead.

The maid's name was Esperanza. She was eighteen years old and reasonably pretty. Her face was narrower than was common in a Santa Sabinan, and it ended in a pointed chin. She had the usual thick and bushy dark hair, combed to stand out like a mane. For the rendezvous with Marcel she had put on a button-through scarlet frock that didn't quite reach to her knees when she stood and which exposed her legs to mid-thigh when she sat. Naturally she had no stockings, but the importance of the meeting was indicated by the fact that she was wearing shoes.

They chatted of nothing much while they sipped araq and iced water. Esperanza's employment in the Pfaff household raised her above the ordinary and made her a person of importance in the village. By definition, all foreigners were rich, and those who became associated with them did well out of it – according to local standards. But Esperanza's position had not gone to her head – she retained her good nature and was very willing to talk about the village and her home in it, her father and mother, her many brothers and sisters, her fiancé and their plans.

Fortunately, her happy chatter was brought to a halt when fat Xavier came out to announce that he was closing for the siesta and asked for 20 tikkoos for the drinks. The look on the girl's face told Marcel that he was being overcharged but it was of no importance, the sum being about two francs.

'A little stroll?' he suggested. 'Show me the beauties of the countryside, Esperanza, away from the village.'

The time was just after two and the intense heat made the dusty road-surface feel like a hotplate underfoot. Esperanza led him along a lane between Xavier's Bar and the next building, though to call it a lane was overstating the truth. It was more of a track, unsurfaced and rutted, just wide enough for an ox-cart and past the three or four houses along it the track began to disappear under grass until, two hundred metres from the road, there was no track at all. The land sloped gently upwards away from the coast and after they had walked for ten minutes they came to a grove of fig-trees.

Esperanza insisted it was too hot to go any further and wanted to sit in the shade. Marcel agreed that it was an excellent idea and took her a little way into the grove, to find a place where they would not be disturbed. She sat down with her back against a fig-tree, her bare legs tucked under her, her short frock leaving two-thirds of her thighs uncovered. Marcel settled himself on the coarse grass at her feet. Overhead the dark-green foliage spread out like a roof, completely hiding the sky. It was very quiet and peaceful – the only sound, the high-pitched chirping of cicadas.

'I have a present for you, Esperanza,' said Marcel, with his most charming smile.

'Oh, Monsieur – you are very kind!' she said. 'What is it?'

From his jacket pocket he took out a colourful silk kerchief he had bought that morning, the sort he knew to be dear to the hearts of girls like Esperanza, and laid it on her outstretched palm. It was bulkier than she expected and she turned back the folds like leaves, to reveal a little sheaf of banknotes. Country girl or not, she flicked the edges with a thumb-nail once and knew what she had.

'Five hundred tikkoos!' she exclaimed. 'Why do you give me so much money, Monsieur?'

There was a calculating look in her dark brown eyes and Marcel guessed what was going through her mind – that his reason for meeting her was not merely to *zeqq* her. That would have cost him nothing, though being a foreigner and therefore rich, he might perhaps have given her 50 tikkoos when he left, to buy herself a present. The money in the kerchief was far too much to be connected with love-making.

'Because you are an enchanting a girl, Esperanza, no other reason,' he answered.

She nodded and let it go at that, certain that his motives would emerge before long. She put the money into the patch-pocket over her left breast, folded the silk kerchief and tied it loosely round her neck.

'Does it look pretty?' she asked.

'Extremely pretty,' he said, taking her work-hardened hand and touching his lips to it.

Esperanza leaned her back against the fig-tree and sat with her knees up and her arms round them, her head turned to one side in thought. Her short scarlet frock was pulled right up her thighs and, since she had no stockings, displayed smooth and light brown skin. Knowing she had his attention, she dropped her hands to the grass and let her knees move apart. Only the very well-to-do wore underwear so that Marcel found himself staring at her dark-haired *kuft*. He put his hand between her thighs to touch the curls for a moment and then laid his palm on her swollen belly.

'It seems that you have been indiscreet with your fiancé, Esperanza,' he said.

'Maybe my fiancé did this to me,' she answered, shrugging her shoulders. 'He gave me my first baby, so I think that this one is also his.'

'Aren't you sure?'

'Sometimes Monsieur Gunther comes home in the afternoon to *zeqq* me when Madame is in town,' she explained.

'Gunther Pfaff? I can't believe it!'

'But it is true!' and she shrugged again and laughed a little at the expression of surprise on his face.

'Tell me about it,' Marcel suggested, caressing her belly.

'What is there to tell? He takes his clothes off and lies on the bed and asks me to feel his *zimbriq* until it stands up. Then I sit on him and *zeqq* him. He says Santa Sabina girls are better because in his country the women lie on their backs while the men do the work.'

'That's the usual way of it with us,' Marcel agreed.

'I know,' she said, 'I saw you doing it to Madame on the veranda. But she did it to you our way afterwards.'

'I saw you with your hand up your skirt rubbing your *kuft*,' he said with a grin. 'Then you went into the house.'

'Seeing you with Madame made me want to *zboca* too. I went to my room and did it to myself twice. With you visiting, it was obvious that Monsieur Gunther was not coming home to *zeqq* me.'

Marcel was still massaging her belly under her scarlet frock. The skin was warm and velvety to the touch.

'If this is a half-German baby,' he asked, 'what will your fiancé say?'

'If I'm not sure whose it is, how can my fiancé be sure?' she countered. 'Besides, he is happy about the money that Monsieur Gunther has promised to give me. After it is born we are going to leave our jobs and open a little shop together.'

'*O sancta simplicitas!*'

'What does that mean?' she asked.

'It means that such simplicity is holy. If only the world's problems could be settled as neatly as you settle yours!'

Esperanza had no idea what he was talking about and asked if he wanted to *zeqq* her.

'Is that wise?' he asked, still stroking her belly. 'Show me your *gublas*.'

She undid the top buttons of her frock and showed him her plump breasts. The ends of the silk handkerchief he had given her hung between them, half-concealing the pink coral *zimbriq*-talisman suspended on a thin silver chain.

'I was watching when you stood over Madame and *zeqqed* her gublas,' she said, 'do you want to *zeqq* mine?'

'Let me see you play with them, Esperanza.'

She squeezed her fleshy breasts together and plucked at their dark tips. Marcel's *zimbriq* quivered and he laid his hand over the long bulge in his trousers.

'Can you kiss them?' he asked.

She bent her neck, forced her right breast upwards

as far as it would stretch and stuck her tongue right out. But the tip of her tongue came nowhere near her coffee-brown bud, however hard she strained.

'Perhaps the other one,' he sighed.

She pushed her other breast upwards towards her mouth, though with no more success, her eyes shifting from Marcel's hand moving slowly over his bulge to his flushed face. She grinned to see the effect she was having on him and her pink tongue flickered in her open mouth.

'Ah, what pretty *gublas* you have . . .' he whispered, delicious little throbs running through him.

Esperanza recognised the signs. She reached out to take his head between her hands and pull him towards her until she held his cheek against her breasts. The warm smell of her flesh was very exciting and the skin under her cheek was smooth as satin. His eyes closed in trembling delight as he felt her hand open his trousers and find his shaking *zimbriq*.

'If you don't want to *zeqq* me, then you came here for this,' she declared, her hand jerking up and down.

Marcel turned his head so that he could kiss her breasts again and again as his crisis rushed towards him. His legs were shaking violently on the grass and, as his hot passion burst from him, he took the firm tip of a breast into his mouth and sucked it, as he had seen the baby do in the bus.

'More, more, more!' Esperanza demanded, her clasped hand pumping him in ecstatic jolts.

In his climactic frenzy, Marcel clung to her and cried out, the sound muffled by her flesh in his mouth. When she had drained him on to the grass between her spread legs, he slid down against her, until his head rested in the crook of her raised thigh. He lay very contented for a while and the girl made no objection.

In the aftermath of gratification, lulled by the chirping of the cicadas, he almost dozed off. But he reminded himself that he was with Esperanza for a particular reason, unconnected with pleasure, and eventually he was ready to start asking her questions. First he ascertained how long she had worked for Trudi, which was over two years, and then he moved on to delicate matters.

'A certain important person who used to be in the Government is now in prison,' he said carefully.

'Monsieur D'Cruz,' she said at once. 'It is very sad.'

'He was a friend of Madame Pfaff,' Marcel stated. 'Did he ever visit her at home?'

'Such a distinguished man!' she said. 'His suits are made of pure white silk! He drove out to visit Madame two or three times, but she went into the city to see him often. Do you know why he was arrested?'

'No, I am trying to find out. Did you listen to what they talked about when he visited her?'

Esperanza's fingers trailed along his belly inside his open trousers.

'What should they talk about?' she asked with a giggle. 'He came to make love to her.'

'Naturally, and I'm sure you watched,' he said with a grin.

'Oh, yes – once she took him into the bedroom and I watched through the window. The other times they were out on the veranda. But he never did it between her *gublas*, like you did. He taught her to do it our way, not the foreign way.'

'He lay on his back, you mean, and she sat over him?'

'Of course – that's the proper way to *zeqq*.'

Esperanza's short frock had pulled up to expose her dark-haired *kuft* close to Marcel's face as he lay with his head on her thigh. He reached up to stroke the long brown lips.

'I have been told that Santa Sabina men of his age can only do it once,' he said. 'They had plenty of time to talk. What did they talk about?'

Esperanza was silent for a time, evidently considering where her loyalties lay – to the Minister who had given her 50 tikkoos each time he visited the Pfaff residence, or to Trudi Pfaff, who paid her wages and gave her status in the village, or to Marcel who had given her a larger sum of money than she had ever owned before and who might well be good for more. Soothed by his caressing fingers, she chose Marcel.

'They talked about pictures,' she said. 'I don't know what pictures they meant, but they had some business together with them. You and Madame talked about pictures yesterday, so perhaps you understand what the business is about.'

'Yes, I know about the pictures,' said Marcel. 'What else?'

'Nothing. They *zeqqed* each other, they talked about pictures, Monsieur put his clothes on and left. That's all.'

'Who else comes to the house?'

'To *zeqq* Madame, you mean? You, and before you Monsieur D'Cruz. No one else. An American Colonel in a beautiful uniform came twice to the house, but it was to quarrel with Madame, not to *zeqq* her.'

Marcel asked what the quarrel had been about.

'It was difficult to understand,' said Esperanza, 'but they were quarrelling about Monsieur D'Cruz. The American wanted Madame to break off her love-affair, because it was causing problems, he said. She said she was not interested in his problems and would do as she wished. What problems there can be about a man and a woman *zeqqing* together, I do not know. Perhaps you can explain this to me.'

'I envy your uncomplicated approach to love!' Marcel said with heartfelt fervour. 'It would take me forever to tell you of the troubles that arise from love-affairs. In Paris there are shops and libraries full of books about unhappy lovers.'

'Then your people must be very sad,' she said. 'But I can believe it, because I have learned a little about the ways of foreigners. I thought the American was jealous of Monsieur D'Cruz and wanted Madame for himself. But I was wrong about that, because when she offered to do it with him, he became more angry than before and shouted at her.'

'She offered to let him make love to her?' Marcel asked in consternation. 'Are you sure?'

'Of course I'm sure – nobody could be mistaken about that. They were in the sitting-room, arguing very loudly, and I was out on the veranda listening to them. Madame told him that the Americans do not rule the world and she would do as she pleased. Then she laughed and said there was no need to get in each other's way because they could both get what they wanted and be friends at the same time.'

'All she offered was friendship,' said Marcel, relieved.

'I peeped in over the window-sill,' said Esperanza. 'She was standing against the piano and the Colonel was on the sofa. She opened her blouse – she was earing the black silk one – and showed him her *gublas*. She lifted them on her hands – just like she did for you on the veranda. Then she sat on his lap and held his face against them.'

Misery seized Marcel at the realisation of how casually Trudi made full use of the sexual attraction of her beautiful body to achieve her ends.

'You say the American refused her?' he asked sourly.

'So strange! He pushed her away and shouted at her that she was a whore. Then he got up and left.'

'He did nothing?' Marcel demanded. 'Did he put his hands on her breasts or kiss them? I must have the truth!'

'So it is you who are the jealous one!' said Esperanza with a chuckle. 'Have no fear – he did nothing at all to her, not even kiss her. This to me was very surprising, because Madame's *gublas* are the most beautiful I have ever seen – as you know.'

'Very beautiful,' Marcel agreed with bitterness.

'Country girls often go uncovered down to the waist when they are working,' said Esperanza. 'Did you know that? Perhaps you should go and look, if you are so in love with girls' *gublas*. All the same, it was difficult to understand why the American Colonel was not interested in Madame's. When I thought about it afterwards, the only explanation I could think of was that he's a *ghanda*.'

'A what?' asked Marcel, who had not heard the word before.

'A man who prefers *buztan* to *kuft*,' she explained. 'He likes to *zeqq* boys instead of women. Do you have them in your country too?'

Marcel agreed that such tastes were not unknown in France.

'But I discovered I was wrong about that the second time he visited Madame.'

'He made love to her?' Marcel asked, his face pale.

'No, he didn't stay long enough for that. He came to threaten Madame that unless she broke off with Monsieur D'Cruz he would inform her husband. She became very angry and told him to get out. She threw a bowl of flowers and nearly hit him.'

'Then what convinced you that he likes women after all?'

'There was a foreign woman with him in his car. I heard them driving up and looked out of the window. They sat kissing and touching each other before he came to the door.'

'Is it really possible to see that much from the window?'

'Oh yes, it was an open car,' she replied. 'The woman was wearing tight blue trousers and a chequered green shirt and while they were kissing, the Colonel undid her shirt and felt her *gublas*. Then after Madame told him to leave and he went back to the motorcar, his friend put her hand between his legs to make him feel better. Then they drove off.'

Marcel considered this new information carefully, his bent knuckle moving up and down slowly between the soft lips of Esperanza's *kuft*.

'The Colonel's friend,' he said, 'was she about twenty-eight or twenty-nine, with chestnut coloured hair and a thin face?'

Esperanza did not recognise his description of Inge Kristensen.

'No, she was younger, about my age, certainly not more than twenty,' she said, 'and her hair was yellow.

Not golden-yellow like Madame's, but a pale straw colour. And it was very long and straight, right down to her waist.'

With some surprise Marcel concluded that the girl in the car was Sherri Hazlitt, the American Ambassador's daughter. And how interesting to know that Errol Hochheimer was pleasuring her at the same time that he was having a love-affair with Inge. It was no wonder that he had looked tired at Madame da Silva's and had been impervious to the naked charms of Mirella. But something was still not explained – why he had taken the girl with him on his visit to warn Trudi off Ysambard D'Cruz.

Engrossed in these speculations, Marcel forgot that he was gently rubbing inside Experanza's soft *kuft* with his knuckle, until she gasped loudly and took hold of his wrist to press his hand against her. *I want to zboca*, she said. He sat up, pressed two fingers into her wetness and massaged her secret bud.

'Do it faster!' she said, showing her teeth in a grin.

Her climax came very quickly when he did as she asked. She gripped his shoulders and shook like a leaf in her spasms, her head nodding up and down and her dark brown eyes wide open.

'Was that nice?' he asked when her trembling stopped and her breathing returned to normal.

'Yes, but it would be nicer still if you *zeqqed* me,' she replied. 'Why don't you want to? Am I too ugly for you?'

'No, no, no – you are very pretty!' he assured her quickly, worried that he might lose her co-operation by annoying her. 'Of course I want to *zeqq* you, Esperanza. But I am apprehensive that to do so might harm the baby growing in your belly.'

They were sitting close together, facing each other. She took her hands from his shoulders and put them in his open trousers to play with him, smiling broadly.

'Everybody knows that *zeqqing* can't do any harm,' she said. 'I do it all the time with my fiancé. Do you think that women are willing to give it up for so many months?'

'I don't know,' he answered truthfully. 'There has never before been occasion for me to ask.'

'You may be the handsome one, but Monsieur Gunther knows more about women than you do,' said Esperanza. 'He knows it's all right to do it and he takes me straight into the bedroom every time Madame goes out.'

'I refuse to believe for an instant that he knows anything about women at all!' Marcel exclaimed in outrage. 'He's a German – all they know about is beer and sausage and war.'

'He must know something you don't know,' she said slyly, 'after all, a woman as beautiful as Madame married him. He was *zeqqing* her for a long time before you became her friend.'

'No, I will not accept this!' he retorted. 'I think that he married him under constraint to escape from whatever calamities were oppressing and restricting her life. She submitted to him out of a proper sense of a wife's duty, but she can never have loved him or have sought his embraces.'

In Esperanza's hands his *zimbriq* had grown full-size and stiff again. She glanced down at it and then back at his face with the same sly expression she had before.

'You are not yet well acquainted with Madame,' she said. 'You have been her friend for only a week or two. You may love her, but I know her better than you do. The fact is that she and Monsieur Gunther quarrel with each other all the time, but she seeks his embraces often – every night that she has not been with you.'

'Impossible!' Marcel said firmly. 'I do not believe it.'

'As you wish. I am the one who makes the beds each morning.'

'They sleep in different beds?' he asked hopefully.

'Yes, but on the days when Madame has not satisfied herself with you, there is only one bed to make in the morning.'

'Ah, the brute! He forces himself on her!'

'No, it is always his bed that is used, not hers. And his pyjamas and her night-dress are undisturbed under the pillows. She gets naked into bed with him and he too is naked. I do not think that they do this just to sleep.'

'The more I hear from you, the more depressed I become,' said Marcel with a sigh, 'I adore her and I thought that she adored me in the same way – but it seems that I am deluding myself.'

'Why do you expect Madame to *zeqq* with no one but you?' the girl asked. 'You go with other women. It is natural to enjoy love with many people.'

'Are you telling me that you would feel no pang of jealousy in your heart if you discovered that your fiancé was enjoying other girls as well as you? What's his name?'

'Porfiro. In the week I stay at night in Madame's house, but on Saturday I come home until Sunday evening and make love with Porfiro. Once or twice during the week he borrows his father's bicycle to come to the house and he creeps secretly into my room after Monsieur and Madame have gone to bed. But this is not enough – he needs to *zeqq* every day. So when he cannot be with me he does it with my sister Josefina and other times for a change he does it with my married cousin Eufemia.'

'And you are never jealous?'

'Why should I be? It is me that he will marry. I go with other men – like you. Except that you do not want to.'

Marcel's *zimbriq* was trembling in her hand. He put his hands into her open bodice and felt her breasts.

'But I do want to, Esperanza,' he murmured, 'and now that you have reassured me that no harm will come of it, I am going to do it to you.'

He pushed her legs flat along the grass and unfastened the rest of the buttons on her scarlet frock to open it and bare her body entirely.

'Take it right off,' he said, easing it over her shoulders, 'I want to make love to you naked.'

While she was removing it he pulled his shirt over his head and then stripped himself completely. It was most exhilarating to be naked in the open and he rolled Esperanza on the green grass and revelled in the feel of her soft flesh. She giggled at his friskiness and ran her hands over his belly and bottom, making no secret of her eagerness to be enfiladed.

The thought uppermost in his mind as he dabbled his fingers into the wet warmth between her legs was that it would not be good for her condition if he lay with his weight on her belly. When she was too aroused to object to his suggestion, he persuaded her to arrange herself on her hands and knees.

'Like two goats! she exclaimed, giggling at the thought.

Marcel found the sight of her on all fours, with her bare rump at his disposal, extremely arousing. Her breasts dangled loosely beneath her and the full curve of her belly was a pleasure to observe. He knelt close behind her and ran his hand up and down the insides of her thighs until she parted her knees wider to give him total access to her dark-curled *kuft*. Viewed from behind like this, it was a plump mound with a long fleshy split between the curls and he fingered it joyfully until he had made it so wet that half his hand could slip inside.

Esperanza turned her head to stare at him over her bare shoulder, a wide grin on her face. He took hold of her round hips, presented the swollen head of his *zimbriq* to the fleshy lips he had so well prepared, and pushed slowly into her.

'This is the first time I have had the pleasure of being in your belly,' he murmured. 'I shall treat it with respect.'

'Not too much respect!' she said at once. 'I'm not ten years old – I want to be *zeqqed* properly!'

When he was well mounted on her rump, he swung his loins backwards and forwards in a strong and steady rhythm that soon had her gasping to the little thrills that ran through her. She attempted to reinforce his efforts, but he held her tightly and would not let her move against him. To be strictly truthful, Esperanza was not exactly plain, but she was no more than an averagely good-looking eighteen-year-old girl and, that aside, there was yet a more serious disadvantage, in Marcel's opinion. Enthusiastic though she was to make love, she suffered from the complete lack of skill and finesse in her approach which characterised Santa Sabinan women.

For her it was a simple question of *zeqq-zeqq* – getting a man inside her and bumping together to bring about a climactic release as quickly as possible. And then to repeat the process until her partner collapsed from exhaustion. Yet even with these serious shortcomings, she was providing Marcel with an experience that was unique as well as delightful. Though it was not so much Esperanza as the pastoral setting that he found enchanting – the emerald-green grass under them, the fig-trees all round, the untainted country air, the drone of honey-bees and the trilling of cicadas. In his delight he felt a warm tenderness for the girl who was making it possible.

When he felt his critical moment approaching, he moved faster and thrust harder into her wet *kuft*. She had been moaning and wriggling her smooth-skinned bottom against him for some time to escape from his hold. The instant that he freed her, she slammed her rump frantically at his belly to trigger off her delayed crisis, and the *zimbriq*-talisman hanging round her neck swung wildly to and fro on its long silver chain. The convulsive energy with which she struggled for her climax made it happen for both of them. Marcel gave a long cry of triumph as he was delivered of a torrent of passion and the naked girl beneath him shuddered and panted in her ecstasy.

'You take so long!' she said when her throes subsided. 'But it was very nice when you let me *zboca*. Lie on your back and I will *zeqq* you now.'

10

The Fastest Gun in the West

Marcel intended the American Ambassador's daughter to believe that their meeting was casual and he went looking for her in the most likely places. There was the Reserved Beach, the Versailles Tennis Club, the Gran'Caffe Camille, five or six acceptable restaurants, the bars of the three passable hotels, the Dance-Bar Rivoli, and a few other locations. On the second evening of his search he spotted her outside the Cinema des Grands Boulevards, shortly before the show was due to start.

She was dressed casually in a long-sleeved pink shirt and silver-grey trousers, the thin shirt accentuating her large breasts. She was talking to a young man of about her own age whose manner suggested that they had only just met and were passing the time while they waited. But though the Santa Sabinan might be a little uncertain of himself with a foreign girl, he was staring at the gleaming-clean straw-coloured hair that cascaded down her back in a way that revealed what he had in mind, if given the chance. Marcel hurried across the road to make his presence known.

'*Bonsoir*, Mademoiselle Hazlitt,' he said in English, giving her his most charming smile. 'We have not met since the Quatorze Juillet reception.'

'That's right,' she answered vaguely, remembering his face, if not his name, 'you're French.'

He had not previously looked at her with such interest as he did now. He observed that she was as tall as he was, that she had a long pretty face and a mole on her cheek under her left eye. Even in the artificial light of the cinema sign, he could see that her eyes were of the palest blue. It was less pleasing to note that her usual expression was that of a certain blankness, as if nothing much was happening behind those pale blue eyes.

'I am Marcel Lamont,' he reminded her. 'It is announced on this poster that an American film from Hollywood is to be shown this evening with Gary Cooper. I adore cowboy films – may I join you?'

'Sure,' she said, her smile friendly, 'call me Sherri.'

Thus emboldened, Marcel bought two tickets, a large paper bag of pistachio nuts and a litre bottle of Coca-Cola, aware that Americans liked to eat and drink while they watched movies. Before long the doors were thrown open and they made their way inside, the disappointed Santa Sabinan vanishing without a word.

The Cinema des Grands Boulevards was open-air. That is to say, a syndicate of local businessmen had leased a piece of wasteland and erected a large white screen at one end, a hut on stilts to serve as a projection booth at the other, and filled up the space between with folding metal chairs. Films were shown for as long as twenty or thirty people would pay to see them, then changed, which meant that a popular film might be on twice-nightly for as long as five weeks and an unpopular one for only two evenings.

For reasons beyond the reach of speculation, Gary Cooper as a tight-lipped and fast-shooting law-man had captured the interest of the local citizens. This was the film's eighteenth evening of showing but the run was nearing its end, for there were no more than twenty in the space that could seat at least five hundred. The price of admission was the same whether a patron sat on the front row directly beneath the tall screen, on the back row under the clattering projector-booth, or anywhere in between. Marcel let Sherri make the decision, and she chose the back row but one. So nearly empty was the cinema that the nearest couple were five rows away.

She made not the least effort to speak French and they chatted in English and munched pistachio nuts while they waited. The poster outside advertised showings at eight o'clock and ten o'clock, but that meant very little, as the employees did nothing until they had as large an audience as possible. By twenty-five minutes past eight the audience had grown to about forty and the uncovered electric light bulbs strung between poles down each side of the cinema went out abruptly.

Most of the movies shown in Santa Sabina were pirated and dubbed into French in the back streets of Calcutta. The result was a comic disaster – Gary Cooper spoke his few words in a high-pitched voice and a French-Canadian accent. The bad men made their evil threats in miscellaneous accents, one recognisably Belgian, and all badly out of synchronisation with the movements of their lips. Not that Marcel paid attention to the travesty on the screen, for as soon as the lights went out Sherri's straw-blonde head was on his shoulder.

He was astonished by such instant familiarity, but he had heard of the informal ways of Americans and he assumed her behaviour to be part of their cinema-going ritual. He scraped the legs of his chair across the trodden earth floor to place it as close to hers as possible, and put an arm round her waist. She responded with a hand on his thigh. Hardly daring to believe his good fortune, he slid his hand up her side to cup her right breast. Without pausing in her munching of the pistachio-nuts, she acknowledged his interest by stroking the hard bulge between his legs with her unoccupied hand.

Gunshots and menacing music sounded from the screen while Marcel unbuttoned her pink shirt and found that her breasts were half-enclosed in a thin brassière of a material he guessed to be nylon. Instantly she reached behind her back with both hands and unhooked it to let him pull it up her chest and free her breasts. Their warm fleshiness was very exciting under his hand, though their buds were still soft.

Her eyes on the screen, she flipped his trousers open, slipped a hand inside and went back to dipping into the bag of pistachios with the other. Marcel was astounded by the total nonchalance with which she had assumed that he would want to feel her breasts and that she was expected to hold his *zimbriq* while they watched the film. If she had been a Santa Sabinan girl, he would have thought nothing of it, but she was the well-brought-up daughter of a well-to-do American family.

Needless to say, his astonishment did not interfere with his enjoyment of the pleasures offered to him by Sherri's obliging nature. He played with her in delight that mounted higher and higher to her casual handling of him while she chewed nuts and watched the screen. As to her thoughts . . . well, who could say in what vague and indefinable dimension of nothingness Sherri's mind might be wandering? Marcel did not even try to make sense of the situation – he was content to close his eyes and let himself drift along in sensations of pleasure.

Her fingers inside his open trousers moved very slowly along the hard shaft of his *zimbriq* and over its sensitive head. It was as if her actions were automatic – almost that her hand knew by instinct what to do, without any need for direction by her conscious mind. Perhaps she had forgotten that there was a man attached to the shaft of flesh she was feeling, but the effect on Marcel was dramatic – through the dizziness that overwhelmed his senses, he felt the muscles of his belly clench and he squirted his ecstasy into Sherri's palm.

'Oh!' she exclaimed. 'I didn't know you'd be so quick! Give me your handkerchief.'

He was unable to reply, his loins bucking upwards from his chair. She found a handkerchief in his jacket-pocket and pushed it inside his trousers to soak up the warm flood of his desire from his underwear. Marcel opened his eyes and looked round the darkened cinema. His raptures had passed wholly unnoticed, the other members of the audience being similarly engrossed in each other. When the damage to his underwear had been to some extent made good he settled Sherri against him with an arm round her shoulders and, while her munching continued, opened her silver-grey trousers and put his hand inside to stroke her flat belly.

Soon his fingers were under the elastic of her small briefs and he felt down between her thighs. Here again she astonished him – where he expected to touch silk-soft curls, he encountered the smooth flesh of a completely hairless *kuft*. She parted her slim thighs on her chair in the most obliging way, and his fingertips felt all the way down and under her – and found the same soft and baby-smooth flesh everywhere.

'But this is charming!' he murmured. 'How did you devise so truly enchanting an idea, Sherri?'

'Don't laugh at me!' she muttered, not at all happy with his compliment. 'I can't help it.'

'What do you mean? I find it adorable!' he assured her, rubbing his fingers slowly up and down the soft lips.

'When I was a kid I got diphtheria or some lousy disease in the Philippines and nearly died,' she said miserably. 'All my hair fall out. It grew back on my head, but not my eyebrows, and I stayed bald down there.'

Marcel took his hand out of her briefs and brushed back the straw-coloured fringe from her forehead. Even in the dark of the cinema, he could see that she had told him the truth – she had no eyebrows at all. They were drawn in brown cosmetic.

'But I do not understand why you should be unhappy about this small misfortune,' he whispered. 'Natural eyebrows have no significance – in Paris the women have them plucked out and then draw them to a shape that pleases them more. And as for having no little fleece between your thighs – believe me, it is very charming.'

'That's OK for you to say – you're French,' she answered.

'Why does that make a difference?' he asked, his hand back inside her tiny briefs to fondle her.

'Everybody knows the French are degenerates,' she told him, 'but when the guys back home get my panties down they think I'm some kind of freak.'

She sounded so unhappy that he said no more. He held her close with an arm round her waist and played with her bare *kuft* to make her feel better. His pride was severely hurt when, after ten or fifteen minutes, he was compelled to admit to himself that he was making remarkably little progress. True, she had become a little moist, but he knew well that any other woman who had received his attentions would have enjoyed a climactic experience by then. Sherri represented a challenge to his manhood – perhaps even a defeat for it!

She herself did not seem to believe there was anything amiss in her lack of response. She lolled comfortably against him, her thighs wide apart, crunching pistachio-nuts and watching the gun-play on the screen. After a while, she opened his trousers again and put her hand inside to feel for his *zimbriq*. Notwithstanding its recent performance, it was long and hard again, for feeling her had aroused him more than it did her.

'You're ready to do it again,' she whispered, 'OK?'

'OK,' he murmured back, amused by the American expression in this context.

She fondled him for a time; she had finished the pistachios and was becoming bored.

'I've seen this movie before,' she said. 'Let's go somewhere for a real drink.'

He took her to the Dance-Bar Rivoli, which was within easy walking distance. Like the cinema, it was open-air – a circular area that had been tiled in red and white to make a dance-floor with twenty or thirty small tables round it, a four-piece band and a bar. A white-jacketed waiter showed them to a table and Sherri said that she wanted araq. Marcel shrugged and earned the respect of the waiter by ordering a bottle of the fiery spirit. Not that he thought he and the girl could empty a bottle by themselves, but at twenty tikkoos a bottle there was no point in ordering by the glass.

In the soft light of the candle in a glass holder on their table, and in spite of the prominent breasts under her pink shirt, Sherri looked younger than she was and as clean as if she had just stepped out of a bath, completely innocent, vulnerable and most desirable. Marcel stared at her, hardly able to believe that his *zimbriq* had spat in her hand not twenty minutes before. The waiter showed him the unbroken seal on a bottle of araq before he opened it and half-filled two tall glasses packed with ice-cubes.

To start Sherri talking, Marcel asked how it was that she was in Santa Sabina with her parents, instead of at university in the United States.

'You think I want to be here?' she asked, her pale blue eyes wide with surprise. 'I hate this place but I'm stuck till I can get my hands on my trust fund next year.'

'Trust fund? An inheritance, you mean?' he asked.

'Have you ever heard of Bust-a-gut Hazlitt, the wheeler-dealer who made the biggest fortune in Texas before World War One?' she asked with pride.

Marcel shook his head, many of her words unfamiliar to him.

'All you need to know about the old buzzard is that he left a trust fund for his grandchildren,' she explained. 'Each of us collects a share on our twenty-first birthday – and mine's next year. Then you won't see me for dust.'

'I understand, but that still does not answer my original question – why you are here in Santa Sabina.'

'Because of Derry,' she said moodily, taking a long pull at her glass. 'Dad and Mom make me live here to keep me away from him – if I make a run for it they'll have me declared delinquent in the courts back home and I'll never get my money. I've just got to sit it out for another ten months.'

'I assume that Derry is a boyfriend of whom your parents do not approve,' said Marcel, topping up her glass.

'I guess you could say that,' she answered with a grin and a shake of her head that sent her long straw-coloured hair whirling about her shoulders in a manner that enchanted him.

'But why – do you wish to marry him?'

'Can't do that,' she answered, 'he's my uncle, my mother's brother.'

'Ah yes, I can see that would cause concern. Is he very much older than you?'

'He's forty-four, but who's counting? When I get my money I'm leaving this god-forsaken island and going straight back to the US to be with him.'

'Is that legal in your country – for a man to cohabit with a niece?'

'How do I know? If it's not, we'll fly down to Mexico or somewhere to live. I might even get my own back by bringing him here – anything goes in Santa Sabina, brothers, sisters, uncles, nieces!'

'Do not make the mistake of believing that because a thing is not forbidden it is encouraged,' said Marcel. 'There are no laws here to forbid sexual intimacy between members of the same family, but it is a Catholic country and I am sure to stay here would be made difficult for you.'

'What about those old-time Cardinals and Popes getting it together with their own kin?' she asked sceptically.

'It may be that high-ranking prelates did such things once,' he answered, 'but no one thought well of it.'

'And don't rich Europeans marry their own cousins and nieces to keep estates in the family?' she asked. 'They're Catholics – don't tell me that's not legal.'

'There have been such alliances,' Marcel agreed, 'but a special dispensation is required for such marriages.'

'Right!' she said. 'You're saying that if you've got enough money, you can buy it. Who do you have to pay off – the Pope?'

Two glasses of araq later, she put her elbows on the table, rested her chin on her hands and confided that she had *fallen for him*, as she put it, meaning her unusually forthcoming behaviour in the cinema, because he looked a lot like Derry.

'Same dark curly hair,' she said dreamily, 'same chin, same dark eyes. I fell for you when I met you at the French Embassy that time, only you took that old bag Eunice Carpenter out into the garden instead. Why do you want to screw her? When you turned up tonight and asked me to the movie with you, it was like a dream come true.'

'If that is how you amuse Monsieur Derry when he takes you to the cinema, then he is a fortunate man,' Marcel assured her, stroking her forearm through the thin pink silk of her shirt. 'How long has this love-affair between you two been going on?'

'I was sixteen when it started,' she said. 'Dad and Mom were abroad and I was living with my aunt and her family in Houston while I finished school. One day she was out shopping or getting her hair fixed or something and Derry raped me.'

'Raped you?' Marcel asked, puzzled and not certain that he had understood her correctly. 'You mean he forced you?'

'He surely did!' she answered. 'We were lazing round the swimming-pool and I went into the house to get a Coke and Derry followed me inside and grabbed me. He said he knew I let boys do it to me and he was going to have me. I wasn't a virgin – he was right about that – but I was afraid of him. Only I couldn't stop staring at the front of his swim-shorts – there was a huge mound in them that terrified me.'

'But did you not scream and struggle to stop him?' Marcel enquired, trying to visualise the scene.

'I was too frightened – it was like a snake mesmerising a rabbit. Derry was big and powerful and I was just a kid. He made me take my swim-suit right off and he laughed at me when he saw I'm bald between the legs. *You got no fluff on your gash*, he said, over and over, till I was in tears. He told me to kneel down and get his pecker out and kiss it. I pulled his shorts down and it was so enormous I didn't think I could get it in my mouth, but he forced me to. He told me to lie down on my back on the kitchen table with my feet on the floor, and he stood between my legs. *Spread them wider!* he kept saying, *Spread them wider!* He got down in front of me and put his hands on my knees to push them apart while he went down on me.'

'My knowledge of English is imperfect,' said Marcel. 'What does that mean?'

'He stuck his tongue up me. God, I hated him for what he was doing to me! But I could feel myself getting excited all the time and I didn't want to, so I rolled from side to side to try and get away from his tongue. But he's very strong and he held me so tight there was nothing I could do to escape. And suddenly it was too late and I was climaxing like crazy.'

'I am sure that excited him even more,' Marcel said, shaking his head in sympathy.

'I'll say it did! Before I'd finished he was on top of me on the table and he rammed his pecker up me so hard I thought he'd split me apart! It made me scream and I punched at his face to get him off, but he was too strong for me. I started to get excited again, though I didn't want to, because I hated him so much. He jabbed pretty hard a few times and I could feel him shooting his stuff – and that made me climax again!'

'Yet in spite of being brutalised by him when you were not much more than a child, you say that you love him and would marry him if that were possible! I find that difficult to comprehend, Sherri.'

'It was exciting because he was rough,' she answered slowly, half caught-up in a reverie of the past. 'He picked me up in his arms as easily as if I weighed no more than a doll. I was sobbing because I hated him and he carried me upstairs and when I punched his face again he put his head down and sucked my nipples so hard it hurt. He threw me on the bed in my own room and made me lick his pecker hard and then raped me again.'

'*Le bon Dieu!*' Marcel exclaimed. 'What an animal!'

'Yes!' she said with enthusiasm, 'I loved him for it!'

'How did your parents come to learn of this liaison?'

'After that first time, Derry did it to me practically every day for the next couple of years. Sometimes he took me for rides in his Cadillac and if we hadn't much time we did it on the back seat and if we had a couple of hours we went to a motel. Then one day Aunt Bea came home early from a bridge-party and caught Derry raping me under the shower.'

'You have my sympathy,' said Marcel. 'I know from my own experience how damaging these unexpected returns can prove. Your Aunt informed your parents, of course.'

'She phoned my Mom in Sri Lanka and she kicked Derry out of the house and filed for divorce. I got sent away to school in Boston, so I couldn't get in any more trouble, but Derry used to fly up to be with me at weekends. I don't know how word got back to Santa Sabina, but all of a sudden I'm on my way here, or else!'

'A remarkable story,' Marcel said, shaking his head sadly while he caressed the back of her hand.

It was clear enough to him now why he had not been able to arouse her in the cinema. He suggested that they should dance and while they moved round the floor to the local version of *Amapola* he held her so closely to him that he controlled her every movement. She made one startled attempt to free herself and then surrendered absolutely, as he had been hoping. Her belly was close to his, her head on his shoulder and her legs were apart to let his thigh force its way between hers. The lighting was dim and he did not hesitate to put his hands on the cheeks of her bottom and squeeze them brutally.

'Oh my God – you're going to beat me up and rape me!' Sherri sighed, her mouth pressed to his ear.

Marcel's introduction to the Dance-Bar Rivoli had occurred not many weeks after he arrived in Santa Sabina and he was taken there by a young woman named Susana whom he had met at the Gran'Caffe Camille. At an appropriate moment during the evening, Susana had shown him the 'sitting-out' area. This facility was provided for patrons of the Rivoli who became so aroused by dancing that they found themselves unable to restrain their ardour. With this in mind – or something not entirely unrelated – Marcel led Sherri off the floor and down the side of the bandstand.

A Santa Sabinan couple coming the other way stood aside and grinned. Marcel said *bonsoir* as he led Sherri past them to where a boy sat on a stool to bar the way. He had a square biscuit-tin on his knees, into which Marcel dropped a 20-tikkoo note, before being waved past. Beyond the door-keeper lay the 'sitting-out' area, an empty space between the band-stand and the back wall of the premises, open to the sky and very dark. It was not a large space, as Marcel knew from his visit there with Susana, and it had wooden benches around the walls.

'Where are we?' Sherri asked.

'Where no one can see us,' he answered, 'or save you from what I am going to do to you.'

As his eyes became accustomed to the darkness, he picked out a couple on the benches against the wall to his right. They were pressed so tightly together that it was impossible to say what stage their love-making had reached. He guided Sherri across to the other side, helped her up on to the bench and told her sharply to stand with her back to the wall. She whimpered a little in bewildered protest and then he had her silver-grey trousers and her tiny nylon briefs round her ankles and stooped to kiss the soft flesh of her bare and smooth *kuft*.

'Oh, no!' he heard her exclaim softly in the dark as he forced his tongue between the hairless lips. 'This can't be happening to me!'

His fingernails sank like cruel talons into the cheeks

165

of her bottom and wrenched them apart while his tongue was flickering over her secret bud – a bud which became firm very quickly under his assault. Her fists beat up and down on his shoulders, as if to stop him – but not for long. The beating slowed and stopped and her hands clutched at his shoulders to support herself as her legs shook. Moments later an ecstatic wail announced the arrival of her crisis.

The duration of her pleasure was gratifyingly long, Marcel considered. When it eventually seemed to be reaching its ending, he stood straight and ripped her shirt open. He forced her big loose breasts out of her brassière and squeezed them hard, making her moan to feel his nails sinking into her soft flesh. He took the tender tip of one breast into his mouth and sucked hard, while plucking roughly at the other.

Between her thighs his fingers probed mercilessly into her hairless *kuft*, forcing it open until she moaned again. She was very slippery inside and he guessed that she was ready to be *raped*. He took a short step backwards and swept her legs from under her with a swing of his arm. She fell sideways, screaming in terror, and he caught her and steered her on to her back along the wooden bench. It was impossible for her to open her legs properly, her ankles being bound together by her trousers and underwear – *So much the better*, thought Marcel – *She is aroused by being made to feel helpless*.

He dragged the bench away from the wall with Sherri lying on it and she began to sob quietly in the dark as he pushed her feet up to her bottom, forcing her knees outward and parting her thighs. The breath flew out of her as if she were winded when he put his belly on hers and let her feel his weight. One long push took him deep inside her and, without the least regard for what she might be feeling, he began to *zeqq* her hard.

That he had done precisely the right thing to arouse her masochistic nature became immediately apparent. She gasped and writhed under him, her loins bucking fiercely upwards to drive him further in. The feel of her smooth flesh under his tongue when she was standing on the bench had already excited Marcel highly, and her noisy enjoyment under him sent him racing towards his crucial moments.

He panted in his exertions while he jabbed and stabbed into her wet *kuft* as if he wished to destroy it rather than pleasure it. And Sherri, pinned and helpless on her back under him in the dark, felt that she was being utterly destroyed and dissolved in paroxysms of ecstasy. The contractions of her belly were so strong that Marcel was overwhelmed and pumped his passion into her in violent spurts.

'I love you, I love you!' she moaned, 'I love you!'

A quarter of an hour passed before they were ready to return to their table by the dance-floor and refresh themselves with iced araq. One of the buttons of Sherri's pink shirt had been torn off in the heat of their encounter, but apart from that she looked as fresh, clean, innocent and desirable as when Marcel first met her that evening, outside the cinema. But in one important respect she had changed – she insisted on sitting on the same side of the table as Marcel, so that she could be close enough to him to hold his hand.

'I love you,' she said softly. 'Do you know that? I started to climax as soon as you put your pecker in me and it went on and on until I was too exhausted for any more.'

Marcel kissed her ear lightly and said nothing. The time was ideal, he thought, to find out what she knew, if he could steer the conversation in the right direction.

'Was it like that with Errol Hochheimer?' he asked, smiling to remember he'd invited the same comparison from Inge.

'It was OK with Errol,' said Sherri, 'but nothing like that. He liked to tie me up and beat my rear end with a rolled-up newspaper. Most times it made me climax, but hardly ever when he stuck it in me. You're fantastic – did you know that?'

'I've been looking for our friend Errol for the last day or two, but I can't find him,' Marcel said untruthfully, 'do you know where he is?'

It was difficult to stop himself from laughing aloud at the thought of Colonel Hochheimer beating Sherri's bare bottom with an old copy of the *Washington Post*.

'He's on his way to the States,' she said.

'But that is most inconvenient – he should have warned me.'

'There wasn't time to get the word round,' said Sherri, 'he talked to Dad after dinner two nights ago and by midnight he was gone. Top secret stuff, I guess.'

Marcel breathed in silently and deeply and took a great leap into the dark.

'But what about the arrangements for moving the shipment before Ysambard D'Cruz breaks down under interrogation and tells them where to find it?' he asked.

'So they find it,' she answered. 'So what? Dad will deny the US had anything to do with it. If a local politician wants to start a private war with guns the Russkies smuggle in for him, that's too bad. The US Ambassador in Moscow will hand in a protest and it will blow over in a couple of days.'

This cynicism in so young a woman appalled Marcel. But he played along in the hope of learning more.

'I hope you may be right, Sherri. But suppose mistakes have been made and there are American markings on the shipment?'

She shrugged her shoulders.

'So maybe the Santa Sabinans get suspicious,' she answered. 'That's too bad. There's nothing they can do about it.'

'I see that you have been well-trained by your father in the doctrine of *Realpolitik*.'

'What's that?'

'An attitude towards international affairs formulated by Germans like Bismark and Hitler – total ruthlessness and a reliance on naked power.'

'I guess, you mean being realistic about people,' she said. 'The world's full of crooks and crazies trying to take you for a ride. I should know – look what my own folks have done to me.'

'They think they are acting in your best interests,'

Marcel pointed out. 'After all, besides being closely related, Derry is too old for you.'

'Who cares,' she sighed, holding his hand against her cheek, 'I know what I want.'

Marcel stroked her long straw-yellow hair and let his arm rest round her shoulders.

'Errol must have liked you a lot,' he said, 'to let you take part in his secret operation. Will you miss him?'

'He only fooled around with me because he was bored out of his mind and wanted a white girl. He rates the people here as coloured, and being from West Virginia he thinks it's wrong to screw with coloured girls. We went to the movies a lot because he liked having his pecker played with and when he drove out into the country on business he took me along. That was OK with me – I've got time on my hands. But I won't miss him now I've got you.'

She gave Marcel an enchantingly innocent smile and put her hand on his thigh under the table.

'Were you with him when he went to inspect the shipment?' he asked, holding his breath in anticipation.

'Sure. Where are you going to take me next to beat me up and rape me – my place or yours?'

'I live in a hotel,' he said. 'It is better if you come there with me. There would be an incredible brouhaha if I were discovered uninvited in the American Embassy – and in bed with the Ambassador's daughter!'

'Brou . . . what? I guess you mean trouble. If I could kick up a big fuss and make trouble for my Dad, I'd do it so fast your head would spin! After what he and Mom have done to me, they've got it coming! What were you were asking about Errol and me?'

'Did he beat your bottom with his newspaper when you went with him to inspect the shipment?' Marcel asked, trying to focus her hazy mind.

'In the caves, you mean? He surely did! He held me face-down over a big rock in the sun and pulled my pants down to beat my rear end. I lay there thinking about Derry till I climaxed – it was pretty good that day.'

'My God – were you thinking about Derry when I did it to you?' Marcel asked, shocked by the insult to his pride.

'Not for a second!' she said, her palm sliding along his thigh in so insinuating a manner that his *zimbriq* stood stiff. 'I wanted it to be you, and it was terrific – a total wipe-out.'

'The caves you mentioned – where are they?'

'In the Sierra Dorada mountains, of course,' she answered. 'The place where they chained the slaves they shipped in from Africa in the old days.'

'Let's go to my hotel,' said Marcel, his hand between her thighs under the table.

11

Nothing So Constant As Inconstancy

It was the middle of the afternoon and the city of Santa Sabina lay in silent and torpid siesta. Marcel was in his shower at the Grand Hotel Orient, refreshing himself under the steady downpour. Not that it was ever possible to take a cold bath or shower, for the water ran inevitably tepid. Baltazar Costa still related the story of the world-famous Hollywood filmstar and *femme fatale* who visited the island in 1929, thinking that she might buy it as a holiday home. She was accustomed to having her own way and refused outright to be defeated by the oppressive climate and lukewarm water.

In consequence, she commanded the hotel owner to half fill his biggest bath with ice and pour fifty bottles of best French champagne over it. Luxury and ostentation on that scale were unknown in Santa Sabina, of course, and the hotelier was astounded. It was Costa's father in those days and he hurried to carry out the lady's order, but finding his stock of champagne and ice insufficient, had to send out to every other hotel in the city. When the bath was prepared, the Great Star retired into it with a handsome eighteen-year-old fisherman she had found down by the harbour that very morning.

When she emerged eight hours later to board her

yacht and sail away, she looked much invigorated but had decided that she preferred Mexico to Santa Sabina for vacations. As for the eighteen-year-old, they found him draped over the side of the bath, sleeping heavily in warm and flat champagne. It took him a week to recover, after which he bought a second-hand fishing-boat with the hundred dollars the lady had given him and became well-to-do by local standards.

Lacking the Hollywood lady's extraordinary riches, Marcel had no choice but to make do with tepid water. His bathroom was small and airless and he left the door from his bedroom open. When he cut off the water and turned to reach for a towel, there in the open doorway stood Concepcion Costa. There was no way of knowing how long she had been staring at Marcel's naked body but he wrapped the towel round his waist quickly. Not for modesty, of course, either his or hers, for she had even less than he, but because he knew how easily the local girls became aroused and he had no desire to become involved.

'Monsieur Marcel,' she said in her excellent Convent-taught French as she jangled the huge bunch of keys that gave her access to every part of the hotel, 'please forgive me – I knocked several times but you did not hear me.'

'Is there a message for me?' he asked. 'Am I wanted on the telephone?'

The tramp steamer for Madagascar was scheduled to sail the next morning and Trudi's plan was to go aboard at the last moment, after her husband had departed for his Embassy. She had said she would be busy all today with her final arrangements and she and Marcel had exchanged tender *au revoirs* in bed the previous afternoon. But naturally he expected that she would telephone to tell him that she was already impatient to be reunited with him.

Not that he thought for one moment that she would be waiting for him in Paris if he followed her instructions to steal the paintings and hand them over to the captain of a Greek ship due in three weeks. He did not believe that Paris was the destination of the pictures and therefore Trudi would have no reason to be there, for he had accepted that her only interest in him was opportunistic. In consequence, he had as little intention of putting the paintings on board a ship for her as she had of keeping her promise to him.

'Monsieur Marcel,' Concepcion said again, 'perhaps I should not be speaking to you. But you have been a guest so long that my father would surely want your interests to be preserved.'

'Does he know that you are here?' Marcel asked curiously.

'He has taken my mother to Selvas for a cousin's wedding and he has left me in charge of the hotel.'

Her self-assurance was greater than would ordinarily be expected in a seventeen year old girl. But then, Santa Sabinans grew up very quickly. Marcel decided it would be better to get dressed and smiled politely at Concepcion as he eased himself past her into his bedroom, towel wound round his waist. She stayed in the open doorway, turning to face him again. With his back towards her, he dropped the towel, conscious that his hasty part was beginning to grow stronger and in great haste wriggled his legs into a pair of casual trousers, not stopping to bother with underwear.

'What are these interests of mine that you wish to preserve, Mademoiselle?' he asked, sitting on the bed to pull white canvas shoes on to his bare feet.

'You must understand that my father has a great respect for you, Monsieur. He always tells us to do all we can to take care of you. Otherwise I would not presume to approach you.'

Marcel was sure now that Concepcion had come to his room to offer herself to him. Not for his gratification, of course, but for her own. He looked at her thoughtfully, wondering whether it was possible to decline without offending her. She was a pleasant enough girl to look at – broad-cheeked, full-mouthed, her skin a very pale coffee colour, her dark hair almost black. In short, she resembled the vast majority of Santa Sabinan girls.

Perhaps he looked a little too long or too closely at the round young breasts pushing out the front of her pink-flowered frock, for he began to ask himself why it was necessary at all to decline the gracious offer she was about to make. Though he would not have admitted it, his reservations about her were being weakened in proportion to the strengthening of what was concealed in his trousers. He saw her moisten her lips with the tip of her tongue, as if she were nervous.

'Your yellow-haired lady,' she said, taking him by surprise. 'The one you make love to in the Shah Jehan suite.'

Marcel looked at her steadily without speaking, wondering whether curiosity or jealousy had prompted the question.

'I regret to inform you of this, but she is there now.'

'But I haven't arranged to meet her today,' he said.

'She is in the suite with another gentleman.'

'That's impossible!' he exclaimed angrily, 'I don't believe you!'

'I hope you will forgive me,' said Concepcion, her voice wavering, 'nobody likes to bring bad news. But I have too much regard for you to permit anyone to make a fool of you. If my father were here I am sure he would have told you.'

Marcel felt as if he had been punched very hard in the belly. His hands trembled so much as he tried to pull a sports shirt over his head that he gave up and sat clutching it.

'Who is she with?' he gasped.

'A foreigner. Someone I have never seen before.'

'I must know!' he said harshly. 'Give me the key and I will go in and confront them.'

'That is out of the question, Monsieur,' the girl said with great firmness, 'the Grand Hotel Orient is a well-conducted enterprise and its guests must not be disturbed. Only consider – if the lady's husband arrived while you were making love to her, would you expect my father to show him into the Shah Jehan suite to catch you at it, however angry he was? Of course not – your privacy would have been protected.'

'But I must know who is with her,' said Marcel in a pitiful voice. 'Help me, Concepcion, I implore you!'

'Only if you swear to make no disturbance.'

'I swear it!' he said instantly.

'This is a serious matter for me, Monsieur Marcel – not one where you can give your word lightly and then break it if you choose. Do you understand what I am saying?'

'Yes,' he answered wearily, 'I have given my word, Concepcion, and I shall not go back on it.'

She studied his face for a few moments, as if weighing up his sincerity. Apparently satisfied that he could be trusted, she came across the room to take the sports shirt from him and hold it up for him to put his arms in. He sat listless while she tucked it into his trousers and fastened his belt buckle, though at another time and in other circumstances a girl's hand that close to his *zimbriq* would have brought it jolting impudently upright. But the shock of what he had been told was so crippling that, as Concepcion saw for herself while she tucked his shirt in, his pride lay miserably small and weak between his thighs.

He followed her without another word out of his room and up to the top floor of the hotel, where the Shah Jehan suite was. She led him along a corridor he had never seen before and unlocked a door with a key from her bunch. The door opened outwards and Marcel found himself looking into a large storage cupboard containing a carpet sweeper, two brooms and an empty bucket. Concepcion offered no explanation as she waved him inside, followed him and pulled the door to behind her.

There was no electric light in the cupboard and with the closing of the door they were plunged into airless darkness. He could feel the heat of the girl's body very close to him and her fingers against his lips to enjoin silence. In another moment a ray of light shone across the cupboard as a peep-hole was opened in the wall facing the door. Concepcion's girlish face was briefly illuminated as she brought one eye to the hole to check on what was to be seen. Then she stood away and touched Marcel's arm in silent indication that he should look.

An atrocious melange of emotions seethed in his breast – furious anger and sickening dismay, a murderous thirst for revenge and a heart-wrenching sense of betrayal. Shah Jehan's elaborately carved bed stood three metres away on the other side of the wall and there was Trudi on her hands and knees, her lush and beautiful body naked, her sumptuous breasts swaying to the rhythm of her movements. These movements were imparted to her body by Mr Hakimoto of the Japanese Embassy, who was kneeling behind her magnificent rump and stabbing vigorously into her *kuft*.

The lovers were sideways on to Marcel and he was spared nothing. Trudi's cries of delight came faintly through the wall as her elbows bent outwards and her head sank until she lay with her face on the cushions and her bottom thrust up boldly for Mr Hakimoto's urgent attentions. Her face was towards Marcel, letting him see her expression of bliss, her staring blue eyes and her mouth wide open to utter little cries of joy.

Mr Hakimoto had removed his large round spectacles and his eyes shone like jet-black buttons. Other than that, his broad yellow face was totally without expression, even in the arousal of this most intimate of embraces. He had no neck at all and his body was squat, though strongly-built. Beads of perspiration trickled down his hairless chest as he swung his loins against Trudi with as much forcefulness as if he were chopping down a tree. His short-fingered hands were palpating the soft and golden-skinned cheeks of her bottom.

The spectacle of betrayal caused Marcel to shake with pent-up emotion and he could not prevent a long sigh of angry despair escaping his lips. Standing beside him in the dark, Concepcion heard it and put an arm round his waist to comfort him a little. He was grateful to her for that, futile though her attempt was, and he touched her cheek briefly with the back of his hand, to show that he understood. Naturally, being a Santa Sabinan, she interpreted his gesture in her own way.

Not that it mattered greatly – he was so distraught that he had only a vague awareness that Concepcion had moved silently in the blackness to stand behind him. The sight of beautiful Trudi naked had aroused him – even Trudi permitting her naked body to be enjoyed by another man! Marcel's *zimbriq* was stiff in his trousers and he was too engrossed in the progress of the treachery being perpetrated on Shah Jehan's ornamented bed to pay attention to what Concepcion was doing. She was pressing herself against his back, both arms round his waist, to open his trousers wide and feel inside.

Mr Hakimoto's short black hair stood up on his head in spikes. He was riding Trudi as if she were a racehorse and it was a question of life and death to be first past the winning-post. If he had had a riding-whip, he would surely have used it briskly on her smooth flanks, to urge her on to greater effort. Nor would she have complained, to judge by the expression on her face. Her eyes were closed in the bliss of nirvana and she was beyond shrieking. In the dark cupboard, Concepcion had taken it upon herself to give what consolation she could to Marcel by massaging his stiffness energetically with one clasped hand and rolling his *castazz* in her other.

'But no – this is ridiculous!' Marcel objected in a swift whisper, waking up at last to what Concepcion was doing to him.

He pulled her hands from him and pushed her away, none too gently, and she made an angry hissing noise. He paid no attention, for a broad smile was appearing on Mr Hakimoto's face, showing all his teeth as his clenched fists thumped up and down on Trudi's bottom, like a drummer beating the *Charge*. Marcel groaned in agony while the happily smiling Japanese rammed himself boisterously into Trudi at the crucial moment.

Unable to endure any more, Marcel moved away from the peep-hole opening to lean his sweating forehead against the wall. But like a man who cannot resist exploring an aching tooth with his tongue, he was drawn to look again, in time to see Mr Hakimoto pull slowly out of Trudi and to observe that, like his body, the Japanese diplomat's gleaming wet *zimbriq* was short and thick. Most obviously it had transported Trudi into a Seventh Heaven for, with the blissful expression still on her beautiful face, she slid down to lie flat on her belly. Mr Hakimoto used a white handkerchief to dry his slowly drooping shaft before lying down with his head on the soft cheeks of Trudi's bottom, as if on a pillow.

So much for the true value of *you are the only man for me*, Marcel thought, and *je t'aime, mon chéri* and the other assurances of unending devotion she had gasped out while he was making love to her on her veranda. For all he knew she had been gasping out exactly the same words to Mr Hakimoto. Perfidious Trudi – she was using her beautiful body as a lure to get men to help her steal the valuable paintings. First Ysambard D'Cruz, then himself, and now Hakimoto. And besides the three he knew of, how many others had she recruited into her scheming by permitting them to enjoy her?

He turned away from the peep-hole and leaned his back against the wall. Concepcion pressed herself against him again and he put his arms round her without thinking – and found that she was naked. In the pitch darkness she had taken off all her clothes, and as his hands roamed over her body, the angry desire awakened in him by watching Trudi betray him transferred to the girl and he knew that he wanted to *zeqq* her to total destruction. Her breasts were soft and vulnerable young delights in his grasping hands, their prominent buds already firm. He felt down across the smooth expanse of her belly and forced his fingers into the lips under her crisp curls.

'Concepcion – I shall *zeqq* you to death,' he threatened, his hands gripping the plump cheeks of her bottom.

By way of reply, she sank to her knees to take his stiff *zimbriq* into her hot mouth and he clasped her unseen head in his hands, spread his legs and leaned back on the wall. Ripples of pleasure through his belly assured him that this was by no means the first time that Concepcion had used her mouth and tongue for this same purpose. He was so aroused that he thought that he was about to reach the peak of pleasure under her skilled ministrations – but that was not her intention.

Satisfied that he was ready for her purpose, she stood upright and parted her legs wide to try to force his hard shaft up into her. But she was too short in the leg for that to be practical – Marcel's *zimbriq* was on the level of her belly-button. She murmured in angry frustration, handling him with unmerciful force in her attempts to insert him.

'A moment, little Concepcion,' he said eagerly, 'let me!'

He picked her up bodily, delighting in the feel of her flesh against his body, until he felt the curls between her parted legs rub over his belly through his thin shirt. She reached down between her thighs to put the head of his *zimbriq* where she wanted it to go and, as he lowered her on to it, her strong legs encircled his waist and gripped tightly. She pressed her face against his, her arms about his neck, and he gave a long growl of triumph – the girl's own weight had impaled her on him to the hilt and the sensations imparted by her warm and slippery *kuft* were very exciting indeed.

'Make me *zboca*,' she whispered fiercely into his ear.

'Ten times!' he exclaimed.

With his shoulders propped against the wall and his hands under her bare bottom to support her, he made deep and rhythmic thrusts into her. Her breathing became fast and ragged on his cheek, for she was so highly aroused that her climactic release came before he was ready. He joggled her up and down on his *zimbriq* savagely, postponing his own pleasure until he could enjoy it in a less awkward position.

The truth was that although standing upright with a girl clinging on looked amusing among the carvings on Shah Jehan's bed, in reality it put a fierce strain on the back and legs that detracted sadly from the enjoyment to be expected from being embedded in a pretty young girl's *kuft*. Not that the girl had any such considerations to detract from her pleasure – she was gasping and squirming against him in a way that indicated she was being thoroughly satisfied. When she was finished, Marcel lifted her off him and lowered her to the floor.

'Was that good, Concepcion?' he asked, his lips touching her soft cheek in the dark.

'Very good,' she answered at once and with enthusiasm, 'make me *zboca* again, please.'

'As often as you want,' he said, feeling a pressure growing in his *castaz* that would soon find its release in an explosion of lust. 'First I must see what they are doing in there.'

He turned back to the peep-hole to see Trudi and Mr Hakimoto lying facing each other, her back towards Marcel and the Japanese with an arm over her hip to stroke her smooth bottom. She seemed to be speaking to him at some length, but either because she spoke quietly or because the wall was thick, it was impossible to distinguish the words. Her hands were not in sight, but Marcel would have been prepared to bet money that she was fondling her Japanese friend's *zimbriq*.

'What are they doing – is she on top of him?' Concepcion murmured close to Marcel's ear, and he smiled wolfishly at this reminder of the Santa Sabina way of making love.

'They are talking,' he replied. 'See for yourself.'

His shaft stood hard and hot out of his open trousers, throbbing to the mounting pressure inside him. He moved aside to let Concepcion put her eye to the peep-hole, stroking her belly with one hand and her plump bottom with the other. She gasped and wriggled and moved her bare feet further apart to tempt his hands downwards and a moment later his fingers were inside her and the force of his emotions was so great that he felt light-headed.

He slid behind Concepcion and pressed tightly against her warm bottom, reaching round her hips with hooked fingers to pull her wide open. She flinched for a moment and then pressed her rump back at him, bent her back and parted her legs until he could get the swollen head of his *zimbriq* under her and force it up into her wet *kuft*. An instant later, before there was time for even a single thrust, the volcanic forces that had been building up in him erupted so massively into the girl that she squealed in shock.

Cataclysmic sensations wiped Marcel's mind blank and his teeth sank into Concepcion's bare shoulder as his passionate torrent spurted like molten lava. It seemed to last for an eternity, but gradually his spasms faded and he became aware of the girl's whimpering as she squirmed in her own release. Eventually his belly stopped shaking and Concepcion became quiet again.

He was so calm now that he had forgotten about Trudi and the Japanese on the other side of the wall, and even when he recalled why he was here in the dark, it did not disturb him any longer. He eased himself out of Concepcion and stood leaning on her back, fondling her *gublas* contentedly. So Trudi went with other men – well, his instincts had warned him of that from the beginning and there were no real surprises after what he had learned from Esperanza. Tomorrow she would board the ship and sail out of his life forever, and good riddance.

'They're going to do it again,' Concepcion whispered, her eye at the peep-hole, 'she's peeling the bamboo.'

'What do you mean?' Marcel asked, not caring what Trudi was doing, but he took Concepcion's place at the peep-hole.

On the embroidered cushions of the bed, Mr

Hakimoto and Trudi were sitting on their heels, Japanese-style, facing each other. She was sliding her clasped hand up and down in the form of stimulation that Concepcion had described, covering and uncovering the purple and swollen head of Mr Hakimoto's stubby *zimbriq*. He was feeling her sumptuous breasts with both hands, a toothy smile on his flat Oriental face.

New sensations of pleasure flicked suddenly through Marcel and, reaching down, he found that Concepcion was sitting between his legs with her bare back to the wall, sucking his *zimbriq*, her fingers stretching his *castazz*.

Mr Hakimoto put his hand between Trudi's spread thighs and turned it over, palm upward. His toothy grin became even broader as he slid two fingers into her pink-lipped *kuft* and tickled her bud. She looked as if she was enjoying what Mr Hakimoto was doing to her and speeded up the peeling of the bamboo, until her companion took her by the hips and lifted her right off the bed and set her down across his thighs. From the happy expression on her face, Marcel hadn't the least doubt that she had been pierced by her friend's thick bamboo staff.

As if to confirm the correctness of Marcel's assumption, the Japanese tightened his grasp on Trudi's hips and rocked her and himself forwards and backwards. But by then Marcel's interest had faded as he lost himself in the sensations which the girl between his legs was providing. She had his trousers round his knees and her fingers probed between his legs, behind his *castazz* and up between the cheeks of his bottom.

Her teeth closed round his *zimbriq* to nip the flesh and the sensations hurled him towards delirium. A finger found the little knot between the cheeks of his bottom, forced a way in ruthlessly and Marcel's hot passion burst from him in spasms that shook him against the wall. He clung to Concepcion's head, jamming it hard against him in a frenzied attempt to push his *zimbriq* right down her throat.

It went on and on, this climax of his, her teeth holding his hard flesh while her tongue lapped over it. When at last his nervous system could tolerate no more of this enormous paroxysm of pleasure, his legs collapsed beneath him and he sank to his knees. The descent dragged his shaft from between her closed teeth with renewed sensations of excruciating delight, until he thought he would faint. Then he was sitting on the floor astride her sprawled-out legs, his head bowed forward to rest on her bare shoulder.

When he came to himself in the dark he knew he had to do it again to keep himself from brooding on the wrong done to him. He put his arms round Concepcion and rested his cheek against hers while he whispered that he wanted to *zeqq* her. She caught her breath and in the dark he felt her fingers tugging at his wet and softening shaft.

'Come to my room,' he said, massaging her *gublas* vigorously.

'No, you come to mine,' she answered. 'Wait while I put my clothes on.'

Naturally, he had never been into the part of the hotel occupied by Baltazar Costa and his family. It lay behind a closed door covered in worn green baize, a long single-storey extension at the back of the building. Concepcion's room was furnished with a brass-framed single bed, a dressing-table under the window and a tall wardrobe for her clothes. The walls of the room were painted plain white and over the bedhead there hung a large crucifix of shiny black wood.

She closed the door but did not bother to lock it. While Marcel was still looking round the room, she had her pink-flowered frock over her head and soon over a chair, she kicked her shoes off carelessly across the brown-tiled floor and leapt on the bed. She lay on her back on the bright orange bed-cover, propped up on her elbows to stare down at the tuft of black curls between her widely spread thighs.

'I am ready for you,' she said, her tone serious, '*zeqq* me to death like you promised.'

Marcel stripped off his clothes, his desires becoming highly inflamed again as he looked at her. At seventeen her breasts were already deliciously round, though not yet full grown. Her skin was an attractive *café au lait* colour, her belly smooth and just slightly curved – but what seized the eye and held the attention was the luxuriant black fleece between her open thighs, the curls so thick that her *kuft* was completely hidden.

'I am sorry you had to see your yellow-haired lady with another man,' she said. 'Is your heart broken? I heard you sobbing in the dark when you were watching them.'

He decided she might be disappointed if he explained that his sobs had been of ecstasy, not of sorrow. He lay between her legs to kiss her belly and then moved up to touch his tongue to the tips of her breasts and rub his belly over her *kuft*.

'It is finished with her,' he said. 'I want to *zeqq* you.'

She grinned and twisted from under him, smacked at his bottom to get him to turn on to his back and sat over his loins in true Santa Sabina style. His *zimbriq* had started to swell and lengthen from the moment she had stripped – and she rolled it between her flat palms to hasten the process.

'My friend Johana says that for a man of your age you are very strong,' she told him.

'A testimonial is always welcome,' he said, 'and doubly so from an expert like Johana.'

Her fingers combed up through her thick black curls to make a central parting and Marcel caught his first glimpse of dark brown lips and, as she opened them, the wetly-pink interior of her *kuft*. She held herself open while she took hold of his stiff shaft and guided it into place. She raised herself and sank down again to push him deep inside her.

'Now you are *zeqqing* me again!' she exclaimed.

'I must dispute that, Mademoiselle,' he murmured, enjoying the sensation of warm and slippery flesh round his *zimbriq*, 'it is you who are *zeqqing* me, I believe.'

'Where's the difference?' she asked, grinning down at him.

She slid herself up and down his impaling shaft as if she were hammering a nail into a plank, her breasts joggling to the energetic rhythm. Marcel lay comfortably on the bright orange bed-cover while she had her way, thinking, so far as he was still capable of rational thought, of the effect this traditional view of their girl-friends must have on the young men of Santa Sabina. In the moments when the sensations of delight were rising to their peak, the Santa Sabinan male saw his woman looming over him, her naked *gublas* flopping up and down and her dark-haired *kuft* slamming at him in a frenzy of desire.

Was it this powerful image and the conviction of being used that drained them of desire so young, he asked himself, just as Concepcion shrilled loudly, her back arching and her head back. For Marcel the moment was equally delightful. Her bouncing had brought him to the brink of ecstasy and the strength of her sudden paroxysm carried him over the edge with her. It was as if they had jumped off a precipice hand in hand and were flying through the air, his sap flicking up into her convulsing belly.

When they were tranquil again, she refused to move off him or let him slip out of her. *You are my prisoner*, she insisted, holding the base of his shaft tightly between finger and thumb to keep it inside her as it shrank and softened.

'I am your prisoner, Mademoiselle Concepcion,' he agreed, 'what do you mean to do with me?'

'I'm going to *zeqq* you again as soon as you are hard,' she told him. 'You are in my room and so you must do as I say.'

The popular wisdom of Santa Sabina had it that girls began to play with their hairless little slits from the age of three and boys no later than five. At six or seven the boys and girls were playing snakes and turtles together, feeling each other at every opportunity. By the time they were eleven, constant stimulation had made the boys able to ejaculate and from then on they and the girls *zeqqed* each other several times a day. Most girls could conceive at twelve, but their mothers made them chew qagga leaves to prevent it, at least until they were fifteen. From then on they were regarded as grown women, responsible for their own fertility.

Concepcion was staring down between her thighs, to where Marcel's limp *zimbriq* would have slipped away from her but for her restraining hand. There was a most serious expression on her broad and pretty face as she considered how best to make it hard again and, certain that she made love more often than he did, Marcel wondered who her partners were. He thought that the young waiter, Teofilo, who served the terrace, might be one of them, because he could frequently be seen on duty with his back leaning against the wall and his eyes closed, snatching a few moments of sleep.

'I can feel your *zimbriq* stretching itself inside me,' she said, 'it wants to *zeqq* again.'

She was squatting over him with her legs folded under her. Holding his shaft inside her, she leaned first to the left and then to the right to straighten each leg in turn and put her bare heels into his armpits.

'Do you know how to play see-saw?' she asked.

Her feet pushed under his arms while she rocked herself backwards and forwards on him and he surrendered once more.

12

The Tranquil Pleasures of the Countryside

After Trudi's ship had sailed, Marcel told Pieter van Buuren that he wanted to get out of the city for a day or two and invited him along on a short walking holiday. The Dutchman agreed readily – *too much zeqqing in this town*, he said with a grin, *I need fresh air in my lungs*.

The truth was that Marcel felt it necessary to use the information he had acquired with great delicacy. Trudi's disappearance would be thought suspicious by the Bureau of Public Information, as the secret police were euphemistically named, and they would be checking on her friends and contacts. He had no doubt that there was a dossier with his name on it, containing detailed accounts of their frolics. A way to clear himself was to uncover a plot, but not too openly, for that would merely serve to deepen suspicion of his involvement.

Naturally, he gave some thought to disclosing what he knew to his Ambassador, but on reflection that seemed imprudent. Having no influential friends in Paris, Marcel was sure that he would be held responsible for any problems that might arise and would be either transferred to somewhere even less desirable than Santa Sabina or be kicked out of the service. What he had in mind was to seem to stumble unawares on evidence of a plot, in the company of a witness whose honesty was above question – van Buuren.

Together they caught the bus to Vilanova at eight the next morning. The rocky coast road to the north-west wound its way along between sea and cliff, the groaning bus negotiating tight curves above a vertiginous drop for most of the time, but by midday they were in Vilanova. They lunched at a restaurant that faced the church of St Dionisio across the central square, where, Trudi had said, there was a very valuable painting – but Marcel had not the least inclination to go and look for it.

An hour later he and Pieter strolled along the town's main street, between shops and houses until the buildings ended, and the street became a lane. It led in the general direction of the Sierra Dorada mountains that formed the northern horizon, ten or fifteen kilometres distant – a range with a profound influence on the island's climate, or so said the experts, making it hotter, wetter and more oppressive than it might otherwise have been.

The lane vanished before they had been walking for more than twenty minutes and they followed a footpath between large and irregularly-shaped open fields. A few were plain brown earth, some were green with growing crops, and othes yellow with ripe *miltsa* – the local corn. An hour out of Vilanova they saw a line of seven or eight women harvesting the corn by hand, naked to the waist with breasts swinging to the rhythm of their work. The *miltsa* grew almost as tall as the women, who bent to encompass an armful and slash through the tough stalks at knee-level.

'Primitive, but effective, I suppose,' said Pieter, staring hard. 'They must develop muscles like weight-lifters.'

The women were all young, which was not surprising for so laborious a task. Marcel eyed the ripple of back muscles, the sway of full brown breasts and the roll of bottoms through the thin cotton of their skirts.

'They are goddesses of agriculture from the dawn of

mankind's history,' he said, 'each one a primitive Venus from a forgotten age. How fortunate the man who possesses one of these semi-divinities and rolls her under him on the earth floor of his thatched hut – in that embrace is to be found the experience of life renewing itself with the cycle of the seasons.'

'Very poetical!' said Pieter. 'But give me a clean and civilised girl every time and keep your sweaty bucolic nymphs.'

The women had stopped work to turn and stare. Marcel called *Bonjour*, and they replied with greetings in their own language, not speaking town-French this far out in the country. The European colonists of Santa Sabina had always preferred the conveniences of living in town and having local bailiffs to manage their farms and plantations. For this simple reason of geography, the amours of the Europeans had not spread their racial characteristics widely, and country dwellers tended to be somewhat darker of skin.

This held true for the group of girls who had abandoned their reaping to crowd round Marcel and Pieter and chatter away incomprehensibly. There were eight of them, all with thick black hair hanging untidily to their shoulders and with skin a lustrous coffee shade that Marcel thought particularly attractive. They were all much of a height and there was a certain similarity in their plump round cheeks and broad mouths that suggested they were from a small village where a handful of families had interbred for centuries past.

It was mid-afternoon and oppressively hot, the time of day when town-people were prostrate in their siesta. One of the girls fanned air over her bare brown breasts and Marcel gazed at her in appreciation.

'There is the proof of what I was saying,' he told Pieter. 'Observe how marvellously unselfconscious are these dear nymphs of the countryside! How innocently they uncover their bodies. Regard with what natural grace this sweet child is wiping her breasts dry with a bandana!'

The leader of the group was in her early twenties, a

year or two older than the others. It was she who was doing most of the chattering now, while the others giggled and looked at the men. She repeated the same phrase several times, tapping Marcel's chest with her finger, until he recognised a word or two of mispronounced French that failed to convey any clear meaning. A moment later Marcel's legs were kicked from under him and he fell heavily on his back. His arms and shoulders were knelt upon by women to pin him flat and he could hear Pieter swearing to find himself thrown and immobilised in the same way.

'What is this?' Pieter gasped. 'Do they mean to rob us?'

'She said something about King of the Harvest,' said Marcel, 'but I didn't really understand.'

A moment later he understood very well when the woman who had tried and failed to explain matters to him sat across his thighs and wrenched his trousers open. Two of the other girls spread armfuls of yellow corn over him from neck to knees.

'I have the honour to inform you that you and I have become Harvest Kings,' he told Pieter, 'a quaint countryside custom.'

The grinning woman on his legs delved with her work-hardened hand into the corn and gripped his precious *zimbriq*.

'No need to pull it off!' he heard Pieter shout in alarm, by which he knew he was receiving the same treatment.

Marcel stared at the plump brown-skinned breasts of the woman gripping his shaft. Young as she was, he guessed from the way her breasts hung low and slack that she had several children. And while he stared, reaching this banal conclusion, she arched her back and waggled her *gublas* at him. It seemed very strange to him that a man should be raped, but the best course was to enjoy it. He made kissing movements of his lips in the direction of her brown-budded *gublas*.

Her response was to strip her loose black skirt up over her head to reveal herself naked and move her knees to straddle his thighs. He pushed his hands under the prickly corn-stalks to throw them off him, but the woman held his wrists to stop him. She spoke the same mangled French words several times until he understood the corn was the robe of the Harvest King.

Evidently the local belief required him to play his part in ensuring that the corn grew tall next season. And he was fully prepared to do his duty – his *zimbriq* had raised its head from among the stalks and was ready. The naked and grinning young woman took hold of it between hard fingers and raised herself on her knees high enough to position it to her liking. She sat down hard and drove it into her, making him gasp.

'Gently for Heaven's sake!' he exclaimed.

But all such injunctions were futile to a Santa Sabina woman impaled on a *zimbriq*. She jerked herself up and down with ferocious energy, her face turned up to the sky and her hands tugging at her own long brown breasts. She was gasping out *zboca, zboca* in a demented way, evidently ordering him to do so. So furious was her *zeqqing* that she soon had her way – his passion spurted from him and the woman mounted astride him shouted in triumph.

Her own crisis took her immediately and she shrilled out *aiee! aiee!* while she rode him in climactic frenzy. On it went, her black-haired head jerking up and down loosely, as if her neck were broken, until her nervous energy was exhausted and she sagged forward on him. He turned his sweating face to look at Pieter, pinned to the ground beside him by three laughing girls. A fourth squatted over his loins, her brown cotton skirt hitched up to her waist and her *gublas* bouncing up and down as she *zeqqed* him furiously. Her victorious shout announced that the Dutchman had been relieved of his essence.

Now that the Harvest King's tribute had been paid, the women became friendly and helpful. Marcel was helped to a sitting position, and the sweat wiped from his face and belly with a red bandana, while another girl gave him a drink of water from a goatskin bag and yet another offered him two or three green figs to eat.

Conversation was next to impossible, the women's combined knowledge of French being no more than twenty words, and smiles and nods served to indicate goodwill.

Pieter had recovered from his sense of outrage and was disposed to give a demonstration of his capabilities. *You take four and I'll take four* he suggested, *between us we'll give them all a treat*. But Marcel talked him out of it, saying that the harvest-women were too rough and untutored for *zeqqing* them to be of any interest.

'You said that they are primitive divinities of agriculture from the dawn of history,' said Pieter with a grin. 'You wanted to roll one of them under you on the earth, you said.'

'Alas, it is we who are rolled on the earth under them,' said Marcel. 'I am sure we can find better, if we go further.'

They agreed to take their leave and asked the women the way to their village. Once this was pointed out, they made their farewells, kissing each of the eight and running their hands over their bare breasts. The women went back to their reapings, singing a work-song together, while Marcel and Pieter headed north in the direction of the mountains. It was another half-hour's walk to the village and they were pleased when at least they were sitting outside a fairly rudimentary inn. For once they drank the vile Santa Sabina beer without complaint.

After a while they were joined by the village priest, a well-fed man of fifty in an old and threadbare black cassock. He introduced himself as Father Isador and spoke good French, though with a strong provincial accent. He was most curious to hear what was going on in the city and what brought the foreigners to his out-of-the-way village. They explained that they were on vacation, but the concept of a walking tour to see the countryside was very strange to him.

'We have nothing of interest for you to see!' he said. 'There are fields and more fields and mountains, that's all.'

'On the way here from Vilanova we met a group of young women reaping *miltsa*,' said Pieter, straight-faced. 'That was very interesting.'

'Did these shameless women make you their Harvest King?' Father Isidor asked at once.

'Yes, both of us,' Marcel answered with a laugh and the priest grinned back at him.

'It is five hundred years since the Portuguese brought the True Faith to Santa Sabina, yet these old heathen customs linger on,' said the priest. 'You must forgive our backward ways – the villagers are good people at heart. Be thankful that only your chastity has suffered today. Once there was a time when the women would have cut off your *castazz* with a sickle afterwards, and then slit your throats to revivify the earth with your blood.'

'My God, we can be grateful that the Portuguese were able to put a stop to that,' Marcel exclaimed.

'The Portuguese could never stop it – nor the French after them,' said Father Isador. 'It was the President's grandfather who finally succeeded in suppressing the murder of passing strangers at the *miltsa* harvest.'

'But Monsieur – that could have been only fifty or sixty years ago!' Marcel objected. 'How is this possible?'

Father Isador nodded and crossed himself casually.

'As I said, old customs linger on for a long time,' he said.

'Apropos of old customs,' said Marcel, 'there are reputed to be caves in the mountains where the Arabs imprisoned slaves in the days before the Portuguese came.'

'Yes, there are caves,' said the priest, 'but it is a desolation. I went there soon after I became priest here.'

'From curiosity, Father?'

'No, I thought that if I prayed there I could banish the old evil that keeps everyone away. But it was only my own youthful pride that impelled me to attempt to cleanse the caves. I failed and nothing was changed.'

'Why do you say there is evil there?' Marcel asked.

'The Arabs raided African villages to capture children

and young men and women. The old and sick, they massacred out of hand. They brought their captives to Santa Sabina, which had another name then, and chained them in the caves. They kept them there until they had been branded and their spirit broken by the whip and bastinado. Through the centuries, the cruelty of the slavers and the despair of their victims soaked into the rock of the mountains. The caves are accursed. I felt that when I was there and not all my praying could alter it.'

'What do you think, Pieter – shall we visit these dreadful caves tomorrow?' Marcel asked.

'Of course we must! Are they easy to find, Father?'

'The track has been overgrown for hundreds of years. You could wander about the mountain-foot for a long time before you found them.'

Marcel produced a 50-tikkoo note and gave it to the priest, saying that it was *for the poor*. Pieter did the same, Father Isidor tucked the money away inside his threadbare cassock and said that he had a granddaughter who would be pleased to show them the way in the morning. He accepted a drink and told them a little about the tranquil life of the villagers, where the only work was in the fields and the only enjoyment in bed.

When they were alone again, Pieter asked whether Marcel believed the story of travellers having their throats and *castazz* cut after they had been *zeqqed*.

'I find it difficult to believe,' said the Dutchman. 'In my experience, the people of this island are courteous and gentle. The priest was regaling us with tall stories, I think.'

'I believe he told the truth,' said Marcel. 'There is only a thin veneer of civilisation over primitive emotions and beliefs. The original people of the island were conquered by Arabs, and made to interbreed with Africans to produce more slaves, then conquered again by the Portuguese and converted to Christianity by torture, fire and the sword. I am sure Santa Sabinans can be murderously savage if provoked sufficiently.'

'And we must not overlook the depravity introduced here by the French in the eighteenth century!' said Pieter slyly.

'What little civilisation they have was taught to them by the French!' Marcel retorted indignantly, 'We freed them from the Portuguese in 1709 and gave them independence as a republic soon after our own Revolution.'

'That shows how little value the island had,' said the Dutchman, 'if you gave it independence.'

'Take this question of Father Isidor's grand-daughter, who will guide us to the caves tomorrow,' said Marcel, ignoring the gibe. 'He is telling the truth, of course, but he is also being discreet. She is his direct descendant, you may be sure.'

'But Catholic priests are celibate!'

'They do not marry, as your Protestant pastors do, but here in Santa Sabina the children start to *zeqq* each other when they are twelve. Training for priesthood does not start until much later – by which time the boys have used up their virility and have no further interest in women. Celibacy holds no problems for them, but by that time they have several children by different girls.'

'This is typical Jesuit hypocrisy!' Pieter objected. 'Where is the virtue in celibacy if they are not tempted? They might as well have had their *castazz* cut off, out in a field!'

He had no reason to complain when Father Isidor's grand-daughter came to the inn at eight the next morning. Her name was Ofelia; she was nineteen and pretty in a sturdy sort of way, and her grandfather had taught her to speak French well enough to be understood without too much effort. She regarded the outing as a holiday and was wearing her best blouse and skirt but, as there was a lot of walking ahead, she had not risked ruining her only pair of shoes and was barefoot. She wore her shoes for Mass on Sundays, she explained. Her dark brown eyes bulged with surprise when they each gave her a 50-tikkoo note and she embarrassed them by kissing their hands in gratitude.

She insisted on taking the haversack of cold meat, cheese, fruit and beer for their midday meal, slung it over her shoulder as if it weighed nothing and led them out of the village toward the Sierra Dorada mountains. As they walked she told them that she was married and had a son nearly two years old, displaying with pride a wedding-ring so thin and narrow as to be hardly more than a hoop of gold wire.

When they saw that their path lay between fields that had been harvested, Marcel and Pieter exchanged a glance of amusement. And of relief, for though it was not yet nine in the morning the temperature was already intolerable and they had a long way to go. Worse – from the village the ground rose uphill all the way to the mountains. They walked for an hour and rested for a quarter of an hour, and when they went on again there were no more cultivated fields, only scrubby grassland that became ever steeper the further they went.

They went on for another hour, rested again, not far now from the mountain foot, and another twenty or thirty minutes brought them to the grey rock-face. Pieter sat down, his normal pink face flushed dark-red from the effort of walking so far, and asked where the caves were. Ofelia shrugged and said she would look around while he and Marcel rested. She left the haversack with them and strode away to the west.

'She's lost,' said Pieter. 'She's never been here before – all she has to go on is what grandpa told her about what he remembers from twenty-five years ago!'

'She will either find the caves or not,' said Marcel, pretending indifference as he settled himself comfortably on his back on the turf with his sun-hat over his eyes. 'If she doesn't, we'll send her home while we push on towards the coast and the next village.'

He was unused to walking so far, his legs ached and he soon dozed off in the shade. When he woke up he held his arm up to look at his watch and saw that it was after midday and that he had been asleep for over two hours. What had awoken him was a loud gasping noise over to his right and he rolled his head on the grass to look. He saw Pieter lying on his back, stark naked, with Ofelia perched over his loins, equally naked, bouncing up and down. They were just reaching the end of their flight together – the girl gave voice shrilly and Pieter jerked up into her in hard spasms.

'Bravo!' said Marcel when he saw their throes fading, and Ofelia turned her head to grin at him.

'I've been entertaining our charming young guide while you slept,' said Pieter. 'She's found the caves.'

'Good! Let's have lunch, shall we?' Marcel suggested.

But Ofelia had a different order of priorities. She unhitched herself from the Dutchman and stood with her hands on her hips and her feet apart to stare down at Marcel. To be truthful, his *zimbriq* had stiffened at the sight of her on his friend. He looked up at her bare and heavy breasts and the black fleece between her thighs, and his impudent part jerked so strongly in his trousers that Ofelia burst out laughing. She fell to her knees beside him to drag his trousers off before she squatted over him and spiked herself expertly on his shaft.

As was to be expected after her bout with the Dutchman, her *kuft* was extemely wet and slippery. Marcel sighed with pleasure as she slid up and down and made her *gublas* and the scarlet talisman between them bounce rhythmically. There was nothing for him to do – and in the extreme heat of midday there was nothing he wanted to do – but lie on the grass and let Ofelia precipitate his climax and her own.

Afterwards they ate lunch naked, as if they were posing for another Manet to paint a new version of the *Déjeuner sur l'Herbe*. Ofelia said that she had found the caves a half hour walk away and made it apparent, by stroking Marcel's bare thigh, that she would like to make love again before moving on. When Pieter said he would like to do it in the caves and chase the ghosts away, she screwed up her nose in horror. A woman from her village had ignored warnings and gone into the caves once, she said, and been thrown down and *zeqqed* by a demon, but she was vague as to when this unnatural event took place.

They trudged on westwards with the sun to their left, and the heat slowed them down until Ofelia's half-hour walk stretched to almost an hour before they reached a dusty grey gorge cutting into the mountain.

'The caves are in there,' she said. 'Not far – how long will you be?'

'But you must come with us,' said Pieter, still hoping to *zeqq* her in a cave, but she sat down with her back to the rock-wall and refused to go any closer, afraid that she might be *zeqqed* by a demon or a ghost.

'There won't be much to see,' said Marcel. 'We shall be back in twenty minutes. Stay here and rest, Ofelia.'

That brought a more cheerful expression to her face and the two men set off side by side up the steep gorge.

'She's not the only one afraid to come here,' Pieter observed, 'there are no tracks in the dust at all – only the ones we are making.'

Marcel nodded and said nothing. To him it was evident that the dusty ground was completely unmarked because it had been swept smooth with branches, for if Sherri was to be believed, Hochheimer had used jeeps to bring in his shipment of arms. The entrance to the first cave was on their right, not more than five hundred metres along the gorge. It was an irregular opening two metres high and twice as wide. Further along the rock-face there was another cave and beyond that another – four in all, though the most distant one appeared much smaller.

Marcel hung back while Pieter plunged cheerfully into the first cave and soon he heard him boom *come and see this!*

The daylight did not penetrate far – five metres from the cave-mouth it was very dim and beyond that it quickly became very dark. What the Dutchman had found were rusty chains hanging from the wall, a long line of them down each side of the cave, stretching away into the distant darkness.

'Good God, this is where the slaves were chained!'

said Marcel. 'The inhumanity of it! I am not surprised that the Santa Sabinans will not come here – this place must be haunted by uncounted thousands of ghosts.'

'Each was allowed less than a metre of space,' said the practical Dutchman, looking at the distance between sets of chains. 'I wonder how many they packed into the cave.'

He went striding into the darkness and Marcel stayed where he was, happy to let the other make any discoveries there were to be made. He heard a shout of either alarm or surprise and in a while Pieter came back, carrying a jaw-bone. 'There are broken skeletons,' he announced sombrely, 'and wooden boxes. I bruised my shin on one of them.'

'Boxes?' Marcel asked, trying to sound surprised, 'Arab treasure chests, I hope. Have we found wonderful riches?'

'No, they're new boxes. Come and see for yourself.'

'I've just remembered – there's a torch in the haversack. I'll go back and get it. Have a look in the other caves to see if there's anything else till I get back.'

When Ofelia saw him emerge from the gorge she decided that he had seen all he wanted of the caves and had returned to make love to her. He explained that he'd come back for the torch, put his hand up her skirt to stroke her briefly between the legs to show his goodwill, and left her disappointed but still hopeful. By shouting at the cave-mouths he ascertained that Pieter was in the second and went in to join him, flashing the beam of light on walls and floor. Rusty chains hung from the rock and though the gorge had been swept of tracks, the caves had not – there were the marks of booted feet everywhere.

Pieter was standing by a stack of large wooden crates, ten or fifteen in all. Marcel ran the light over them, looking for identification-marks or shipping-marks, and was startled by what he found.

'But those letters are Russian!' he exclaimed. 'What do you imagine can be in the crates?'

'These are the sort of boxes that guns are shipped in,'

said Pieter, 'but we have no tools to break one open and look.'

'Guns?' said Marcel, pretending surprise. 'Who would store Russian guns in a cave? If our Soviet colleagues intend to invade Santa Sabina, surely their soldiers will come ashore fully armed and shooting? Let's go and look in the first cave and see what you fell over.'

The first cave held ten large wooden crates with markings in an alphabet more familiar to them.

'These are American,' said Pieter, 'Look at that – a crate full of sub-machine guns, I'd bet six month's salary on it!'

'American guns, Russian guns – what can it mean?' Marcel asked, genuinely puzzled and unable to reconcile what they had found with what he had imagined.

'It means trouble,' said Pieter, 'Let's go outside and think it over. There's an unpleasant atmosphere down here that has nothing to do with guns.'

'You didn't believe me when I said there are thousands of ghosts in here!'

'Ghosts don't bother me,' said Pieter in a hushed voice, 'but after listening to Ofelia I've got this nasty feeling that there might be female demons who throw men down and *zeqq* them, and I'm sure they bite your *castazz* off when they'd finished.

They went outside and sat on rocks at the cave-mouth while the Dutchman lit one of his small cigars. He seemed uneasy and on edge and so Marcel made a start.

'It is obvious that we have found an illegal cache of arms,' he said. 'Perhaps it is a small part of the Cold War. It would seem that the two so-called Super-powers have each sent enough weapons to Santa Sabina to overthrow President da Cunha.'

'If it were either one or the other, I could understand it,' Pieter complained. 'Do you think that someone has managed to fool the USA and the USSR and got weapons from both?'

'It is equally possible that the Americans and the Russians have fooled themselves into arming a political adventurer in exchange for promises of future co-operation,' Marcel replied.

'Of course! Everyone wants permission to build bases and exploit the minerals in these mountains and drill for oil and heaven knows what else. D'Cruz must be the leader of a planned *coup d'état* – that's why he's been arrested. But they haven't found his arsenal, so someone else might take over from him.'

'It is very possible,' said Marcel. 'Many others must be involved, including some of the army. But I must remind you that as foreigners our position is delicate. Shall we report our discovery or continue our walking tour and forget what we have seen?'

'We have no choice in the matter,' said the Dutchman. 'We must report it to our superiors. What they do about it is for them to decide, but it is then out of our hands.'

'Yes, you're right,' Marcel agreed, 'I think we must abandon our little vacation and go back without delay.'

'There is something I do not understand,' said Pieter. 'How were these weapons brought here? Not through the port of Santa Sabina, obviously, and not through Vilanova.'

'They must have been landed in a cove or on a beach on the west coast where there are few villages and brought across country,' said Marcel, that being what Sherri had told him.

'It is very funny,' the Dutchman said, grinning suddenly. 'Only imagine – two ships arriving on different nights on the same deserted coast, one Russian and one American, each thinking that they alone have thought of this plan. Each side unloads boxes of guns and hauls them to these caves, guided by an associate of D'Cruz, who makes sure they use different caves to store their boxes!'

'An excellent farce for a film-director,' Marcel agreed, 'but not one that will be made in Hollywood, I think. Come on, we've got hours of walking ahead of us.'

201

'We must act responsibly,' the Dutchman agreed, 'but on the other hand, a short delay will do no harm.'

'A delay for what?'

'Our pretty guide is waiting patiently for us to come back,' Pieter said with a grin. 'For the sake of a few guns it would be unfriendly to rush off without giving her a good *zeqqing*.'

'It is a long and boring way back to Vilanova and the bus,' Marcel agreed. 'You are right, we owe Ofelia something.'

'When all is said, the political future of Santa Sabina will not change, whether da Cunha or D'Cruz is President,' Pieter observed. 'In my opinion Ofelia's happiness is more important.'

'She expects us to do our best for her,' said Marcel, 'and I never yet disappointed the expectations of a pretty woman. I suggest we postpone political considerations until dusk, when it will be a little cooler to walk back to the village.'

'Dusk,' said Pieter, looking at his watch, 'that gives us a good four hours to apply ourselves to making Ofelia the happiest girl in all Santa Sabina.'

When she saw them approaching down the dusty gorge Ofelia jumped up and waved. From the smiles on their faces she guessed what they had in mind and took off her clothes, so that by the time they reached her she was naked. She lay down on the grass, her legs apart and her hand on her black-curled fleece while the two men stripped. Marcel lay on one side of her, Pieter on the other, each with an arm under her head and a hand on a soft brown breast and she, with a happy grin on her face, took a stiff *zimbriq* in each hand.

13

To Encourage the Others, as Voltaire Put It

After Marcel and Pieter van Buuren had reported their find to their Ambassadors, events moved at a pace wholly untypical of Santa Sabina. The French and Dutch Ambassadors discussed the matter with each other, consulted their home governments, met again to concert their action and made a joint official visit to the Minister for the Exterior, Annibal Palmella, and the startled Minister took them to see President da Cunha. Four days later Ysambard D'Cruz was put on trial, accused of treason and eighty-three related offences concerned with the importation and possession of arms, conspiracy with foreign powers unknown to overthrow the government and the constitution and so on. Several army officers and business men, members of the Chamber of Deputies and the Secretary-General of the Santa Sabina Workers' Party were arrested.

The island's only newspaper, the *Daily Chronicles*, announced that there had been a most serious plot, in which D'Cruz and others had been involved with foreign enemies of the State. The newspaper was owned by the President, who had inherited it from his father along with the Presidency, and naturally it spoke out firmly against this evil attempt to destroy democracy itself. Indeed, it called upon the President, the judiciary and all others concerned, to show no mercy to the treacherous malefactor D'Cruz and his lickspittle Imperialistic warmongers, Neo-Colonial running dogs, Fascist hyenas and Communist dupes.

To the surprise of the diplomatic community, the trial was completed within one day, even allowing a break for lunch. D'Cruz pleaded guilty to all charges, having no doubt been advised that it would be the worse for him if he caused problems. The only evidence heard was that of the Army Major who had been sent to collect the guns from the caves. The court was ringed with troops, not because any disturbance was expected, but to let them show off the fine new weapons they had unexpectedly acquired.

Santa Sabina's best advocate, Maître Drago, represented D'Cruz and did the best he could in impossible circumstances. His impassioned plea for mercy was greatly admired as an exercise in sustained rhetoric and on behalf of the three presiding judges, the senior judge congratulated him on his eloquence before sentencing D'Cruz to death. The appeal against sentence was heard after lunch, Maître Drago pleading before the same panel of judges, for there were no others. The appeal was rejected and the execution fixed for the next day but one.

Marcel's Ambassador sent for him the next morning and handed him a large and black-edged invitation card.

'You are invited to the execution of D'Cruz tomorrow.' Marcel exclaimed, aghast. 'But this is barbarous!'

'It is the way things are done here,' said Jean-Jacques Ducour with ill-humour. 'All Ambassadors at present in Santa Sabina have been invited – as a warning not to meddle in local politics. Have you ever witnessed a public execution, Lamont?'

'I? Of course not – how could I?'

'During my years in the service of France I have had the misfortune to witness official executions in various parts of the Orient,' said Ducour. 'I have seen men beheaded, hanged and shot to death by firing-squad. But I do not propose to attend the garrotting of D'Cruz. You were responsible for bringing it about, therefore it is only just that you attend in my place. The Santa Sabinans have been advised that I am indisposed.'

'But Your Excellency . . .' Marcel stammered in consternation.

'Allow me to suggest that you wear a dark suit and tie,' said Ducour, giving him a bleak smile of dismissal.

However appalled Marcel might be at the prospect of attending an execution, the Santa Sabinans themselves treated it as a public holiday. The main square in front of the cathedral was packed with chattering, cheerful people of all ages, and it was necessary for the army to keep a way open for official guests to reach the stand. The soldiers looked very smart in new uniforms issued for the occasion, with brand-new American-made automatic rifles slung over their shoulders.

The wooden scaffold on which D'Cruz was to meet his end had been built in front of the Cathedral of St Sabina the Younger, Virgin Martyr, and at right angles to it were larger platforms for invited guests. One was draped in the red, yellow and green colours of the Republic of Santa Sabina, and here President da Cunha was receiving the diplomatic corps. The platform on the other side of the scaffold had tiers of seats and was occupied by Departmental Ministers, members of the Chamber of Deputies still at liberty, civil servants, Army officers and others who might benefit from a reminder of where their duty lay.

It was to the President's platform that Marcel presented himself in place of the French Ambassador at ten in the morning. As befitted the occasion, the President was sombrely dressed in a black tail-coat, striped trousers and a shiny black top-hat. He was a round-faced man in his forties, with the comparatively light complexion of Portuguese ancestry and the beaked nose of Arab blood. Marcel bowed and presented his Ambassaador's apologies that illness confined him to his bed. The President looked at him closely while they shook hands.

'I owe you a debt of gratitude, Monsieur Lamont,' he said. 'But for you the situation might have become very serious.' Marcel mumured his thanks and moved on to make room for the next in line to shake da Cunha's hand. Though the Presidential viewing-platform was not equipped with chairs, it had a bar at the back where servants in green velvet livery were dispensing drinks. And President da Cunha being a widower, his sister was present to discharge the duties of hostess, as she regularly did at official functions. Marcel kissed her hand and accepted a glass of champagne.

Mariantonetta da Souza was a woman in her late thirties, who had preserved the slenderness of youth by rigorous dieting and exercise. Her complexion was the olive tint of Santa Sabina's leading families and her hair the usual near-black. Her clothes were superb, for she had learned from the French Ambassador's wife to have them made in Paris. For the execution she was wearing a long-sleeved frock of fine black silk and a broad-brimmed hat with a single black-dyed ostrich feather standing up from the band.

'I am so pleased you are here, Monsieur Lamont,' she said. 'But for you, my brother might be mounting the scaffold while Ysambard D'Cruz stood here to watch.'

'I am glad to have been of some small service, Madame.'

'My brother intends to honour you with the Grand Cross of the Three Orders of St Sabina. Has Monsieur Ducour told you?'

'Not yet, Madame. I was not alone of course, a Dutch friend was with me. He is not here today, I believe.'

'He will be honoured too, but our historic links with France are closer than with the Netherlands and the President will award your colleague the Sash and you the Grand Cross.'

Marcel bowed gracefully in gratitude that the honour would get his name off the Bureau of Public Information suspect list. The Bureau's agents were everywhere, especially today – down in the crowd posing as citizens celebrating the triumph of democracy, on the platform opposite, under cover as civil servants and, it went without saying, here on the President's platform. He was certain that every one of the liveried servants handing round champagne was an agent in disguise.

A great gasp from the thousands in the square announced that D'Cruz had been brought from prison and was being helped up the steps of the scaffold. His wrists and ankles were chained and it was only with the assistance of a soldier on either side that he got up the steps and turned to face the crowd. For his momentous public appearance he was wearing a pale blue suit with a black silk tie. Two priests in full robes had followed him up the steps and stood in readiness.

Conversation on the President's stand came to an awkward and uncomfortable halt as the diplomatic corps were at last forced to stop pretending that this was a cocktail-party. They stood silent, Europeans, Americans, Russians, South Americans and Japanese in dark suits, Indians, Pakistanis, Arabs and others in exotic garb of many colours, and the Chinese in the drab blue boiler suits of professional Maoists. President da Cunha had advanced to the front of the platform to glare thoughtfully across at the pinioned D'Cruz. A moment later Madame da Souza went to stand beside her brother, her face expressionless.

An official in the black robe of a court usher read out the sentence of death from a large document with a crimson ribbon hanging from a wax seal and asked D'Cruz in a loud voice if he knew of any reason why the sentence should not be carried out. D'Cruz's reply was lengthy but inaudible. Marcel thought that a great pity, since he would have been interested to know what reasons a man in so deplorable a predicament could advance. Whatever they were, they were not acceptable, for the official announced that the sentence would be carried out at once.

As with most things in Santa Sabina, *at once* did not mean at once. It was the turn of the priests to step forward, Prayer Books in hand, and start to recite the Service for the Burial of the Dead, alternating in their reading. D'Cruz did not appear to be listening to them. He was very pale, as he had every right to be, and shivers shook his body from time to time. He and the President were related and without doubt there had been urgent and secret negotiations between his family and da Cunha to get the death sentence commuted to exile. But it was obvious that the President had decided to make an example of his cousin, as a warning to others.

The priests were still intoning their Latin when the executioner took charge. He came from the back of the scaffold, a burly middle-aged man of dark complexion, wearing a neat black suit and an incongruous bow-tie. Under his instruction the soldiers flanking D'Cruz took the chains from his wrists and helped him courteously out of his jacket before leading him to a heavy wooden armchair waiting for him in the centre of the scaffold. There was a hideous and nerve-wrenching pause while the executioner's assistant strapped D'Cruz's wrists to the chair arms and removed his silk tie.

The thousands in the square were silent, the only sound the droning of priests promising D'Cruz Resurrection to Life Eternal, while the soldiers knelt to strap D'Cruz's ankles to the chair legs. Marcel watched in mounting horror, unable to believe that he was watching a man being executed in public. He saw the executioner station himself behind the chair and position D'Cruz's head so that it rested against a thick square pole that stood up from the chair back.

Marcel was praying silently for the macabre ceremony to be over. He tried to distract himself by staring at Madame da Souza's bottom, round and firm under the thin black silk of her Paris frock, but his gaze kept moving back to the scaffold. The executioner had put a broad leather collar round D'Cruz's neck and was buckling it behind the post. D'Cruz's mouth hung wide open, though he was not saying anything, or if he was, nobody heard it above the prayers. Even now that everything was ready, the final horror was delayed while the executioner carried out a last check of wrist and ankle fastenings.

Satisfied that all was as it should be, he resumed his place behind the chair. There was a sigh from the crowd when they saw the assistant hand him a length of polished wood as thick as a wrist and the length of a forearm. He slid it into the loops of the collar behind the post, held it by the ends and paused to take a deep breath. An instant later he was twisting with all his might, D'Cruz's eyes bulged and his face turned dark red and then almost black, as he was choked.

In an agony of guilt, Marcel cursed the day he had allowed himself to become involved in this affair. To condone the theft of a painting or two by Trudi Pfaff, however reprehensible, was one thing, but seeking out the weapons' cache had brought about this dreadful spectacle. The executioner twisted harder, until he broke D'Cruz's neck.

Under cover of the roar that went up from the crowd Marcel stumbled to the back of the platform and snatched a glass from a servant. He downed it in one long swallow, not caring that it was neat gin, and deaf to the stentorian announcement from the scaffold that the sentence of the court had been carried out. In another moment he was surrounded by others reaching for drinks with trembling hands and avoiding each others' eyes, though the Chinese Chargé d'Affaires seemed to be comparing notes with a white-robed Arab.

Madame da Souza moved away from the front of the platform as the undertaker's men unstrapped the body and lifted it into a black coffin they had brought with them. She stood beside Marcel and took a glass of champagne from a servant who appeared instantly at her side with his tray.

'A disagreeable occasion, Monsieur Lamont,' she said, 'and the first public execution since my brother became President.'

'I hope it may also be the last, Madame.'

'When my father was President there were never

fewer than five or six a year. I was a child when I was taken to my first. My brother had great hopes that father's severity had discouraged insurrection, but it seems to be otherwise.'

'My condolences, Madame,' said Marcel, captivated at last by the swell of her breasts under her frock.

No doubt there was a Monsieur da Souza somewhere, but he did not appear to be present today and, truth to tell, Marcel had never heard any mention of him. Madame da Souza became aware of the direction of Marcel's gaze and her manner became a little less formal.

'You must not think us barbarous because we enforce the law strictly,' she said, smiling briefly at him. 'A special Mass will be said in every church in Santa Sabina on Sunday. I shall attend here in the cathedral – will you escort me to it, Monsieur Lamont?'

'I shall be honoured,' he answered, bowing slightly. 'It is a Requiem for D'Cruz, I take it.'

'Oh no, his family must arrange that in private – after all, he was a traitor. By order of the President the people are to attend a Penitential Mass on Sunday.'

She moved on to speak to other guests and Marcel slipped away when he felt it safe to do so without giving offence. In addition to the acute discomfort of his conscience, he was perspiring heavily from the increasingly unpleasant heat of the day and wanted to get out of his dark suit. Down in the square, the crowd was dispersing with much cheerful and noisy chatter, small children borne on their fathers' shoulders and unattached women looking for likely young men.

It was impossible to hurry in such a press of people. Marcel sauntered along with them and was almost out of the square when he felt a tap on his shoulder from behind and a girl's voice said *Hi, Marcel!* It was Sherri Hazlitt, her waist-length and straw-blonde hair making her stand out among the dark-mopped Santa Sabinans round her. But in a sleeveless blue shirt and exceptionally short white shorts, she was dressed with as little regard for the grim event of the day as they were. She slipped an arm round Marcel's waist as they walked along.

'I saw you up on the platform with the big shots,' she said, smiling at him. 'I waved to you but you didn't see me. I guess you were too busy watching that poor slob.'

'This has been the most ghastly morning of my life,' said Marcel. 'I am shocked that you are here – your father was not among President da Cunha's guests, I noted.'

'He's been called to Washington to explain what's going on. I really owe you, Marcel – you dropped the old man right in it when you blew the whistle on the local revolution. Maybe they'll even sack him and I'll get to go home to the US.'

'I am happy for you,' Marcel said morosely.

'You don't *sound* happy. Maybe that's because you're hot and sweaty in that suit. Let's go swimming – you'll feel a lot better when you've cooled off.'

'Everyone seems to know of my part in these wretched events. I am not disposed to face the world on the Reserved Beach.'

'No, that's for old bags who get a thrill out of beachboys staring down their cleavage,' said Sherri. 'I know a place where we'll be all alone. We won't even need swim-suits.'

The thought of taking off his hot suit and plunging into the sea was irresistible. They walked to the American Embassy on St Agata's Square, where she casually commandeered a Jeep. At her direction the Marine corporal driver took the Vilanova road, stopping at a stall on the way while she bought cheese, bread and bottles of beer. She had the Marine set them down at the eleventh kilometre stone and told him to come back at five.

The road had been cut about halfway up the cliff, with a steep slope upwards to the left and an equally steep drop, covered in scrub, to the right. But as Marcel saw, there was the beginning of a track slanting downwards, almost parallel with the road, and it was along this that he followed Sherri. The path fell steeply – concealed from above by thorny bushes. It ran round the outside of a rocky spur and emerged at last into a little cove. There was a narrow strip of sand between large rocks, where the waves ran lazily in to expire on the tiny beach with hardly a murmur.

Sherri stripped naked and ran out whooping into the sea, waving her arms in the air while Marcel was ripping off his constricting tie and shedding his clothes. A moment later he ran after Sherri, waist-deep in the sea, then slid forward and swam strongly away from the shore. Naturally, the water was warm, so there was no bracing shock, but the feel of the sea on his body calmed his mind after the terrible events of the morning.

When he had washed away his burden of guilt, he swam back and started a game of splashing and ducking with Sherri. Evidently she passed a lot of her time on beaches, for her slender body and long limbs were a beautiful golden colour, as were her big round breasts, bobbing up and down in the most exciting manner as she leaped and plunged. Soon the game developed into a kind of swimming-wrestling and the rub of their bodies together quickly brought Marcel's *zimbriq* upright. Sherri shrieked like a virgin to feel it press against her belly as she twisted in his grasp and his hands slid wetly over her *gublas* and between her thighs to touch her hairless *kuft*.

But her shrieks were merely playful, not the cries of arousal, and so he edged her closer inshore as they struggled. She guessed his intention, turned in his arms to break away and ran for the beach. With a great leap Marcel overtook her and brought her down on her hands and knees on the wet sand, his belly against her bare bottom and his arms clasped around her waist to prevent her escaping from him.

'Oh my God!' she moaned. 'You're going to rape me!'

The swollen head of his *zimbriq* was rubbing between the cheeks of her bottom, as if desirous of plunging itself into the forbidden entrance. Marcel held her close, enjoying the sensation and content to let matters take their course. But when she realised the extent of the threat to the natural order of things, she uttered a scream of horror and struggled against his hold. *Not that, not that!* she cried loudly.

He held her tightly and was rewarded by feeling her bottom buck hard against him as her helpless terror precipitated her ecstatic surrender. Rubbing against her smooth flesh had taken him a long way towards his own crisis and Sherri was still shaking and gasping when he found the smooth lips between her legs and pushed into her. The sea ebbed and flowed round his knees as he stabbed strongly ten or twelve times and emptied his passion into her wet *kuft*. *Oh, yes, yes, yes,* she moaned, her bottom smacking against his belly as she reciprocated his convulsive thrusts.

When they had their breath back he helped her to her feet and they walked hand in hand up the beach and lay on a flat rock. Sherri was on her back with her arms folded under her head and her legs slightly apart – a posture that invited the most intimate caresses. But remembering how touchy she was about the bareness between her legs, Marcel took care to keep his face close to hers while he caressed her body.

'Know what I miss most here?' she asked. 'Somebody to talk to. I guess that's why I went along with Errol, even though he was pretty weird sometimes. I didn't mind playing with him in the cinema as long as he gave me a good smacking afterwards, but he never raped me properly, not like you do.'

'Why was that, do you think?'

'Don't know,' she said with a shrug. 'Maybe he thought I'm not worth the effort. With you it's for real – you'd never let me get away after you'd got hold of me and jerked my panties off. You're like Derry – when he'd got his pecker in me nothing would stop him, not even Aunt Bea walking in on us.'

'You mean that he continued with his wife watching?'

'She grabbed his hair and tried to pull him off, but he kept right on slamming into me till he squirted his stuff. I'd already climaxed once, when he rammed it in me, and when I saw the look on her face, I climaxed again and it was wild!'

'But it is strange that Hochheimer, whose profession is force and deception, could not achieve this for you?'

'He likes it the Santa Sabina way with the girls on top but he hated to go with the local girls. On top's no use to me, so he got me to do him by hand. Maybe he wasn't tough enough for his mission.'

'*C'est la vie*,' said Marcel, speaking most philosophically as he stroked her warm belly. 'It is often the case that those who rely on ruthlessness and naked force are weak. As for me, I prefer making love to making revolution.'

'Naked force . . .' Sherri sighed. 'It happened to me one time in a motel in Los Angeles and it was out of this world!'

Marcel asked her to explain what she meant.

'I met this guy in a bar and he asked me back to his room. He was tall and husky – maybe thirty-five – he said he was a salesman and had a wife and three kids, but so what – he looked as if he could do great things to me.'

'I can guess,' said Marcel. 'He beat you and raped you.'

'No, this guy was different. He made me strip off and put a black rubber suit on – something like a scuba-diving suit with a zipper down from the neck to between the legs, and it had a head section.'

'A hood, you mean, to cover your hair and ears?'

'No, it was more like a black balloon. It covered my head and face and there were just a couple of holes for air. He cinched a belt round my waist and fixed my arms to it and there I was – blind, dumb, deaf and helpless.'

'But how bizarre! There was nothing he could do to you – he couldn't feel your breasts or your *kuft*.'

'My what?' she asked blankly.

'*This*,' he said, slipping his fingers into the bare wet slit between her legs. 'You must have learned some of the Santa Sabinan language?'

'Oh, sure,' she said, 'they speak French, like you. That's my *con* you're feeling.'

'But their other language – the older one?' and seeing her look of total incomprehension, he said. 'No matter. My point was that your strange friend in the motel had denied himself all possibility of pleasure by wrapping you in rubber.'

'That's what you think! He found plenty to do – he started by throwing me on the bed while he took his clothes off.'

'How do you know he did that, if you could not see?'

'Because I saw him later, when he'd finished with me,' she answered. 'He jumped on me stark naked and wrestled me around on the bed – like he'd get a bear-hug on me and squeeze the breath right out of me and then fold me over till my head was right down between my legs and I could feel by back breaking. He kept rolling me over and over him and clamping his legs round my head. My God, he was strong – I guess he got a thrill from the feel of the rubber against his skin.'

'How long did this strange conduct continue?'

'It felt like hours and maybe it was half the night. When he was good and ready he turned me on my back and lay on top of me. I thought he was going to yank the zipper down and stick his pecker in me, but that wasn't his way at all!'

She paused at this most dramatic moment and in an agony of suspense Marcel urged her to continue.

'He just lay there panting on me and rubbing himself against my belly through the suit, for the longest time. He was so heavy I was being squashed to death under him and I couldn't get my arms loose to push him off. I was about dead when he started shouting and screaming and shot his stuff on the rubber.'

'But what an extraordinary way of making love,' said Marcel. 'I cannot begin to understand what bizarre thought in the mind of this man led him to transform you into a non-human object for his desires. You must have been very frightened.'

'I was scared because I didn't know what he'd do

next,' she agreed, 'but it was an exciting sort of scariness. I felt I was being used as if I were a store-window dummy and that was a great turn-on. So was the feel of the rubber right up between my legs. I climaxed while he was wrestling me around, and then a second time when he lay on top of me and rubbed himself against the suit. It was terrific the second time – I wanted him to do it again, but he made me take the suit off and kicked me out because he wanted to sleep.'

Marcel looked with a certain wary compassion at the golden-skinned and beautiful young girl lying beside him on the rock. Her long straight hair was dark and heavy from the sea-water and lay under her, making her look younger than twenty years. It seemed to him that for all her advantages of family and position, Sherri had suffered more sexual exploitation than most girls of her age. On the other hand, he reminded himself, she is not at all intelligent and perhaps for this reason does not regard what men do to her as exploitation or see herself as a victim.

Indeed, if she enjoys the unusual experience of being bound, gagged and half-stifled in black rubber for the gratification of a passing madman, or becomes aroused when she is mocked and abused sexually by her uncle, then in what sense can she be described as a victim? And yet, no doubt because Marcel's attitudes towards women were old-fashioned and unprogressive, it seemed to him indisputable that at twenty she ought to be in love with a handsome young man and finding the traditional ecstasy in his embraces. But as he had discovered in the dark of the cinema, traditional caresses failed to stir her.

'You must not leap to conclusions,' he said, stroking the delicate pink bud of her right breast with a fingertip, 'and I certainly do not. But I remember that at the Dance-Bar Rivoli you told me more than once that you loved me. Was this merely an expression of gratitude for the pleasure I gave you, or had it another meaning? What was in your mind when you said it?'

'I said it because I meant it.' she murmured, staring

down to where his stiff *zimbriq* was nudging at her waist. 'I go for you in a big way, Marcel.'

'I am honoured,' he said, his hand between her thighs to fondle her *kuft*, 'but you have also told me that you love Derry. What am I to believe, my dear – that you love us both equally, or that you find me an acceptable substitute for Derry, as you did the person who wrapped you like a parcel and brought himself to an emission on it?'

A puzzled look replaced the normally blank expression of her pretty face. While she grappled mentally with his question, Marcel rolled on to his belly and kissed the hairless and well-developed lips between her thighs.

'You're so sweet,' she murmured inanely as the tip of his tongue slipped into her delicate pink slit. 'Kent was a one-nighter. I never saw him again after that one time.'

Marcel was lying between her parted legs, his hands under her bottom to squeeze the tender cheeks while his tongue fluttered against her secret bud. His hard *zimbriq* was squeezed between the rock and his belly and he was happy to hear Sherri sighing in modest arousal.

'That's how Derry made me climax the first time he raped me!' she sighed. 'He held me down while he stuck his tongue up me! I hate you for doing that to me!'

In Sherri's mind the emotions of hatred and love – or at least of hatred and sexual arousal – seemed to be in unusually close proximity. Her hips rolled from side to side to escape the insistent throbbing of Marcel's tongue in her open *kuft*, but he held her legs under his armpits and continued until she writhed and cried out in her crisis of release.

'Who do you love, Sherri?' he demanded while shudders of pleasure still shook her slender body.

Marcel had a good opinion of himself, of course, as is normal for young men. He was vain of his looks and his appeal to women and this was a game he was playing with the American girl to please his vanity.

'I love Derry,' she moaned. 'Do it to me again!'

'But I am not your uncle Derry, Mademoiselle,' he taunted her, his thumb deep in her wet *kuft* while his finger probed between the cheeks of her bottom. Her pale blue eyes opened to stare up at him wildly.

'It's you I love, Marcel!' she gasped. 'Do it to me!'

'Are you sure of that?' he asked, his fingers gripping with cruel force inside her and she screamed out *yes*!

He took hold of her ankles and stretched her legs upwards and outwards and stared down at the bare, wet slit he meant to use for his pleasure. He raised her bottom and slid his bent knees under her until he could rub the head of his *zimbriq* against the delicate pink folds between her thighs.

'What are you doing to me?' she moaned. 'You'll split me apart with that enormous thing!'

His vanity inflamed by her words, he pushed relentlessly until the wet lips of her *kuft* parted and let him slide swiftly into her. The moment she felt herself enfiladed, she abandoned all restraint and struggled heroically to prevent him from completing his intention. She rolled about on her back, threw her arms in the air, moaned and screamed aloud – in short, she gave a most convincing demonstration of how an outraged young woman behaves when she is being violated.

But flat on her back with her legs in the air and her ankles held firm in Marcel's hand, she was as helpless as a sheep in the grip of a shearer. Marcel plunged and gasped in rapture making her big round breasts roll up and down her chest.

'Do you love me, Sherri?' he gasped, hardly able to get the words out as his crisis came rushing towards him.

'I hate you!' she moaned.

Her bare feet hooked round the back of his neck and her bottom rose off the rock to drive him in deeper.

'Tell me again!' he gasped.

'I love you, I love you!' she wailed, her body

squirming in ecstasy, and at once Marcel's desire exploded in her belly.

14

The Gates of Paradise are Opened Wide

When Marcel arrived at the Presidential Palace on Sunday morning and was ushered into the apartments of Madame da Souza, he found her alone in a large sitting-room, furnished in the style of Louis XV. She looked very chic in a tailored black suit and she was holding a long-stemmed glass. After he had kissed her hand and murmured politenesses, she patted the sofa cushions beside her and a manservant brought him a glass of excellent champagne. She listened to his idle chatter with flattering attention, leaned back and crossed her knees to reveal a glimpse of shapely thigh in fine black silk.

If she had been any other woman Marcel would have raised her hand to his lips in a kiss of adoration and allowed nature to take its course. But it had to be remembered that a President's sister was no ordinary woman. Even so, when she deliberately made her breasts prominent by stretching an arm along the sofa-back he saw that, President's sister or not, Mariantonetta da Souza was indicating that his advances would be well received.

For his part, he had no objections to abandoning attendance at Divine Service in favour of love-making in the Presidential Palace, but even as he leaned forward to embrace her, she raised her arm to consult her tiny diamond-encrusted wrist-watch and announced that the Penitential Mass had started and they must leave.

'Will the President be there?' Marcel asked, somewhat at a loss what to make of her attitude, and was told that he restricted his attendance to Easter, Independence Day and the Festival of St Sabina.

A limousine took them to the cathedral and just inside the magnificent bronze entrance door, Madame da Souza led Marcel to a small wooden door flush in the wall and waited for him to open it for her. It gave on to a spiral staircase, lit by window slits in the impressive thickness of the outside wall. Marcell closed the door behind him and followed her up to a small landing and another door like the one below.

This one she opened herself and, once they were through it, bolted it so that her devotions would not be disturbed. They were in a kind of loft measuring three metres each way, its floor, walls and ceiling all of polished teak. It was lit by candles in gilded wall-brackets flanking religious paintings, and two ornately-carved wooden chairs were the only furniture.

'What is this place, Madame?' Marcel asked.

She smiled and took his hand in her gloved hand to lead him to the front of the small room. There was a long brass handle which she pulled down, and the wooden slats of a venetian blind swivelled open to give a perfect view down the length of the cathedral below them.

'It is called the Viceroy's Loggia,' she explained. 'When Santa Sabina was a colony of Portugal, there was once a Viceroy who loved a lady who was not his wife. He had left a wife behind in Portugal, you understand. Not that this mattered to anyone, except that this Viceroy was religious. The stories say that before he made love he and his lady went down on their knees at the bedside to ask for God's blessing, sometimes five or six times a night. But their piety was not enough for the Bishop, who became angry when they attended Mass together, and so the Viceroy had this Loggia built, where he and his love could make their prayer without being seen.'

'What a charming love-story!' said Marcel.

In the distant chancel the elderly Cardinal-Archbishop sat on a raised throne under a gold-embroidered canopy. His eyes were closed, and no doubt he was immersed in pious meditation, not merely dozing. The high altar had been draped with black for the Penitential Mass and officiating priests were taking turns to recite prayers while altar boys in snow-white surplices over crimson robes swung golden thuribles and sent thick clouds of intoxicating incense drifting upwards.

Below the open slats was a broad ledge on which lay silk-bound hymnals and Prayer Books. Madame da Souza knelt on a thick crimson and gold cushion, crossed herself elaborately, put her elbows on the ledge and closed her dark eyes. Marcel thought it polite to kneel beside her and do the same. The organ was playing and the choir was singing something devotional that sounded morbidly doom-laden.

It was impossible not to admire the tailored suit that Mariantonetta da Souza had chosen to wear for this solemn religious occasion. Her three-cornered hat had the merest wisp of black veil and went perfectly with her elegant jacket and skirt. The cut was so chic that no one could have mistaken it for anything but the creation of a master Parisian couturier. As she bowed her head in her devotions, the collar of her white silk blouse peeping enticingly above the black at the nape of her neck and, below the jacket, her skirt stretched with exquisite smoothness over the curve of her bottom.

Libera me, Deus, ab hominibus malis . . . the choir sang and Marcel knew there could be no doubt who was meant by the evil man from whom they were praying to be delivered – the former Minister of Commerce and Fine Arts, the late Ysambard D'Cruz, buried with a broken neck in his family plot in the cemetery. It was strange to think that he was being hounded beyond the grave at the insistence of President da Cunha.

Mariantonetta was so still that Marcel assumed that

she had been overcome by an attack of piety but she disproved that by reaching for his hand and squeezing it. Her black gloves lay on the ledge in front of her, between the Prayer Books, and her long-fingered hand was warm and dry to the touch. He started to raise her hand to his lips to kiss it, but she had other ideas. She steered his hand under her black skirt and up between her legs. Marcel gave a small sigh of delight as he felt the bare skin of her thighs above her stocking-tops – so tender and so exciting to his fingers.

'We cannot be seen from down there,' she whispered.

She slid her knees apart on the thick cushion to let him feel up between her thighs until his questing fingers touched lace and then the silk of her knickers. He sighed again and she sighed with him this time and closed her eyes when his fingers found their way into the open leg of her knickers and touched her curls. At once he forgot that he was contemplating sacrilege and abandoned himself to the pleasures of the moment.

The President's family were the pinnacle of what might be described as the aristocracy of Santa Sabina – the landowners who monopolised the lucrative offices of Church and State. They referred to themselves as *The Hundred Families*, and maintained their exclusivity by marrying only among themselves. Of course, the precocity and promiscuity of the islanders being what it was, many babies were born with an unacknowledged claim. None of which was of importance, except that this was the first time Marcel had ever had the honour of feeling an aristocratic *kuft* and he was enjoying the experience with snobbish delight.

The warm lips between Mariantonetta's thighs were already loose and open to the touch. She unzipped his trousers and rubbed his stiffness with such enthusiasm that his entire body quivered with excitement. Under her skirt, his fingers were inside her warmth to flicker lightly over her swollen bud.

'Kiss me,' she murmured, turning her head towards him.

He pressed his mouth to hers and felt her wet tongue

insinuate itself between his parted lips. It was a long kiss, her hand sliding up and down his shaft until he could stand it no more. He moved behind her and knelt between her silk-stockinged legs. As if they had rehearsed this scene together, Mariantonetta put her arms flat on the ledge and rested her face on the back of her hands while Marcel pulled her skirt up her thighs and over her rump with trembling hands.

He eased her silk knickers down her thighs and fondled the round cheeks he had uncovered, loving the smoothness of her *café au lait* skin, and stroked her black-haired *kuft* with light, quick touches. Mariantonetta's head was turned sideways on her hands and he could see her face over her elegantly clad shoulder. Her eyes were wide open and shining as he presented his *zimbriq* to the awaiting slit and pushed in strongly.

Below in the cathedral the congregation were also on their knees, the choir was silent and the organ provided a doleful meditative music. Marcel's arms were round Mariantonetta's waist to hold her tight while he rode her to a slow and stately rhythm. A golden sensation in his belly advised him that his moment of crisis was here – he stabbed passionately into Mariantonetta's slippery *kuft* and spurted tumultuously.

Her beautifully coiffed head jerked up off her hands and her faint shriek was lost in a sudden thunder of organ music and the *fortissimo* anthem of the choir. Her climax was brief and, when it was over, she straightened her back, pulling herself off him, and turned on her silk-stockinged knees until she faced him.

'You did that very well,' she said, her fingers caressing his face gently.

'It was enchanting,' he replied, 'but very wrong of us to do it here – let's go back to the Palace and do it again.'

He was holding her hand against his cheek while he kissed the inside of her wrist, and an exquisite trace of expensive French perfume lingered there.

Mariantonetta held his wet and dwindling *zimbriq* on her open palm and stared at it as if committing its shape and size to memory. It was impossible for Marcel not to look at it himself, shrugging his shoulders in regret that it was diminishing, but before long he was so flattered by the avid interest of his elegant companion that it ceased to shrink, twitched a few times on her hand and began to grow longer and thicker.

'Good,' she murmured, 'very good, my dear.'

Her hands on his shoulders pushed at him and he understood what she wanted. He submitted gracefully, stretching himself on his back on the polished wooden floor, with one of the cushions under his head. Mariantonetta stood up to remove her black silk knickers, her back to whatever was going on in the church below, placed a foot on either side of him, pulled her skirt up round her belly and lowered herself to sit astride his loins. She unbuckled his belt and pulled his trousers to his knees.

Her wide open thighs offered him an unimpeded view of her *kuft*, and he sighed in appreciation when she held the head of his *zimbriq* to her wet slit and sank down to drive it right up into her belly. Bewitched by what he had witnessed, Marcel looked up and found she was staring at him with an expression he did not understand. She leaned forward with her hands flat on his chest while she started her up and down ride and he was very surprised – not to say gratified – at the steadiness of her movements. Perhaps it was only the ordinary women of the island who *zeqqed* their men in furious haste, he thought.

He reached for the buttons of her jacket, to open it and put his hands up her blouse to play with her breasts. But before he had undone even one button, he gasped and almost choked as his rider clamped her disregarded knickers over his mouth and nose.

'*Grg, grg!*' he gurgled, groping for her wrists.

He was trying to convey that he couldn't breathe and she was choking him, but half of her knickers had been drawn into his mouth by his attempt to breathe, and articulate speech was no longer possible. He put his hands against her *gublas* and pushed hard but she ignored him. And though he did not notice the change while he was dying of suffocation, her slow slide up and down his shaft changed to a fast and furious *zeqqing*.

He bucked and squirmed to unseat her, labouring to breathe through the silk that blocked his nose and mouth. His flailing hands found Mariantonetta's hair and he tried to drag her head upward. But he was already too close to unconsciousness to achieve more than pulling off her little three-cornered hat.

Everything slid away from him, and he knew that he was going under. His hands fell from her hair and his struggles became feeble. The glaring redness before his eyes faded into a grey that deepened rapidly to black and he was unconscious.

He came to himself slowly, wondering where he was and what was happening. He was on his back on a wooden floor and a woman beside him was dabbing his face with perfume from a small bottle. Then his memory reassembled itself and he looked into her eyes and asked her why she had tried to kill him.

'It was a little experiment,' she said, smiling. 'You are so beautiful that I couldn't resist. I hope you don't mind.'

He knew that it made not the least difference whether he minded or not what Mariantonetta da Souza did. She was far too important to concern herself with the opinions of casual lovers – or anyone else, for that matter, with the exception of her brother. And so he suppressed his anger and asked her what experiment she meant. She tucked his shirt up to his neck, soaked her tiny handkerchief in perfume, and wiped it over his belly and chest. The rapid cooling was very refreshing.

'They say that when a man is hanged his *zimbriq* stands up by itself and he squirts his seed,' she said, 'but I've never been close enough at public executions to find out for sure.'

'And so you decided to experiment by choking me to death?'

'You're not angry with me, are you? The idea came

into my head the moment I saw you lying here on your back.'

'Angry? Heavens, no! Why should you think that?' Marcel exclaimed, confounded by her total lack of anything like an apology. 'Was your experiment enlightening?'

'Oh yes,' she answered. 'You got thicker and harder all the time you were struggling. I could hardly believe it.'

'And then?' he asked, curiosity getting the better of him.

'You squirted like a fountain at the moment you passed out.'

'I remember nothing of the sort, merely the unpleasantness of being stifled, but I am pleased that I provided you with some small enjoyment,' he said, sitting up on the floor.

He pulled his trousers up his legs and tucked his shirt in. Mariantonetta held up the fragile black knickers she had used in her perilous experiment and shook her head.

'You've ruined them,' she said, 'look at the teeth-marks!'

She screwed them up into a tiny ball and put them in her handbag, found the hat he had torn from her head in his extremity and replaced it at a jaunty angle. She stood up to smooth down her skirt and then returned to her position of devotion, on her knees looking down into the cathedral.

'Come and kneel beside me,' she said, 'I want you to see something.'

Apart from a certain familiar lethargy resulting from the violent discharge of which he had no recollection, Marcel felt no ill effects from being half-choked. He rearranged his clothes decently and did as she requested. A priest in mauve robes was preaching from a high pulpit and the gist of his message was that all men were desperately evil.

'I've often wondered,' said Mariantonetta, giving Marcel a sideways glance, 'whether the Viceroy had this Loggia built so that he and his lady could spite the Bishop by making love right under his nose. What do you think?'

'Religion varies with temperament,' he answered. 'One would have to know more about the Viceroy to guess that.'

'The Viceroy's lady was not the daughter of Portuguese settlers but a very beautiful Santa Sabinan,' Mariantonetta explained. 'Her name was Santita and when news came from Portugal that the Viceroy's wife had died, he married Santita in this church. My brother and I are descended from them and that is why the Presidency has been in our family since our country became a Republic. I am certain that Santita and her Viceroy made love here many times – how else could she revenge herself on a meddling Bishop?'

'How else?' Marcel echoed softly.

'Down there to your right,' she said, her hands together in an attitude of prayer, 'in the chapel of St Anastasio – what do you see above his altar?'

Marcel craned his neck to see into the small sidechapel halfway along the cathedral. Two candles were burning in golden candlesticks on the marble altar and at least twenty others on a wrought-iron stand to one side of it.

'There is a painting – though I must confess that I have never heard of St Anastasio before. He must be popular to have so many candles lit to him.'

'I lit them myself early this morning for Ysambard, when I prayed for his soul,' she said.

'You did?' he asked in surprise. 'At least they make it possible to see the painting . . . oh, I think I understand!'

'Good,' said Mariantonetta. 'Our Anastasio is a handsome young man with curly dark hair, a little like you. And as you can see, though the picture is very neglected and dirty, he is shown at his moment of martyrdom. He has been stripped naked, except for a little loincloth, and he kneels with his hands raised in prayer, while the executioner stands behind him and strangles him with a noose. Do you see that?'

'Now I understand what prompted your experiment with me,' said Marcel, astounded that he had very nearly become a martyr for no better cause than a woman's curiosity.

'Good,' she said, turning her face towards him briefly to grin, 'but in a painting destined to hang in a church as an object of veneration, the artist cannot show whether Anastasio had a stiff *zimbriq* when they strangled him, or whether he wet his little cloth in his death-throes. I have often wondered.'

'And now you know,' said Marcel.

'Yes,' she agreed, 'and something else I know – that dusty old picture was painted by the Italian artist Veronese four hundred years ago. After poor Ysambard suffered the same fate as Anastasio there were only two people in the whole world who knew that. Now I have told you, there are three again.'

'The other person being . . . ?'

'The yellow-haired woman you used to *zeqq* in the Grand Hotel Orient. She was the expert who recognised the paintings and arranged to get them out and sell them abroad. As you know.'

'Then D'Cruz did confess,' said Marcel in a resigned tone. 'Well, I thought he would and advised Frau Pfaff to go.'

'He was too infatuated with the German woman to betray her. He said nothing to the interrogators about her.'

'What was the reason for his arrest?' Marcel asked.

'When the first painting arrived in Europe it was shown to an expert for authentication as the work of El Greco and by chance he was one of the few people in the world who knew it belonged to the cathedral of Santa Sabina. He enquired by cable if the picture was still here and the Cardinal-Archbishop was puzzled enough to mention the enquiry to my brother.'

'Why did he do that? Surely the painting is the property of the Church, not of the State.'

'Church or State, it's family business,' she said. 'The Cardinal-Archbishop is our great-uncle. My brother put Ysambard under house-arrest while enquiries were made. I was terrified that Ysambard would implicate me as well as his German woman.'

'I do not understand – what had you to fear?'

'You are a foreigner and do not know our ways,' she replied smiling and frowning at the same time. 'Ysambard couldn't carry out the German woman's schemes without a powerful ally.'

'But he was Minister of Commerce and Fine Arts!'

'In our Republic all power is in the hands of the President. Friends are appointed Ministers to give them an income and keep their families well-disposed. To succeed in a plan as ambitious as stealing valuable pictures from churches, Ysambard naturally came to me for assistance, with an offer to share the money.'

'Naturally,' Marcel echoed, ironically.

'We grew up together,' she said, 'we played snakes and turtles with each other when we were small and *zeqqed* each other as soon as we were big enough. We were friends, until he plotted to get rid of my brother and make himself President. I do not think he would have harmed me, but who can be sure?'

Marcel had once held the view that Santa Sabinan politics were as trivial and boring as the squabbles of any small French village. He was now of the opinion that the island's politics were as intricate and cut-throat as those of the Byzantine Empire in its decadence.

'In effect, the plot to acquire the pictures is now your plot,' he said suavely, and began to consider his own position.

'Mine and yours,' she said. 'Your yellow-haired woman left you in charge of getting the rest of the pictures out of the country. When are you arranging to do that?'

'I have no intention of doing it. I promised Frau Pfaff that I would, only so that she would get on the ship and go away.'

'You are still angry because she let the Japanese *zeqq*

her, I see. You foreigners become absurdly upset over these little amusements. She needed him because she did not entirely trust you to send the pictures to Europe after she'd gone. And I do not trust *him*, and so he has been neutralised.'

'What do you mean?' Marcel asked in alarm, fearing that Mr Hakimoto might have been relieved of his pendants.

'But I know I can trust *you*,' said Mariantonetta. 'If you have any thought of spoiling my plan to become extremely rich by selling a few old paintings nobody will miss, dismiss it at once. It would be such a pity if a beautiful young man like you met with the same misfortune as the Japanese. I insist that you carry on with the German woman's excellent arrangements.'

'How has Hakimoto been neutralised?' he asked fearfully.

'Information reached the Japanese Ambassador that Monsieur Hakimoto consorts with foreigners in suspicious circumstances. He was photographed naked and with a stiff *zimbriq*'

'Making love to Trudi Pfaff – and taken through the peephole in the hotel wall,' said Marcel sourly.

'Oh no – the other naked person in the photograph was a young man from the Soviet Embassy, Monsieur Nikita Gorki.'

'Impossible!' Marcel exclaimed, remembering all too clearly the Japanese making love to Trudi. 'Your photograph is a fake.'

'Fake or not, it was enough to plant concern in the mind of his Ambassador and Monsieur Hakimoto is returning to Tokyo very soon. Until he does, he will be watched night and day by his own people, as well as mine, and he will not be able to do anything about the paintings. That leaves you a clear field.'

'Me?' he exclaimed in horror. 'Never!'

'Darling Marcel, consider how unfortunate it would be if a photograph reached your Ambassador showing you and Monsieur Hakimoto naked together. He will not be here to substantiate your denials. Or imagine a photograph is found of you and that handsome young Communist Monsieur Gorki naked together. Would anyone believe that you were not a security risk?'

'But it's madness to think of taking the other paintings now that the plan is known!' Marcel said in disbelief.

'On the contrary, it is perfectly safe. Only one picture is known about – the El Greco that reached Europe, and that is blamed on my poor Ysambard, who can no longer be questioned. No one will suspect anything now.'

Down below in the cathedral, the choir raised their voices in a most mournful anthem. Three priests, resplendent in white lace over purple, prostrated themselves in penitence before the black-draped altar. Marcel was beginning to feel trapped.

'I don't understand why Trudi didn't tell me about the picture of St Anastasio,' he complained.

'She meant to cheat you over that one,' said Mariantonetta. 'She must have arranged for somebody else to move it, perhaps Monsieur Hakimoto. But you and I will have our share of it.'

'It seems we are partners in this venture,' said Marcel, seeing no way out. 'Then let us seal the agreement.'

He pulled her to her feet, led her to the carved wooden chairs standing side by side in the middle of the Viceroy's Loggia and urged her to sit down. She sat straight-backed on the mauve cushion, her shoulders back and her chin up, arms resting along the padded arms of her chair.

'Since you were a little girl,' said Marcel, sinking to his knees before her, 'multitudes of men have told you that you are beautiful and very desirable, Mariantonetta, I am sure.'

He undid the four buttons of her jacket quickly and then lingered over the mother-of-pearl buttons of her white blouse, tantalising her and himself, until at last it was open and her full breasts, innocent of any brassière, were revealed. He felt them in dreamy pleasure for a long time, then bent forward to kiss them avidly.

'I like your way of sealing agreements,' she murmured, holding her blouse wide open for him. 'In fact, there's a lot I like about you. I thought you were finished for today after you played St Anastasio for me, but I underestimated you.'

The warm fragrance of her skin and the expensive perfume she applied between her breasts and under her chin made Marcel almost giddy as he touched his tongue to her dark buds.

'I shall surprise you yet,' he told her.

He kissed her mouth and felt her tongue between his lips while his hands slid up her thighs under her skirt. She tried to part her legs for him, but the skirt was too narrow, and she unfastened it at the waist and raised her bottom to slip it down to her knees. Marcel pulled it the rest of the way down her legs and threw it on to the other chair, where her handbag lay with her crumpled knickers in it. She spread her legs wide to display her tight dark curls and, while he was admiring them, reached forward between her knees to open his trousers and free his stiff shaft.

He put his hands flat on the soft flesh of the insides of her thighs, up above her stockings, and she drew in a long breath of anticipation and moved her bottom forward to the edge of the chair. Within her almost black curls, the fleshy lips of her *kuft* were wet and open and, intoxicated with pleasure, he sank to his haunches and pressed his mouth to them in a long kiss. When he heard her breathing become fast and irregular he pressed the tip of his tongue into her to touch her secret bud.

Mariantonetta was in a delirium of sensation, her hands clutching the arms of her chair, her head thrown back, while she enjoyed a long succession of urgent little spasms rippling through her belly and shaking her bared breasts. Certain that she was past caring what was done to her, Marcel stood up, put an arm under her knees and one under her shoulders to lift her, sat himself on the chair and lowered her to his lap facing away from him, her legs dangling either side of his joined thighs.

She was murmuring *oh, oh, what are you doing* . . . while he peeled off her jacket and blouse and threw her three-cornered hat to the floor. Her body was still shaking to little spasms as he slid his hands under her bare bottom, lifted her to get his shaft to the wet lips between her legs, and let her own weight drive it up her as she sank back to his lap. He reached round under her arms to grasp a breast in each hand.

'Now, Mariantonetta, dear lady,' he said, gloating a little, 'you do not see me down on my knees to worship you. Nor am I on my back to be your victim. I have stripped you naked and spiked you on my *zimbriq*. I have your *gublas* tight in my hands and you can do nothing but dangle across my lap while I make use of your *kuft* for my amusement.'

Her arms and legs jerked loosely, as if she were receiving an electric shock from the shaft thrust into her belly. As for Marcel, though he greatly desired to prolong his triumph over Mariantonetta, he too was galvanised into an involuntary response by these extravagant raptures of hers. An intense sensation stabbed through his belly, somewhere down near the root of his palpitating *zimbriq*, a sensation so exquisite that he cried out as if he were in torment. Though he had been in Mariantonetta only a very short time, he cried out incoherently and erupted in a blaze of delight.

After that emptying out of himself he lay back half-fainting in the antique chair, unable to move and only just able to breathe. Mariantonetta had collapsed against him, her head back on his shoulder and her face turned up to the ceiling. His hands released their grip on her breasts and lay listlessly on her parted thighs. The *zimbriq* which had performed so prodigiously now dwindled, all its strength used up, until it slipped out of the wet *kuft* it had delighted. The languor that had overcome Marcel transformed itself into gentle sleep.

He was awakened by the unseen choir pleading with God to be merciful and he wondered what penance would be required if he confessed to making love in church. Whatever it was, he would have no regret, he decided, for the last hour had been one of the most exciting he had ever experienced. He stroked Mariantonetta's breasts delicately until she stirred on his lap and sat upright to listen to the music for a moment.

'The Mass is over,' she said. 'We're just in time for the benediction.'

She slid off his lap and dragged him across the Viceroy's Loggia, to kneel on the crimson cushions.

'Someone may see you!' Marcel exclaimed as her bare breasts swung over the ledge where the Prayer-Books lay.

'I've told you – they can't see us from down there. Santita had it designed for that very reason,' she answered.

'But you are naked,' Marcel protested, hurriedly tucking his limp *zimbriq* out of sight in his trousers.

'Does God love His children any less when they take their clothes off?' she asked.

The choir was silent and from the marble steps of the high altar a priest in gold-embroidered vestments raised his hand to pronounce a blessing on the congregation. Mariantonetta bowed her head devoutly, her hands together and her lips moving silently. Marcel found it impossible to pay attention to the priest while Mariantonetta was crossing herself with a fervour that made her bare breasts wobble in the most charming way.

There began a slow procession of priests, assistants, servitors, altar boys, incense-bearers and other participants in the penitential rites. Two men in white surplices lifted the venerable Cardinal-Archbishop onto a gilded palanquin and two others joined them in raising its carrying poles on to their shoulders. Meanwhile, the procession was making its way down the central aisle, led by a man in scarlet and lace carrying a gold crucifix high before him. Behind him came two young men swinging golden thuribles to waft blue-grey incense smoke to left and right over the kneeling congregation.

Next came the Cardinal-Archbishop, a small and thin old man nearing ninety, and behind him, two by two, assorted clerics in magnificent robes of every shade of scarlet and purple. As the palanquin was about to pass under the Loggia the Cardinal-Archbishop stared upwards and his gold-rimmed spectacles glinted as he raised his hand and sketched a blessing, a smile on his wizened old face.

'He knows we're here!' Marcel exclaimed in consternation.

'He knows I'm here because the blind is open,' said Mariantonetta, 'but he doesn't know I'm naked. And he doesn't know I've had three blessings from you to his one.'

15

Gratitude is Often a Hope for Further Favours

With Trudi out of the way, Marcel's intention had been to ignore the arrival of the ship and go nowhere near it, leaving the Captain high and dry with his forged Old Masters and no one to pass them to. But the intervention of Mariantonetta da Souza had changed all that. To protect her profit she would have the ship watched to make sure that Marcel did what was required of him and open defiance of her was impossible. A woman with the resources to command the forgery of a photograph of Hakimoto in bed with a male Communist was capable of anything.

After much agonised thought, Marcel constructed a plan which he hoped would extricate him from his predicament, a plan involving Trudi's maid. He arranged it so that the bus to Selvas dropped him at the fifth kilometre stone in mid-afternoon – the time of greatest lethargy, when even the most inquisitive eyes were closed in the afternoon siesta. He strolled up the drive from the road to the Pfaff house, rehearsing in his mind the strategy he had formulated to save himself from becoming Mariantonetta's unwilling accomplice.

Gunther Pfaff's conspicuous German car was not parked in front of the villa, but its absence was unnecessary to assure Marcel that Pfaff was at work –

he had persuaded a colleague to telephone the German Embassy before lunch to make sure. But to be absolutely certain that the maid was alone, he went round the side of the single-storey building, looking into each window in turn. The sitting-room was empty, as was the dining room and the kitchen and there was nobody on the long veranda.

He started back along the other side of the house and found a small room he guessed to be the maid's from the large wooden cross on the wall over the bed – the bed on which her fiancé consoled her on the nights he rode over from the village on a borrowed bicycle. The room was empty and untidy, a sign perhaps that household arrangements had deteriorated since Trudi's departure. When at last he located the maid she was in the main bedroom, a pretty room of pink and grey with, as she had told him, two beds.

He peeped cautiously over the window-sill and saw Esperanza standing in front of the wardrobe, her back towards him. She was stark naked and the cheeks of her brown-skinned bottom rolled humorously as she reached up to take out frocks and hold them against herself before the full-length mirror. Her domed belly ensured that none of the clothes that Trudi had abandoned in her flight would fit the maid in her present condition. It was barely three weeks since Marcel made love to her on the grass between the fig-trees, but he could see that her belly had grown fuller and her breasts bigger.

After she had looked through all the frocks, Esperanza went across to the dressing-table, giving Marcel a glimpse of her dark-curled fleece and a keen reminder of the pleasure she had given him under the fig-tree. She took a pair of crocus-yellow silk pyjamas from a drawer and tried them on. The buttons at the trouser-waist would not fasten over her belly and she wore the jacket alone to admire herself in profile and full-face in the mirror.

Marcel's thoughts became diverted from the real object of his visit into more frivolous channels by the provocation of the maid's bottom and *kuft* exposed below her yellow pyjama-jacket. He felt a strong urge to slide his hand up between her bare thighs and his *zimbriq* stiffened pleasantly. He watched a little longer as Esperanza took several pairs of knickers in various colours and styles from the dressing-table and held them against herself. Evidently Trudi had travelled light, confident of replacing everything with new and better when she reached Europe.

Esperanza chose a pair of French knickers in a delicate shade of cinnamon silk and pulled them on, making the elastic stretch over her swollen belly. Not content with the dressing-table mirror, she went across the bedroom to the full-length glass to see the result and smiled in pleasure at what she saw. Underwear was unknown to the ordinary girls of Santa Sabina, as Marcel had good reason to know, but it seemed that the little maid had ambitions in that direction. After her confinement, of course. It was very apparent that she found the touch of silk on her skin to be enjoyable, for she ran her hands slowly and luxuriously over her belly and bottom, her dark eyes half-closed and a little smile on her broad face.

Perhaps she found the silk a little too enjoyable for her tranquillity for, to Marcel's delight, she put her hand into the open leg of the knickers to touch herself between the thighs. And soon she was rubbing her *kuft*, with every sign of enjoyment, her mouth open and her legs trembling slightly. But in this, as in *zeqqing*, moderation was not a part of the Santa Sabinan character. She had not stroked herself more than nine, ten times between the legs before her feet slid wide apart on the parquet floor and her hand was jerking frenetically inside the cinnamon silk knickers.

Marcel's *zimbriq* was bulging uncomfortably stiff through his trousers and, without thinking what he was doing, he caressed it gently through the thin material. He felt perspiration on his belly under his clothes and saw little beads tricking down Esperanza's full breasts as she strove to reach her goal, her whole being concentrated on this overwhelming need to *zboca*. By his estimation it took no more than thirty seconds of feverish stimulation before her head went back and her climactic moan reached him through the window.

As always with the island girls, her ecstasy was of brief duration. Not that it ended the matter, of course, – she stood on shaking legs, grinning at her reflection in the mirror for a little while before wriggling out of the knickers and flinging herself on the bed closest to her. She was on her back, her belly curving up like the dome of a cathedral, her legs spread wide and her hand between them to gratify herself again. From Marcel's point of view this was disappointing, for she was sideways onto him and he could see nothing of the fast stimulation of her dark-curled *kuft*.

Before she could exhaust herself in solitary pleasures, he made his way round quickly and quietly to the front door and rang the bell. While he waited his imagination projected in feverish pictures what was happening in the bedroom. It was highly improbable that Esperanza would consent to be robbed of her ecstasy by an inconvenient visitor – she would speed up her rubbing and bring on her crisis even more quickly before she jumped up to pull on her clothes and answer the door.

By his wrist-watch it took her three minutes to accomplish all that. She opened the door wearing her uniform of plain white blouse and black skirt, and she looked flustered. Indeed, having been harried through her moments of sexual delight, it could hardly be otherwise, but in addition to that, she was so surprised to see who the caller was that her mouth fell open.

'But . . . this is not possible . . . you ran away with Madame!' she stammered. 'Have you brought her back, Monsieur?'

'I did not go away with Madame,' he said, trying to sound as reassuring as possible. 'She went alone and she will not return. I want to talk to you, Esperanza – may I come in?'

She let him into the house, still confused and uncertain. Their previous meeting had been in her own time,

240

her day off, on neutral territory, and she had known perfectly well how to behave towards him, to the extent of inviting him to *zeqq* her. But here she was in Gunther Pfaff's house and responsible for it, in his time, as his employee. When Marcel made himself comfortable on the sitting-room sofa, she remained standing, her hands folded over her swollen belly.

'Sit down, Esperanza, we are friends, you and I,' he said.

In spite of his most charming smile of invitation she stayed where she was, looking most uncomfortable, until he reached for her hand and pulled her down beside him.

'Then who did Madame run away with, if not you?' she asked.

'No one – she went alone.'

Esperanza looked at him in total disbelief, convinced that a woman as beautiful as Trudi Pfaff did nothing alone or at her own expense. But before they became involved in a lengthy and futile discussion of the matter, Marcel put an arm round the maid's shoulders and began to unbutton her blouse to bare her breasts. To his surprise, she took hold of his fingers to stop him and the expression on her face was one of puzzlement. Her unaccustomed hesitancy in accepting a man's advances was not due to modesty or chastity, thought Marcel, but to an awkward sense of duty to her employer, who was now Gunther Pfaff.

He had been long enough on the island of Santa Sabina to know how to proceed in such rare circumstances. He smiled and abandoned his attempt to undo her blouse, dropped his hands to his lap and opened his own trousers instead. His *zimbriq* still stood upright from observing Esperanza naked through the window and he let it thrust boldly upwards. She sighed in resignation as she watched him take the fleshy pink shaft between his fingers and stroke slowly up and down.

'I came all the way here to see you, Esperanza,' he said, 'but you are not pleased to see me. You refuse to even let me see your *gublas*. I was mistaken – we are not friends, after all. I shall go back to the city and never come here again.'

At the sight of a stiff *zimbriq* she surrendered at once, as he knew she would, and unbuttoned her blouse to show him her heavy breasts.

'Of course we are friends and you may feel them all you like, Monsieur Marcel,' she said, massaging his *zimbriq* with a clasped hand. 'Have you come to *zeqq* me?'

'But of course!' he breathed as he squeezed her breasts and ran his thumbs over their prominent brown buds.

He understood what Santa Sabinan girls liked to hear from men and obliged her willingly.

'I woke up this morning thinking about you and how nice it was when we made love under the fig-trees,' he said. 'I left my work and caught the bus to come here and *zeqq* you.'

'Was your *zimbriq* as hard when you woke up as it is now?' she asked, her hand smoothing up and down it.

'Every time I think of you it stands up like that,' he said. 'Let's go into the bedroom and lie down properly.'

She giggled as she used his *zimbriq* as a handle to lead him out of the sitting-room and towards her own room, but Marcel put his arms round her waist from behind and steered her into the main bedroom. The wardrobe doors hung open and on one of the twin beds lay the silk knickers which had excited Esperanza's fancies and the crocus-yellow silk pyjamas she had tried on.

'You want to make love in here?' she asked, rubbing herself against him like a cat while he felt her breasts. 'You want to *zeqq* me on Madame's bed – is that it?'

Standing close behind her, Marcel stripped her blouse off, unbuttoned the waistband of her black skirt and pushed it over the swell of her belly until it slid down her legs to the floor and she was naked. His stiff shaft lay between the plump cheeks of her bottom while he stroked her belly.

'Have you decided yet whose this is, Esperanza?'

She laughed and said she had thought about it a lot and done her calculations about the dates and could now be certain that it belonged to Monsieur Pfaff.

'And what does he say?' Marcel enquired, his hands below the overhang of her belly to part the loose lips of her *kuft* and feel the slippery warmth inside.

'He is very pleased about it,' she answered, breathing a little quickly from the throbs of pleasure Marcel's fingers were inducing. 'Perhaps it is because he gave Madame no babies. He has promised to pay me money every month until his child is grown up. Can you imagine such a thing!'

'And your fiancé has no objection to this arrangement?'

'Not him! He thinks that after this baby is born and we have our shop I should come back here and let Monsieur Gunther *zeqq* me till I get another baby from him. Then he will pay me twice as much money every month. Porfiro says we can be rich without working.'

She leaned back against Marcel as her pleasure grew, her head on his shoulder and he could smell the musky scent of her thick mop of almost black hair. His fingers moved with quick precision inside her wet *kuft*.

'And what do you say, Esperanza?' he asked.

'I say that I'm going to *zboca*!' she exclaimed urgently.

Her warm bare bottom was grinding against his *zimbriq* and she held his wrist to force his fingers deeper into her while she gasped out her brief ecstasy.

A moment later she turned in his encircling arms and seized his trembling shaft in one hand and his *castazz* in the other.

'You too,' she sighed, 'you are going to *zboca* right away – I can feel your *zimbriq* throbbing in my hand!'

She pushed him backwards onto the bed, and fully dressed as he was, straddled him clumsily. What she had said was true – the rubbing of her smooth-skinned bottom against the sensitive head of his shaft had aroused him almost to the moment of crisis. He cried out as he felt himself swallowed by her clasping wet flesh and, before she had slid up and down on him more than twelve or fifteen times, his desire fountained upwards into her swollen belly. And she, the spasms of her first release hardly over, exclaimed *harder, harder!* and went into climactic convulsions again.

They lay in each other's arms after that and, if Esperanza seemed to need an uncharacteristic little rest, it was because she had enjoyed four climaxes in not much more than a quarter of an hour, Marcel reminded himself. In the languor of her content she would be well disposed towards him for providing a hard shaft for her gratification at a time when she needed it. For himself, the release she had given him was pleasant enough in its way, but so short and sharp that it might almost have been a giant sneeze. Nevertheless, it suited his purpose to lie with an arm around her shoulders and stroke her big bare belly while he approached the purpose of his visit.

'I have a little present for you, Esperanza,' he said, 'but when I saw you I wanted to *zeqq* you so much that I forgot to give it to you.'

'Monsieur is too kind,' she said, doubtless recalling that at their last encounter he had given her 500 tikkoos.

'It was my intention to give you the same as I did before,' he said, spinning out the suspense, 'but you are so sympathetic that I would like to make you a present of 1000 tikkoos.'

'That is very kind indeed,' she said thoughtfully. 'Perhaps there is some small service I can perform for you in return, as a mark of my gratitude.'

As an intelligent girl, she understood that the princely sum of 1000 tikkoos was not dispensed for friendship alone. The 500 she had before had been payment for information about Trudi Pfaff's visitors and she knew that for 1000 something more than domestic tittle-tattle would be required.

Marcel explained slowly and carefully the little service she could perform to earn his undying gratitude, irrespective of any cash that changed hands. When she went home to the village at the weekend he wanted her to go to confession in the usual way and, apart from whatever other sins were on her conscience, to tell the priest that since the execution of Monsieur D'Cruz she had become worried that she might have been involved indirectly in a sin against Holy Church itself.

'But what do you mean?' she asked, twisting her neck to stare at him in great surprise. 'What is it I have done?'

Marcel told her that when her confessor asked for an explanation, she was to tell him that D'Cruz had been a friend of Madame Pfaff and, on one of his visits, she had by chance overheard them talking about paintings. It meant nothing to her, of course, and she forgot about it. But after Madame ran away from her husband, she had been cleaning out cupboards and drawers on the instructions of Monsieur Pfaff, and had found something which made her remember the conversation about paintings and caused her concern.

Esperanza's heavy *gublas* rolled sideways as she raised herself on an elbow to look down at Marcel's face.

'Everything you have said so far is true,' she said, 'except the part about finding anything I did not expect. I have found only the clothes Madame left behind and I shall ask Monsieur Gunther to give them to me. What can it be I am supposed to have discovered that is a sin against Holy Church?'

'Hidden in Madame's bureau you found some papers which you intended to throw away as rubbish, but you glanced casually at them and saw that they contained information about paintings. I have these secret documents of Madame's in my pocket to give to you before I leave.'

'But what are these paintings in which Madame took so great an interest?'

'The shameful truth is that Madame Pfaff and Monsieur D'Cruz were planning to steal valuable paintings from churches and sell them in Europe. The papers I have brought for you list the paintings and the churches and give the name of a ship which is shortly to arrive here to take them away. If you hand the papers over to your priest, he will absolve you from any guilt of complicity and take whatever action is required. That's all there is to it and we shall be friends forever.'

'But now that Monsieur D'Cruz is dead and Madame has gone away, surely the paintings are safe and there can be no reason to do as you suggest,' Esperanza objected.

'I wish it were so! But others know about the plan and will try to take the pictures from the churches,' he answered truthfully. 'Your priest will report the matter to his superiors and precautions will be taken.'

'If you know all this, why not tell the police?' she asked.

'I am a foreigner,' Marcel said at once, 'and it is better that I play no part in the affairs of Santa Sabina. As for the police – this is the business of the Church and it is for the ecclesiastic authorities to decide whether to involve the police. Will you do this little act of friendship for me?'

She thought it over in silence for some time.

'What if I get into trouble?' she asked eventually.

'There is no possibility of that or I wouldn't ask you to do this for me. You overheard a few words and found some papers you do not understand and since the matter seems to concern the Church, you think it best to pass the papers on to your Confessor. No one will blame you for obeying your conscience.'

'Will Monsieur Gunther get into trouble?' she asked. 'I would be a fool to risk losing all the money he has promised to pay me for the baby.'

'He knew nothing whatsoever of the plan to take the pictures and he will not get into trouble,' Marcel declared confidently, though he was by no means sure that Pfaff would entirely escape censure for his runaway wife's misdeeds.

'It is important to you, this affair of the paintings,' said Esperanza, her dark brown eyes intent on his face. 'You want your revenge on Madame and the man she ran off with. Was he a good friend of yours who betrayed you? She must have gone to his home to *zeqq*, because no one but you came here.'

Marcel started to insist that Trudi had left the island on her own and that there was no question of revenge, but seeing Esperanza shrug her bare brown shoulders in disbelief he thought it easier to humour her by confirming her tale of love and revenge.

'A man I thought was my friend,' he said, 'but he deceived me and persuaded Madame to run away with him. But he shall not have the paintings!'

'Just as I thought!' said Esperanza. 'He has stolen your woman but you will not let him have the paintings as well. Now I understand. Of course, if my Confessor or a policeman asked me difficult questions, I might have to tell them that you and Madame also talked about paintings after you *zeqqed* her.'

'I will not deny that it is of some importance to me to get this matter finally settled,' Marcel agreed, 'and naturally I rely on your discretion as a good friend.'

It was obvious to him that the conversation was taking a new turn and Esperanza was about to reveal the side of her nature that had procured an income from Gunther Pfaff for the next fifteen years.

She fondled his soft *zimbriq* a little while she told him that she liked him so much that she would lie to the priest for him when she went to confession. She hoped he realised that to lie in confession was a fearful sin and she would be in serious trouble if it were ever found out. God would forgive her, of course, but not the priest. But she would accept this terrible risk because she found Marcel so sympathetic in every way. As for her discretion, that could be relied on completely by a rich friend who liked her enough to give her 2000 tikkoos.

Marcel pretended to hesitate and then agreed, pleased to have secured her services for not much more than 200 francs. To impress her he made her swear never to betray his confidence before he gave her the false papers he had prepared and counted out the money into her hand in large and colourful 100-tikkoo notes. She put it on the bedside table and stretched out again with a broad smile on her face.

'I've had so much good luck since I started to work here,' she said. 'First Madame paid me nearly twice what maids usually get from foreigners – in return for my discretion about her visitors, of course. Then Monsieur Gunther decides that he must give me money every month for years because he *zeqqed* me a few times. And you, my dear friend, give me presents of money for the small services I can do for you.'

'There seems no point in marrying your fiancé,' said Marcel, but his irony was lost on the girl.

'He will be no more use for *zeqqing* soon,' she answered in all seriousness.

'How old is he, your Porfiro?' Marcel asked curiously.

'Almost twenty. Last Sunday when I was at home with him he could only do it twice all day. And my sister Josefina told me that he had been with her only three times all week.'

'What about your married cousin who also obliges him during the week – I can't remember her name,' said Marcel with a grin. 'Did she have more encouraging news to report?'

'Eufemia – no, she said that Porfiro hadn't been near her at all since I saw her last.'

'Poor Esperanza! When you and Porfiro are married you must content yourself with being *zeqqed* only once a day,' Marcel said, suppressing his urge to laugh.

'Why must I do that?' she demanded. 'You will still come to see me sometimes, I hope, and I know that Monsieur Gunther will want me. Shall I tell you what I'm thinking of doing after the baby is born? Nobody knows about this except my mother, but I know I can trust you because you are so generous to me.'

'I am honoured to be taken into your confidence.'

'With the money you have given me I can buy the bar where we met in the village, instead of the shop Porfiro wants. Xavier is my uncle and I know he wants to go and live in the city. Porfiro can run the bar while

I stay here and get paid to look after the house for Monsieur Gunther.'

'Who will look after your baby?'

'My mother. She already looks after my first – one more will make no difference. It would be a great pity to leave Monsieur Gunther now that Madame has deserted him for another and he needs me so much.'

'A great pity,' Marcel agreed, straight-faced, 'I am sure he relies on you to comfort him in his loneliness. And if he puts another baby in your belly, what of it – he is rich and can afford to maintain you.'

Esperanza grinned at him and rolled his *zimbriq* between her fingers to make it stiff again.

'When we met before you *zeqqed* me like a goat,' she said, 'and it was very nice.'

'Memories can be deceptive,' he said, 'I think we should try it again now and make sure.'

'I don't think my memory is wrong,' she said, heaving herself clumsily up off her back. Marcel took her hand and led her across the space between the two beds.

'Let's do it here,' he suggested.

'It will please you to make love to me on Monsieur Gunther's bed?' Esperanza asked with a half-smile.

She sat on the side of the bed with her hands under her bare thighs and her feet swinging while he took off all his clothes and let her see that his *zimbriq* was hard again.

'You have no respect for Monsieur Gunther and you do not care who knows,' she observed. 'You *zeqqed* his wife in his own house, and now that she has left you both and he has me, you want to *zeqq* me on his bed. Not that I mind – I like you a lot more than I like him.'

That I believe, Marcel thought – you like me 2500 tikkoos worth, which amounts to undying love here in Santa Sabina. He grinned at his own thought and bleated *meh* like a goat.

Esperanza laughed and got on to the bed on her hands and knees, her heavy belly and breasts swinging below her. He knelt close behind her to stroke her bottom and separate her dark curls to finger the wet brown lips of her *kuft*, his thick shaft jerking in anticipation.

'Now, my little nanny-goat,' he said, mounting her with easy agility, 'you have been singled out from the herd to satisfy my desires, do you understand? I shall ride you until you collapse beneath me.'

'*Meh!*' she bleated in excited agreement, '*meh!*'

With the single exception of Mariantonetta da Souza, it was hard for Marcel to regard the Santa Sabinan women he made love to as anything more interesting than the fortunate possessors of a slippery and available *kuft* in which to release his desire. And responsibility for this regrettable failure of sympathy could, in his analysis, be attributed to their total lack of interest in the finesse of love-making and their almost immediate physical response. All they wanted from a man was his stiff *zimbriq* inside them for the brief time it took them to achieve their climax and all they offered was their constant availability.

Esperanza was no different from the rest of them – she could arouse him quickly and drain him equally quickly with a minimum of enjoyment for either of them. Except that with her he had happily found ways of improving upon nature. Out in the open, among the fig-trees, she had been more satisfying, because of the pastoral setting. And letting her do it to him on Trudi's bed had provided a *frisson* of perverse delight that had added to his sensations – in his fantasy Trudi had come naked into the room and seen him laying on his back and Esperanza squatting naked over him, impaled on his shaft.

He had pictured Trudi rushing to the bed, consumed by a rage of jealousy, her sumptuous breasts joggling wildly up and down, to drag the girl off him by her hair. Esperanza believed that he sought revenge on some imaginary man for the loss of Trudi, but the truth was that he wanted to revenge himself on Trudi for the gross disappointment she had made him suffer. And so while he was being *zeqqed* by Esperanza he had imagined a triumphant grin on the maid's face at having scored over her employer, and on her bed.

But above all it was the expression of outraged fury he had pictured on Trudi's face, as she saw herself betrayed by two people she thought she controlled, that had brought on his climatic spasms. With each gush of ecstasy into Esperanza, he had felt a surging sense of victory over the woman he had seen betray him with Hakimoto. He had found it most satisfactory to lie underneath the maid and picture Trudi's chagrin but when they changed beds and he played at goats with Esperanza, his fantasy ranged ever further into the secret realms of sweetly perverse revenge.

In his mind's eye blonde and naked Trudi was lying on her back on her husband's bed and dark-haired Esperanza was kneeling over her, brown-tipped and heavy *gublas* brushing sensually against pink-tipped heavy *gublas*, and thick dark curls rubbing over neat blondish curls. The image aroused him so much that he was sure he was sliding in and out of two wet *kufts* at the same time – Esperanza's and Trudi's – not merely doubling his pleasure but multiplying it enormously. Although Esperanza could know nothing of the lurid visions flickering across the screen of his mind, she was gasping loudly in keen enjoyment of the insult to Pfaff – using his bed to make herself available to another man.

Marcel felt her body shuddering beneath him as her easily-aroused passions flared up towards the point of explosion. By his count, she reached a climax of sensation three times before he spurted his essence into her. When he did, he was so feverishly excited by his fantasising that what he experienced was cataclysmic in its intensity – a *total wipe-out*, in Sherri Hazlitt's bizarre American phrase. His senses swam away from him and, as his throes faded, he lay panting in exhaustion on the little maid.

Esperanza too was exhausted – and with good reason. To *zboca* four times within an hour was a little too much for a girl in her delicate condition. Without saying a word, she let her arms and legs collapse slowly to sink down beneath Marcel and, when he extricated himself from her, she lay on her side and closed her eyes. It was very obvious that she was about to fall into contented sleep, and so he carried her to her own room, tucked her money and the false papers under her pillow and planted a grateful kiss on her bulging belly.

Before leaving the house he tidied up the two beds they had made use of and put away in a drawer of the dressing-table the yellow silk pyjamas and the knickers Esperanza had been trying on when he arrived. Then on a sudden and unaccountable whim, he emptied the whole drawer out on to Trudi's bed and spread out the flimsy intimate garments and sat staring at them. At her hasty departure she had left behind two other pairs of knickers besides the cinnamon-coloured ones that had excited Esperanza – a pair of small briefs in magenta silk and another in primrose edged with ivory lace.

Marcel knew that he would never see her again, but the deep emotions her love-making had stirred in him would not fade. He took the little magenta briefs in his hand and felt the thin silk with trembling fingers, the thought in his mind that this fragile silk had many times concealed Trudi's pink-lipped *kuft* and neat blonde tuft of curls. He smiled as he kissed the silk and then folded the tiny briefs with reverence and tucked them into his jacket-pocket to take away with him as a souvenir of lost love.

16

When Everyone is Wrong, Everyone is Right

Less than a week after Marcel's arrangement with Esperanza, the shipping column of the *Daily Chronicles* carried the information for which he had been waiting. The steamship *Andromeda*, 5000 tonnes, was due to arrive the next day and a telephone call to the harbour master established that, assuming there were no maritime disasters or other unforeseen delays, it was expected in the late afternoon. His heart quaking, Marcel accepted that the moment had arrived to put into effect the plan he had worked out to save himself.

The instructions Trudi had given him before she left Santa Sabina for ever had been to go aboard the *Andromeda* after dark, establish his identity with Captain Nikopopolos and take away the fake paintings. They were large and a vehicle was required. After that it became more complicated and involved substituting the fakes for real paintings, aided by various church employees, and then delivering the authentic pictures to the ship before it sailed again.

Though he had made promises to Trudi to speed her departure, he had no intention at all of keeping them. But flaws were already making themselves apparent in his stratagem to avoid becoming implicated. Esperanza had performed her part in the confessional – he knew that because he had taken the bus out to the Pfaff villa after the week-end to check on her.

Perhaps Gunther Pfaff had annoyed his maid in some way and her loyalties were frayed, for this time Esperanza did not hesitate to share the sofa in the sitting-room with Marcel. Naturally, while she was telling him what he had come to hear, he unbuttoned her white blouse and fondled her soft breasts and she unzipped his trousers and stroked his *zimbriq*. Soon they both took their clothes off to play little goats, that being the most comfortable way for her in her present condition.

She was on her hands and knees on the sitting-room carpet, moaning with delight, her heavy *gublas* swinging beneath her and Marcel plunging into her slippery *kuft*. His eyes were closed tight and in his imagination it was yellow-haired Trudi naked on her knees for him, not Esperanza, and the smooth warm flesh clasping his shaft was not the little maid's *kuft* but blonde Trudi's red-painted mouth. He was two seconds away from squirting his passion down her pulsating throat when a car drew up outside the house.

Though he was seized by dread at the prospect of being discovered in an intimate embrace with Pfaff's maid, he was unable to prevent nature from taking its appointed course. Sharp jolts sent his desire spurting into his ecstatic partner, though all his pleasure in the imaginary humiliation of Trudi vanished. By the time he was rational enough to pull out of Esperanza he could hear a key in the front-door lock. He grabbed up his clothes, Esperanza grabbed hers, and together they ran silently on bare feet into her room.

'He mustn't find you or I'll lose my job!' she said in a vehement whisper. 'Don't make a sound!'

They could hear Pfaff calling for her while she scrambled hastily into her blouse and skirt.

'Wait for ten minutes and go out the back way very quietly,' she said. 'I'll keep him busy, come and see me again soon.'

She trotted out of the room, calling back to Pfaff that she was here and hadn't expected to see him home so early. Marcel got dressed and sat on Esperanza's narrow bed, his heart pounding with anxiety. After only five minutes he opened the door halfway and listened. There was no sound at all from the front of the house and he decided it was safe to leave. He went out by the veranda and, though it would have been more prudent to follow the slope down behind the house and make a wide circle round to the road, he could not resist going by the side of the house to look in through the windows.

As he had already guessed, Esperanza had chosen the obvious way of keeping Pfaff busy to give him time to get clear. They were in the sitting-room together, on the same sofa where she had been sitting with Marcel not half an hour ago and she had taken off her skirt and opened her white blouse to display her *gublas*. Pfaff had removed his trousers but neither his jacket nor tie and was lying full-length on the sofa with Esperanza astride his thighs with his upright *zimbriq* in her clasped hand.

The brisk massage continued for some time before Pfaff's hands groped blindly for the maid's bare breasts. She impaled herself on his spike and began to *zeqq* him, not in a typically energetic Santa Sabina way but slowly and with caution, both hands clasping her swollen belly to stop it from bouncing up and down too vigorously. Marcel was sure that he was safe from being seen for a while, and went boldy but quietly down the drive to the main road and walked to the fifth kilometre stone to wait for a bus.

It had been a narrow escape, but it was still an escape. More serious was the question of a companion for the visit he planned to the port. It was absolutely necessary that he was seen near the *Andromeda* by whoever was reporting on him to Mariantonetta. But it was equally necessary to provide himself with a reason for being in the vicinity of the ship, so that he had an alibi if, as he thought most likely, the uniformed police had been called in by the church authorities to arrest everyone in sight.

What he had in mind was to invite Sherri Hazlitt to dinner and take her to Paladio's Restaurant, down on the quayside, and probably within sight of the berthed *Andromeda*. Afterwards they would stroll about a little, like lovers enjoying an evening together as, in a sense, they were. He had chosen the daughter of the American Ambassador as perfect for his purpose. But when he met her at the Gran'Caffe Camille to make the arrangement, a second and more serious flaw appeared in his stratagem.

Sherri threw her arms round him and kissed him in great glee. She informed him with a huge grin that her father was in deep trouble with the State Department over the frustrated *coup d'état* and that Errol Hochheimer had been reassigned by the CIA to tourist monitoring in Alaska. Needless to say, none of the benefits and military bases on Santa Sabina were forthcoming that Ysambard D'Cruz had promised when he would become President. Neither for the US nor the USSR, thought Marcel.

And the joke was, said Sherri, hardly able to contain her mirth, President da Cunha was pressurising the embarrassed US State Department to give him a multi-million dollar loan on a non-returnable basis. The upshot was that Daddy would not be returning to Santa Sabina and his future in the diplomatic service was extremely uncertain. In the Embassy at this very moment Mrs Hazlitt was busy packing so that she and Sherri could leave for the US almost immediately. No doubt the same scene is being enacted at the Russian Embassy, Marcel thought.

'I owe you a big one, Marcel,' Sherri chortled, 'you really dropped my old man in it when you blew the whistle on Errol's revolution. I'm practically on my way back to Derry!'

'Ah, I am pleased for you,' he said, charmed by her bubbling happiness, 'even though I shall miss you.'

'I'm going to miss you too,' she answered, and threw her arms about him again, her impetuosity sending her beautiful long yellow hair flying. 'I love you!'

'No, you love Derry, *ma chérie*. I had the honour of amusing you in his absence, that's all.'

'You're wrong,' she insisted. 'I truly love you and if you ever come to the US I'll prove it by leaving Derry for you.'

Though her good fortune had totally ruined Marcel's plans for a visit to the port, at least it gave rise to an orgy of enjoyment. She went back to the Grand Hotel Orient with him for the evening and stayed all night as well. The mood was set when he undressed her to her tiny lime-green briefs and forced her to kneel under the tepid cascade of the shower and plead with him not to make her expose her hairless *kuft*. He loomed naked over her, his *zimbriq* jutting out like a tree-branch, as he ignored her little broken cries of anguish and ordered her to take her briefs off and show him.

When she still refused, he took her by the ankles and hoisted her legs into the air so that she lay helpless with water cascading on to her breasts and face while he stripped off her soaking briefs and parted her legs to gloat over the bald lips between them. The ignominy she felt at being stared at like that excited her so much that she gasped out her plea over and over again to be spared from being ravished and Marcel knew it was the right moment. He took her from behind, exactly as he had on the sea-shore, holding her very tightly round the waist while he rammed into her.

After they had dried off Marcel recalled what she had told him of Errol Hochheimer's idiosyncrasies and made her lie face-down over a chair to have her tight-cheeked little bottom smacked with a rolled-up copy of the *Daily Chronicles*. Her response was one of gratifying enthusiasm and, after only ten or twelve smacks, her feet jerked off the floor and she moaned loud and long as she approached her climax. Like that she was irresistible, of course, and Marcel threw away his frayed newspaper and went down on his knees to wrench her long legs apart and kiss her smooth *kuft*.

'No, I don't want you to do that!' she wailed.

She tried to break his grip by kicking and to thwart

her he forced her legs wider apart and slid his tongue into her.

'I hate you – don't do that!' she moaned, hardly able to speak for the climactic spasms that racked her body.

Marcel rubbed the tip of his tongue strongly over her hidden bud while she ran the whole gamut of ecstatic sensation. After her shuddering slowed to a tremble and she lay panting over the chair, he lay over her upturned bottom to penetrate her slippery *kuft*. It was a position of extreme awkwardness, acceptable only in the height of sexual arousal – Sherri's belly on the chair-seat, her head drooping down and her long hair hanging to the floor. Every thrust threatened to dislodge her from the chair and throw them both to the carpet.

But Marcel was furiously excited and cared nothing for the dangers of the moment as he stabbed into her with ungovernable force. As for Sherri, her face-down posture and the simulation of rape not only revived her ecstasies but lifted them to a higher peak of delirium. Her bottom writhed under his belly, her feet and hands beat against the floor convulsively, and she shrieked *I hate you, hate you, love you!* Massive sensations of pleasure burst through Marcel and he fountained his hot essence into her in jolting gasps of delight.

Later on, when they had rested a little and were sharing a bottle of champagne sent up from the hotel bar, she asked him to make love to her straight, by which she meant lying on her back with her legs apart for him, and to show that she meant it seriously she played with his *zimbriq* until it stood up again. He slid into her easily. She was still wet from their acrobatics on the chair, but though he became very excited almost at once, he could not help but be aware of her lack of response. He stared down at her face and saw the usual blank expression, though his hard shaft was probing deep into her.

'Ah, my poor Sherri – it is no good for you,' he said and lay still on her belly, reluctant to continue.

'It's OK,' she replied casually. 'Go ahead and finish – I want you to enjoy yourself.'

'But it disappoints me to think that I am not pleasing you.'

'It doesn't matter,' she said. 'It used to be like this with every guy I went with. I just wondered if anything had changed, but it hasn't. I can feel you poking away inside me but it does nothing for me. But it's you, so I don't mind.'

But I mind, Marcel thought, understanding what she had left unspoken – *it used to be like this before Derry's brutality made me excited enough to climax*. By asking him to make love to her like this she was bracketing him with the failures before Uncle Derry took over. At once he pulled out of her and knelt upright to take hold of her legs and jerk them up off the bed, dragging her body closer to him, until he could hook her knees over his shoulders and stare down at her exposed *kuft*.

'What use is this to a man?' he demanded in contempt as he fingered it. 'No hair, no curls, just a bald slit!'

'Don't say that!' she whined. 'You know it's not my fault – I can't help how it looks!'

Marcel drew her so close to him that she was balanced upside-down on her shoulders, her back pressed to his belly. He pushed his fingers into her as far as they would go.

'You should put lip-stick on it,' he said in disdain. 'Then you can pretend it's another mouth, instead of the delicious attraction women offer men.'

'Let me go!' she exclaimed, almost in tears. 'You've no right to do this to me!'

'You gave me the right,' he answered, 'when you asked me to make love to you and then proved you couldn't do it.'

Sherri's heels were drumming hard on his back and, as he looked down between her big sprawling breasts at her face, he saw her eyes roll upward in her head as her shame changed into sexual arousal and she began to shake. She struggled furiously to break away from his hold and stop him staring into her open slit while she climaxed, but he gripped her even tighter, enchanted to think that the hard stare of his eyes achieved more than the hard push of his *zimbriq*. She was still twitching in ecstatic sensation when he draped her over the back of a chair and emptied his urgent desire into her from behind.

But however enjoyable their last night together, the fact was that Sherri was not available for the dinner-outing that was an essential part of his scheme. He telephoned Inge Kristensen the next day, though he had not seen or spoken to her since the day of the storm and she was delighted to hear from him and told him that she had never stopped thinking about their fantastic afternoon together. He had opened her eyes to the true joys of love-making, she declared, and all her previous experience was, in comparison, no more that a few spasms, shallow and soon over. She made it clear she wished to be *zeqqed* again by him, as soon and as often as possible.

So far, so good, but when Marcel invited her to dinner and promised stupendous ecstasies to follow, she explained that it was impossible to leave her husband and children in the evenings and suggested an afternoon instead. Marcel promised to arrange a meeting to extend her experience into new realms of unimaginable delight and put the telephone down. And indeed, he thought, recalling with delight the thick chestnut fleece between her thighs, why not? With Trudi gone and Sherri about to go, Inge could perhaps be coaxed into some interesting performances in her quest for the type of sexual cataclysm brought on by her fear of the thunder-storm.

The immediate problem remained and he wondered if there was any possibility of Jaqueline Ducour accepting his invitation to dinner. To the best of his knowledge she was at present without a suitable companion for her little games and if he offered very sincerely to submit to her caprices, perhaps she might be tempted. After all, he was sure that he was the most handsome young man whose *zimbriq* she had teased for her pleasure. But in the end he was compelled to admit to himself that Jaqueline was admirably discreet in her preying on young men and would refuse to be seen alone in a restaurant with him – especially Paladio's, where it was certain there would be people she knew.

Eventually he swallowed his pride and set out to visit Eunice Carpenter, to see if there was a possibility of making up their quarrel. He arrived at her apartment about six in the evening, summoned up his resolve and knocked. Eunice opened the door wearing a polka dot frock in black and white.

'Oh, it's you!' she exclaimed. 'What do you want?'

Without a word, Marcel pushed her into the apartment and kicked the door shut behind him. He forced her back against the wall and kissed her hard while he reached under the hem of her frock to get his hand into her loose knickers.

'What the hell do you think you're doing!' she gasped.

She twisted her face away from him and tried to push him away, and by then Marcel's fingers were attending expertly to the fleshy lips of her *kuft*.

'Get off me!' she said angrily, pushing at his shoulders. 'Get off before I scream for help and have you arrested!'

'You are wearing your knickers this evening,' he said. 'That means no party. How sad – you enjoy *zeqqing* so much that every evening should be a party for you.'

Her knee came up sharply to mash his *castazz* and disable him, but he had been expecting the move and all she achieved was to graze the outside of his thigh. The rapid lift of her thigh forced his fingers up into her, and he caressed her bud lightly. As she dropped her knee again, his other hand found its way into her knickers, to prise her wide open.

'I told you I never want to see you again,' she exclaimed and, though her voice was unfriendly, her feet moved apart.

'That terrible night we parted – it was impossibly hot and we became irritable, even in our pleasures,' he murmured. 'I have pleaded for your forgiveness more than once, but you have refused to see me. So here I am, dear Eunice, and I want us to forget that night and be good friends again.'

'You never wanted me – you were only using me,' she said, her tone accusing, though her *kuft* was wet to his touch and her legs were trembling just a little.

'Using you – yes, for my pleasure, I admit it frankly,' said Marcel, 'and in return you used me for your pleasure. There is nothing wrong in that – men and women are made for each other's pleasure. When we make love I feel the ecstasy of your climax and you feel the ecstasy of mine. This is how it should be.'

He knew that he had won her over when he felt her fingers groping along the long bulge in his trousers.

'You lied to me,' she gasped as she forced her hand down the front of his trousers and into the slit of his underwear.

She grasped his *zimbriq* and jerked it up and down with such violence that Marcel feared she would rip it from his body. A moment later her head went back against the wall and she shook and moaned in a crisis of sensation, her loins bucking against his busy fingers. For Marcel too his own moment had come – the violence with which she was handling him brought a torrent of passion spurting into his trousers.

His mouth found her open mouth and they exchanged gasps of delight, legs shaking under them, until gradually Eunice's back slid down the wall and she was squatting on her haunches, her face level with Marcel's belly. With trembling fingers she unzipped his trousers, pulled out his wet *zimbriq* and kissed it again and again with so much fervour that instead of dwindling into limpness it retained its firmness and became harder still. He pulled Eunice to her feet and took her into the bedroom, where they embarked upon the most prolonged and pleasurable reconciliation possible.

By nine the next morning he had *zeqqed* her seven times – on her back, on her knees, face-down, over an arm-chair, under the shower, on the table and, in the silent middle of the night, draped over the railing of her balcony in search of a cooling breeze. And since Eunice also enjoyed being aroused by hand, she experienced thirteen climaxes in all and was so delightfully fatigued in the morning that she decided to take the day off. She wanted Marcel to stay with her and consolidate their reconciliation, but he claimed that he had to be at the Embassy and promised to take her to dinner that evening.

Naturally, he was proud to have done better than Pieter van Buuren, who after a night with Eunice, had lain unconscious for half the next day, but he needed sleep. At the reception desk of the Grand Hotel Orient Concepcion Costa gave him a friendly and knowing little smile, well aware that he had been out all night and pleased that he had recovered from the pain caused by the betrayal and flight of the yellow-haired German woman. He returned Concepcion's smile with all the charm he could muster after his Marathon of lovemaking and asked her to ensure that he was not disturbed.

He slept until five, shaved and showered, composed a short anonymous letter and went out again. The doubtful beggar with the mandolin was outside the hotel and Marcel walked slowly round the Square before turning into a narrow street of small shops that ran north towards the cathedral. The shopkeepers were beginning to put up their shutters and halfway along the street he spotted the sort of girl he was looking for. She was sixteen or seventeen, he guessed, pretty enough in the olive-skinned and mop-haired Santa Sabina way.

When he spoke to her, she assumed that he wanted to *zeqq* her, that being the usual reason for men to approach girls. She said her name was Mira and flicked her green skirt up to give him a quick glimpse of her bare thighs. Marcel explained that a friend of his had just arrived from a long sea voyage and was in desperate need of the company of a pretty girl. *Five weeks without zeqqing!* Mira exclaimed, aghast at this outrage to human nature. Marcel said that if she took pity on his poor friend she would never regret it and to reinforce his appeal to her good nature he produced a 20-tikkoo note.

Mira took the cash with a grin and promised to relieve his friend's anguish. Marcel gave her the letter and told her she would find Captain Nikopopolos on board the *Andromeda*. Before she hastened off to the port on her errand of mercy, Mira told him that if he were outside her father's fruit shop tomorrow, it would be her pleasure to relieve his anguish too.

By eight that evening, shaved, showered and dressed in his best white suit, Marcel had collected Eunice and they were on the terrace of Paladio's restaurant. He chose a table at the front, in clear view of anyone keeping an eye open for him, and was reasonably certain that a man in a white straw hat and sunglasses who walked past three times within half an hour must be a member of the Secret Police acting on instructions from Mariantonetta da Souza.

Eunice's conversation over dinner was fascinating. She had made up her mind that Marcel was an agent of the French Secret Service and that his job at the Embassy was a cover, exactly as Colonel Hochheimer's had been at the American Embassy. But where Hochheimer failed in his mission, Marcel had triumphantly averted a Russian-backed uprising that would have turned Santa Sabina into a repressive Soviet-dominated People's Republic. He listened in amazement to this farrago and congratulated himself on the correctness of his assumption that the way to change Eunice's mind was through her *kuft*.

'You're a hero,' she said, her big loose *gublas* heaving with emotion under her cream frock, 'it was in the *Daily Chronicles* that they awarded you the Order of St Sabina and there was a picture of you with President da Cunha.'

'In the Presidential Palace on Saturday afternoon,' he said. 'My Ambassador is wildly jealous and pretends not to be.'

It seemed unnecessary to tell Eunice that immediately after the ceremony with the President, Mariantonetta had taken him to her private apartments. In the course of an hour and a half he had *zeqqed* her four times, wearing only the golden Order round his neck on its colourful ribbon.

Eunice said that she understood perfectly that a Secret Agent was required to be utterly ruthless, which was why he had manipulated her sexually. But in the course of espionage work that was forgivable – and, in fact, it was extremely exciting. As soon as she had come to grasp the truth of the situation, she had lain awake night after night with a wet *kuft*, longing to be manipulated by him again. The only reason she had rebuffed his approaches after the night she realised he was a spy was that she knew she would not be able to resist him if he asked her to act against the interests of Britain!

Marcel kept a careful eye on the time while his ego was massaged lovingly over the food and wine. At a quarter past ten he paid the bill and proposed a stroll in the night air before they returned to Eunice's apartment. She would have preferred an immediate return and, standing in the entrance to Paladio's terrace, she contrived to rub his hand down between her thighs for a moment, to make him touch her plump mound while she chuckled and said *no knickers tonight*.

Marcel kissed her cheek and stroked her *kuft* for a moment through her thin frock, giving the Secret Police agent time to leave his hiding-place and start following them.

'We have all night when we go back to your apartment,' he told Eunice as he walked her slowly along the water-front. 'We shall be naked together and everything will be permissible. But before then, let us see if we can capture just a tiny something of the thrill of the forbidden.'

The *Andromeda* was the last of three ships moored along the quay, a scruffy vessel with rust-streaks on the hull and soot-marks on the funnel. A bare-chested seaman with tattooed arms stood on watch at the top of the gang-plank, a cigarette cupped in his hand. Marcel led Eunice past the ship, fondling her fleshy bottom through her frock, for the benefit of the deck-hand, who was watching them closely, and any other eyes observing their progress from places of concealment.

He suggested to Eunice that they should turn back and she sighed her agreement, her arm tightly round his waist. Her legs were a little unsteady, not because of the wine she had drunk at dinner, but because Marcel's fingers were well down in the cleft of her bottom and his soft rubbing through her frock was making her highly excited, as he intended it to. When they were well away from the *Andromeda* and almost back to Paladio's, he pulled her into the doorway of the Customs House.

'Customs, Mademoiselle,' he said, 'is there anything you wish to declare to me?'

His hands were up her frock to stroke her *kuft* and the little knot of muscle between the cheeks of her bare bottom.

'I declare . . . I'm being *zeqqed* forwards and backwards at the same time,' she sighed, 'and I love it!'

He had positioned her so that he could look over her shoulder along the water-front to the *Andromeda*. As he expected, three more sailors had appeared on deck and were manhandling two packing-cases down the gang-plank. Each crate was about two metres square and flat, and Marcel had not the least doubt they contained the fake paintings. His unsigned letter delivered to Captain Nikopopolos by Mira said that a consignment for Madame Pfaff would be collected at ten-thirty and it should be on the dock-side for instant loading.

Eunice's legs were as far apart as her frock would allow and she was squirming in delight as Marcel's fingers between her thighs probed her moist depths front and rear. *Oh yes, yes*, she gasped, her parted legs shaking beneath her in her climactic spasms. Over her shoulder Marcel could see that the packing-cases were on the dock-side and the sailors had been joined by a black-bearded man in a sea-captain's peaked cap. All was going to plan, so far, and he would have crossed his fingers but for the fact that they were busy in Eunice's apertures.

The gesture to avert ill-fortune was not required – he heard the engine of a vehicle on the quay-side behind him and felt a sudden surge of joy. Moments later it drove past, one of the twenty or so ancient motor taxis in the city of Santa Sabina. At this time of evening it waited for customers outside Madame da Silva's on the Avenue of the Constitution and a telephone call to the establishment had summoned it to fetch Captain Nikopopolos from his ship to Madame's. Needless to say, the call had been made by Marcel from Paladio's, just before he and Eunice left to take their little stroll.

As the taxi drew to a stop alongside the *Andromeda*, Marcel raised Eunice's frock high enough to bare her from the waist down and opened his trousers. She was still quivering in the after-throes of climactic delight as she took his *zimbriq* between her fingers and guided it between her thighs. He bent his knees and then slowly stood up straight again.

'Ah!' he sighed, while he pushed into her, hands clenched on her bare bottom to steady her for his slow thrusts.

The arrival of the empty taxi triggered off shouting and confusion down by the *Andromeda*, uniformed policemen appearing out of nowhere to seize Captain Nikopopolos and his contraband. Eunice was so far gone in ecstasy that she heard nothing of it, her plump belly pushing rhythmically against Marcel while she moaned softly under her breath. Marcel's thoughts were intent on the drama alongside the *Andromeda*, though he continued to *zeqq* Eunice in a distracted sort of way.

So this is how it ends, he thought – *all that golden desire for blonde and beautiful Trudi Pfaff has brought me to this – I stand here on a quay-side smelling of fishing-boats and rotten bananas waiting for the police to discover me pleasuring an overweight and middle-aged Englishwoman.*

He remembered his afternoon on the veranda with Trudi and he sighed to feel Eunice's fat belly pushing hard against him. He slithered in and out with deliberate slowness, until he saw two policemen coming along the quay-side towards the Customs House and then he started to *zeqq* her fast and hard. She moaned and shook and Marcel had only just time to complete the release of his pent-up emotion into her wet *kuft* when a policeman tapped his shoulder and announced that he was under arrest.

'But why?' he gasped. 'It is no crime to make love!'

He pulled slowly away from Eunice, holding her frock bundled up round her waist so that both policemen had ample opportunity to observe her bare belly and his wet shaft sliding out of her.

'A thousand pardons, Monsieur,' said the police corporal with a grin. 'I thought you were look-outs for the criminals we have just arrested further along the quay.'

Marcel zipped up his trousers and produced his diplomatic passport. While Eunice sorted through her handbag for hers, he explained that they were taking a stroll after dinner at Paladio's and, overcome by the moonlight and their natural passions, had paused for a moment or two in the privacy of the Customs House doorway. The police corporal read out their names and passport numbers for his subordinate to write down.

'You are correct, Monsieur,' he said, still grinning as he gave the passports back, '*zeqqing* is no crime, though it must be awkward standing up. I wouldn't do it like that. But you and the lady are foreigners and I suppose you do things differently in your country. *Vive l'amour!*'

Eunice giggled and repeated *vive l'amour* while Marcel tucked her arm under his, wished the policemen *bonsoir* and led her away from the scene of his triumph.

NEXUS BOOKS

A LIBRARY OF THE FINEST EROTICA

There are over 80 books in the Nexus collection of sensual writings

Fact and fiction, novels and short stories, by writers from both America and Europe.

Tales of unbridled sexuality and forbidden passions to satisfy the tastes of the most demanding gourmet of eroticana.

For a complete list of Nexus books, please send a stamped addressed envelope to

NEXUS BOOK LIST
CASH SALES DEPARTMENT
WH ALLEN & CO LTD
175–179 ST JOHN STREET
LONDON
EC1V 4LL

Nexus books can be ordered from bookshops, or from the Cash Sales Dept at the above address.

NEXUS